UNRAVEL

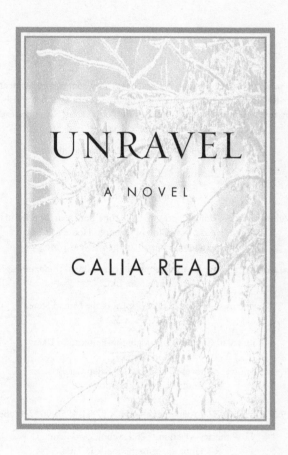

UNRAVEL

A NOVEL

CALIA READ

BALLANTINE BOOKS TRADE PAPERBACKS
NEW YORK

2014 Ballantine Books Trade Paperback Edition

Copyright © 2014 by Calia Read

Published in the United States by Ballantine Books, an imprint of Random House, a division of Random House LLC, a Penguin Random House Company, New York.

BALLANTINE and the HOUSE colophon are registered trademarks of Random House LLC.

Originally published in eBook form in the United States by Calia Read in 2014.

Library of Congress Cataloging-in-Publication Data
Read, Calia.
Unravel : a novel / Calia Read.—Ballantine Books
Trade Paperback Edition.
pages cm
ISBN 978-0-553-39477-1 (paperback)—ISBN 978-1-4953-0097-4 (eBook)

1. Witnesses—Fiction.   2. Psychological fiction.
3. Romantic suspense fiction.   I. Title.
PS3618.E219U57 2014
813'.6—dc23   2014023993

Printed in the United States of America on acid-free paper

www.ballantinebooks.com

4 6 8 9 7 5 3

Book design by Karin Batten

Title page: iStockphoto.com by Sangfoto

TO LORI

Every storyteller deserves to
have someone like you.

UNRAVEL

1

BREATHE ON GLASS

I GAZE OUT THE WINDOW AT THOUSANDS OF SNOWFLAKES FLUT-
tering to the ground. I press my face against the pane, aching for
freedom. But it isn't a thin layer of glass that's blocking me from
the outside, it's the truth.

Most people believe the truth is a delicate little bird. They
think it's harmless.

But I know something they don't.

If they dare to move their hands away from their body, they'll
discover that the little bird is gone. It's torn their skin apart and
traveled to the core of their soul, right where it hurts the most.

And that's why I'm here and they aren't.

I press my forehead against the window and breathe on the
glass. Mist forms and my tally appears. I put another mark on
the glass. Thirty days.

Thirty days since I'd been involuntarily admitted to Fairfax Mental Health Institute.

Seven hundred and twenty hours of opening my eyes every morning to an unfamiliar room. Seven hundred and twenty hours of having nurses coming in and out of my room every hour. Seven hundred and twenty hours of being monitored around the clock like I'm a toddler and can't be trusted.

I watch a fly moving across the window, frantically trying to find a way out into the world.

"I've already tried, dummy." I tap my finger against the window. "They have these suckers bolted tight."

The fly stops moving, as if it can hear me. Sooner or later, it's going to find a way out. I feel envy, thick and powerful, flow throughout my body. I want to slam my palm against this insect, killing any chance of its escape.

This is what my life has been stripped down to. I'm envious of a fucking fly.

Loudly, someone knocks on my door.

One, two, three . . .

Three is the magic number for my nurse. It's as if those few seconds will allow her to brace herself for what she'll discover on the other side.

Mary stands in the doorway. I take in her short brown hair and colorful scrubs. "You have a visitor," she says.

I move away from the window. My heart beats the same monotonous rhythm every day, but in seconds it speeds up. The tone sounds different. It isn't dull. It's interesting and new and exciting. It's beautiful. And it can only mean one thing.

Lachlan Halstead.

Before I leave the room I look over my shoulder. The fly's gone.

"Lucky," I mumble under my breath as I walk out of my room.

Anyone who ever doubts whether madness exists need only look right here. It drifts throughout every room. It slides down the sterile hallways and attaches itself to every patient, stripping them of their hope and covering them with despair.

Some people don't react. But the ones that do, scream. Their shouts echo throughout the building. The nurses run down the hallway and a few seconds later those screams turn into moans and then stop. When I first arrived, those screams sent a chill down my spine. But now I'm used to it.

As Mary and I walk down the hall, a nurse and a brunette patient pass by. My steps get slower. I stare at the brunette. Her hair is cut short. Her skin is pale, but underneath the fluorescent lighting its tone takes on a yellow hue. Her body is emaciated. There are track marks all over her arms, telling their own story. She meets my gaze. Her soul shines through her eyes, and asks, "How the hell am I still alive?"

I have no answer.

Mary stops at two locked doors. She enters a four-digit code and the doors slowly open. It's like we're entering hell. The rec room is the most depressing place in Fairfax Mental Health Institute. This is where everyone is shoved together.

Mary pushes me forward. The blinds are open, letting sunlight pour in and making the tan linoleum floors blindingly white. Tables are spread throughout the room. A few people are sitting down, playing board games or watching the television mounted on the wall. The news plays so softly the captions are on.

But most people do nothing. They stare straight ahead, their eyes vacant.

There are so many minds around me that are wasting away. But I have someone that keeps me coasting above insanity, and he's only a few steps away from me.

My body relaxes as I watch Lachlan. He's sitting at a table next to the windows. His thick brows slant low as he scans the outdoors. His tan hand reaches up and loosens his dark blue silk tie. His brown hair is still cut short, with a few strands brushing his forehead.

If I blink, he's just a boy with a cocky smile that comes from a child's naivety. Wiry frame. The best friend that stole my heart. When I open my eyes that image disappears, and in front of me is a man. His cockiness has evaporated into experience. His body has filled out. And now, not only does he own my heart, he possesses my soul.

He's always been an extension of me, and you cannot be that close to someone and expect your pain not to spread. I know that my sadness is his sadness.

I move across the room. Lachlan is still looking outside. I squint my eyes and follow his gaze to the naked tree closest to the window. It's the same tree I always look at. Its branches have been stripped of their leaves and bow from the cold wind. For the last week, I've watched a frozen water drop on one of the lower branches. It hangs there, looking ready to fall.

The weak branch sways in the air, but the water drop remains. If the ice drop can hold on, then perhaps I can hang on to my small bit of sanity.

I pull out the chair across from Lachlan.

His eyes meet mine. It's a shock to my nerves. My blood rushes straight to my head.

"How are you?" he asks.

My feet rest on the edge of the seat. I place my chin on my

knees, refusing to look away from him. He visits frequently. But those visits seems to stretch farther and farther apart.

"I'm the same as two days ago," I say.

Lachlan stares at me levelly. His eyes are sharp. They miss nothing. "Have you been talking to your doctor?"

I look out the window, away from his gaze.

An exhausted sigh escapes him. Lachlan drags his hands through his hair. "I miss you, Naomi."

"I miss you too." My voice cracks.

"You know you don't belong here, right?"

I nod.

"Then you need to try and get better." Lachlan looks around the room like he's watching a circus. His jaw hardens. "It fucking kills me to leave you here."

I reach across the table and place my hand on top of Lachlan's. His eyes become hooded as he looks at it. He turns his hand over and his fingers move across my wrist, making my skin burn. With his palm faceup, he swallows my hand in his own. "You love me?"

I look Lachlan dead in the eye. "You know I do." My words should have given him hope, but now he just looks deflated. "If you love me, then you need to get better."

"I'm trying," I insist. I try to move my hand.

Lachlan's grip tightens. "No, you're not."

"I can't ignore everything that's happened," I say in an intense whisper.

He leans in, his face inches from mine. "I told you I wouldn't stop fighting. I told you that you weren't in this alone, and you crumbled."

I jerk my hand back. He lets go. I can handle a lot of things, but hearing those words come out of his mouth feels like someone has cut a piece of my heart off.

He stares down at the table, where our hands were once intertwined. "This is destroying you," he murmurs. "The Naomi I know would have never just given up so quickly. She would have fought to stay in the present."

"I am fighting. Look around you, Lach," I say. "How do you think I've lasted this long here?"

"You know why you're here?" he asks sharply.

I don't say a word.

"You're here because you fell apart."

I flinch because, true or not, I can't go up against Lachlan's words. He's going to come out as the sane one. His words will make sense before mine ever will.

My heart thunders in my ears, and my vision blurs. I see a woman with sad eyes, staring at herself in the mirror. And I see Max lying beside me in bed. In one quick move I'm above him, and he smiles up at me, his hands gripping my waist.

And then the image disappears. I groan and press the heel of my hands into my eyes.

"Naomi, look at me."

I lower my hands. Lachlan sits across from me, staring at me intensely.

His hand is around my neck. His thumb brushes across my skin and my body jolts.

"Are you with me right now?" he asks.

Yes . . . no . . . maybe. Every day is an unknown for me. Every day I wake up feeling like I'm surrounded by a heavy fog and I know I'm missing a piece of myself, and I don't know where it is.

I answer Lachlan honestly. "For now I am."

There's a two-second pause as he looks me in the eye. A pause that makes my stomach twist and my blood roar through my veins. His mouth opens, but nothing comes out. He looks like he's battling his feelings, but I watch as he loses. His eyes lock with mine and then he kisses me hard on the mouth.

Instantly, I come alive. And that's what a good kiss should do. It should speak to you the second your lips connect.

You don't think.

You react.

You feel.

For Lachlan and me, it's always been this way. All I can hear from this kiss is, *"Remember me. I'm real."*

I respond the only way I know how, the way Lachlan showed me in the past. His hands hold my face in place. The pressure of his lips declines when I move my mouth against his. He makes a noise and grips my face tighter. It triggers memories of who I used to be. Behind my eyes, memories start to play on a projector. Each one has Lachlan. The two of us in a field, lighting rockets. Staring at the stars and talking until the sun comes up. I see myself smiling and carefree and so happy.

For a brief moment, I feel at peace. Lachlan's tongue slips between my lips. A shudder moves through me as I open my mouth wider. My fingers move up his arms, toward his neck. Just when hope starts to flicker in me, Mary clears her throat.

Lachlan pulls away first. His pupils are dilated; his lips are swollen from our kiss. I lick my lips, trying to get a piece of that kiss back. Mary clears her throat louder this time. I glance up.

"Mr. Halstead," she says, "I think it's time for you to leave."

He removes his hand from the back of my neck. My skin instantly feels cold. My arms drop heavily onto the table as I watch Lachlan stand up.

He looks at Mary. "Give me just a minute," he says.

Mary's eyes move between the two of us. She sighs. *"One minute,"* she warns, and walks away.

Lachlan leans close to me. I keep my gaze on the table, but

the smooth surface starts to blur as tears pool in my eyes. Something terrible is brewing. I can feel it.

"I can't keep doing this," he says.

I look at him. I see the pain in his eyes. "I need you to visit me," my voice cracks. "It's the only thing keeping me going."

Lachlan looks out the window. My fingers reach out and I grip the collar of his shirt, forcing him to look directly at me.

"You can't leave me."

A tense silence wraps around us. He looks at me through his eyelashes, his expression grim. One by one, his fingers wrap around my wrists. Firmly, he pulls my fingers off his shirt.

"I'm not leaving you. That's the last thing I want. But I don't think I'm helping you. I think I just make everything worse," he says slowly.

"You help me," I insist. "Whenever you visit things are better."

Lachlan says nothing.

"You're just having a bad day. I'm having a bad day. Tomorrow things will be better, and—"

His head turns. I see the look in his eyes. It doesn't matter what I say. He isn't going to change his mind.

Everything around me has been a chaotic mess, yet he has stood firm. And now he's shredding my world.

This must be what hell feels like. It has to be. My lungs are constricting. I can't breathe. I rub my eyes with my palms, moving my head back and forth in denial. If Lachlan stops coming, I'm afraid of what will happen. My sanity is being held together by a threadbare string. I'll break before that frozen water drop does.

Feeling his hand on my shoulder makes me shake. He squeezes once. I force my hands to stay on the table.

His hand drifts away. There Lachlan goes, walking out of my life.

I turn in my chair. "Wait!"

Lachlan turns around.

At this point, I'm desperate. I know I'm losing him. "Do you remember what you said to me a year ago?" I ask.

His jaw tightens. He looks away and I know he's trying not to respond to my question, but he can't help himself. Even when you're angry, love tugs at your soul in the most painful way. It makes you care—makes you feel—when that's the last thing you want.

He nods stiffly.

"Then, please, don't do this," I say.

He steps forward.

"Lachlan," Mary calls out behind him.

He stops.

I plead with my eyes. Seconds pass and I think he's going to tell Mary to fuck off. I think he's going to say he didn't mean what he said. But he slowly backs away.

The world rips out from under my feet. I'm in a free fall, frantically trying to grab onto anything that will save me.

Lachlan's figure starts to become hazy. My skull feels like it's been cracked in half. I grip the table and slump forward. Tables and chairs disappear into thin air. The walls crack and shatter to the floor. New walls, the rich shade of brown, burst from the ground. The tan linoleum floors fade into plush, white carpet.

The windows shatter around me. A cold gust of air bursts into the room. I curl my fingers around my head and moan. Shards of glass rotate through the air. They miss my body by inches before they disintegrate. A large window fits into the wall with a loud suction noise. Sunlight fades away, replaced by the soft glow of moonlight.

Then everything stops.

My eyes open. I blink once and slowly stand up.

The rec room is gone.

I'm facing a mirror, staring at my reflection. I don't look the same. I look refreshed, happy, and even beautiful. My blond hair is styled in finger waves, one side pulled up with a golden barrette. My cheeks have color and my eyes have life in them. I'm back to being Naomi.

My body is covered in a dress that clings to my body. Turning to the side, I see my entire back is exposed. Quickly, my attention goes from the dress to the male sitting in the corner of the room.

Max.

My lips curve up and my heart races as I watch him. He rests his ankle against his opposite knee. His expression is relaxed and the dimple in his right cheek makes him appear boyish. But his full lips curve up into a masculine smile that is anything but.

He stands to his full height and I watch as he slides his black blazer over his wide shoulders, covering up his white shirt and black suspenders. His black bow tie is undone, hanging around his neck like a black ribbon.

His hair is unruly. But he doesn't care. That's the thing with Max. He breaks past every single rule and takes his own road.

He adjusts the collar of his jacket as he walks up behind me. His body swallows me up. The top of my head grazes his chin.

I cherish this moment like a lifeline and I hold on for as long as I can. It never lasts long. But each time I see him, I become convinced that it will be different, that he won't disappear on me.

I take in the strong jaw below his sharp cheekbones. His skin is free of stubble and tan from the sun. He steps closer and his fingertips brush against the bare skin of my back. I shiver.

"Beautiful," he murmurs.

I stare at us in the mirror. He lifts a brow. His lips curl up in a lazy smile.

Pulling my hair to the side, he wraps both of his hands

around my arms, encouraging me to lean against him. I go willingly, and when my shoulder blades touch his chest, I practically sigh. He stares at me through the mirror and slowly leans down to kiss me on the shoulder. His teeth graze my skin. I make a noise and tilt my head farther to the side.

He asks the same question Lachlan asked minutes ago. "Do you love me, Naomi?"

My body still reacts at the way he says my name. I can barely swallow, so I nod as he moves in closer and breathes me in.

I do love him. In the most twisted, impossible way.

Max tilts his head and smirks, as if he knows what I'm thinking. His hand moves from my neck and drifts lower. I watch as his large, tanned hand stops where my heart beats. His palm lays flat against my skin and his fingers spread.

His eyes droop to half-mast as he watches my reaction in the mirror. The tip of his nose brushes against my cheek. My hands fist up, and I watch in fascination as he kisses the curve of my cheekbone.

"If you love me, then don't give up," he says, his voice a low whisper.

"I promise I won't."

I know what's next. And I'm desperate for this time to be different. So I lean even farther into him and smell his scent. For me, stuck in this place with its sterile walls and musty scent, it's refreshing. It wraps around me before it disappears.

Just like that, he's already fading. My voice is stuck in my throat and I reach out for him, but my hand just slashes through the air.

He's gone and I'm falling.

My back hits the back of my chair. I jump in pain and shock. My heart pounds in my rib cage, and I take deep, shallow breaths, trying to calm my heart.

"Naomi. Are you okay?"

I flinch and look up to find Mary staring at me.

Her face is etched with concern as she waits for me to answer. I swallow loudly and shake my head. Painfully, my fingers dig into my thighs while my body shakes with pent-up frustration.

"I'm fine."

"It's time for your medication," she says.

I stand up and nod before I follow her back to my room.

I'm running on adrenaline, and a sweat breaks out across my forehead.

Even though he's gone, I can still hear Max. I can still smell him. I can still feel his hands on my skin.

I know I'm not making Max up. I know I'm not imagining anything. And what scares the hell out of me is that all those facts change nothing.

The only fact that matters is that everyone thinks I'm a total head case. And now, the one person who has consistently been there for me is losing hope.

Tonight, I would rather take the drugs than think about what is stacked against me.

Tomorrow, I'll accept that in order to unravel my story, I'll be destroyed first. Like the frozen water drop, it's inevitable that I break.

Going, going . . . gone.

2

BELIEVE ME

"WHAT FEELS GOOD TO YOU?"

I roll onto my side and rest my head on my hand. Max lies on his stomach. Across from us, the window is open, letting in the summer heat. Bright sunlight pours into the bedroom. It trails across the floor, up onto the bed, and slants across Max's back. I trail my fingers across his tan skin before I lean close.

What feels good to me? I answer by kissing him hard on the mouth. Good. Max responds, his hands curving around my face, holding me in place as he sits up.

He moves above me, his lips never leaving mine. His body lowers and we're skin to skin. He breathes through his nose and I wrap myself around him.

The hands that I love trace the outline of my body. His breath is warm against my skin, kissing my jaw and moving farther down.

And then he's ripped from my embrace. He reaches back for me. Right before he disappears, I see the look of fear in his eyes. It's not for himself. That fear is for me.

"Get out of my head," I moan. "Get out, get out, get out!"

I press my palms against my eyes forcefully until spots form. I keep pressing, hoping the image of Max will dissolve.

How long can a memory replay before your mind short-circuits? I can feel my mind trying to keep up with all my Max memories. It works faster and faster. Starts to overheat. And then *boom*. It explodes.

Right now, it doesn't seem like such a bad option. I want a blissful moment where I can just . . . *be*.

No memories.

No words.

No pain.

Silence.

I stand up from my bed and pace. A frustrated groan escapes me. I'm tired of being stuck in this place. This small room. I stare at the four cream-colored walls that surround me. They're blank. No pictures of family, no posters. Nothing. Other than the television, the only thing I have for entertainment is the big, square window.

I'm tired of it all.

It's like being trapped in a box. And every day that I'm trapped, the sides close in just a little bit more.

Most days, I can handle this place. But now that Lachlan is staying away, I'm afraid. He was my only source of support.

Mary knocks on my door. Nine a.m. sharp. I expect to see her usual somber face, but today she looks at me with a light in her eyes. "Good. You're up." She hands me my morning pills. "You're seeing a new doctor today," she says.

I frown as I swallow them all. "Why?"

I think Dr. Woods is full of shit. He thinks I'm a whack job. We have a silent understanding; he prescribes me medicine, and I pretend to listen to his advice.

"Why? I don't know why you're seeing someone new." She nudges her head toward the hall and I can't tell if she's lying to me. "Are you ready?"

No, I'm not ready. I hate change and I don't want to start all over again with a new doctor.

"Has Woods given up on me?"

"Naomi . . ." She sighs and looks away. "I've already told you I don't know why you're seeing someone new."

"Mary, if you're going to lie to me, make sure your delivery is right. Make me believe it."

She gives me a blank look, but one corner of her mouth pulls up. Just a little. "Just come on, will you? You're going to be late," she says.

"So . . . this new doctor. Does it have a name?" I ask as we walk down the hall.

"It's a she, not an it. And her name is Dr. Rutledge. She's new here and excited to meet you."

I toy with the ties of my gray sweatshirt, processing this new information. "Will I be the first to suck the hope out of her?"

"No, you're not the first." Mary looks over at me, a warning in her eyes. "She's very nice."

Being nice means nothing here. I give her nine months before she's either handing me off to another doctor or packing up her pretty diplomas and hightailing it out of here.

We stop in front of a closed door. I stare at the bronze name-plate. In black letters is the name *Genevieve Rutledge, M.D.*

She will be just one more person who will judge me and I'm not ready for that.

"Are you going in?" Mary asks.

I don't want to answer all the stupid questions. I don't want to deal with her gaze quietly assessing me.

"Naomi?"

"Yeah. I'm going, I'm going." I say the words but my legs refuse to move. My hands stay rooted at my sides, as if weights are attached to them.

Mary loses her patience. She knocks loudly on the door before she walks away. I watch her, and for the first time, I wish I could follow.

"Come in," a voice calls out. She sounds happy. Rutledge probably has it all together. If I don't crush her hopes, someone else in this place will.

Trying to be as quiet as possible, I slowly open the door. Her office throws me off. Dr. Woods's office felt designed to intimidate. Every time I walked in, I swear I had to walk miles before I reached his desk. It felt like a walk of shame.

But this office is warm. The tan walls are decorated with her diplomas. No shocker there. But there are touches of femininity. Plants near the window, a decorative rug spread out across the floor. Even a candle is lit on her desk. For a second it makes me forget where I am. The moment the small brunette behind the desk stands, I remember.

First impression of Dr. Rutledge? In her early thirties. Pretty face. She smiles, revealing a set of straight, white teeth. She's way too happy to be here.

"Hello, Naomi. I'm Dr. Rutledge." She holds her hand out to me.

I look at it like it's poison. Cautiously, I reach out. My hand is barely in hers before I snatch it back.

She doesn't blink. "Please, have a seat."

I sit. My knees bounce up and down as I look everywhere but at her. I can feel her eyes on me. I glance back at her diplomas.

Her full name, Genevieve Marie Rutledge, is printed in the middle of each certificate.

I picture her being the youngest of a large family. Four or five siblings. Her parents are hardworking. And they were just so proud when she graduated medical school. They looked on as she received her diploma with glassy eyes and thought, "She's going to change the world!"

Her chair squeaks lightly as she sits down. She flips through a manila folder and plucks a pen from her immaculate desk. Her papers are organized. A laptop faces her. Everything has a place.

She threads her fingers together and flashes me her million-dollar smile. "How are you, Naomi?"

It would be so easy to judge her if she did something to make me suspicious. Dr. Woods always wore a white lab coat. Never a wrinkle, and always buttoned. It was so formal and stiff that it instantly put a wall between us. He was the doctor and I was the fucked-up patient. But Dr. Rutledge doesn't wear a white lab coat. She's dressed in navy-blue slacks and a cream-colored sweater. I can smell her perfume. It smells good. Something I would spritz on my wrist if I weren't in a loony bin.

"I'm okay."

She smiles again. It's starting to make me nervous. Dr. Woods never smiled this much.

"How did you sleep?" she asks.

"Okay."

Her happy demeanor remains as she asks me a question that no one's ever bothered to ask me.

"Why do you think you're here?"

"What?"

"Why do you think you're here?" she repeats.

My gaze shoots to the ground. The silence becomes awkward. "I don't know," I finally say.

She nods and writes on the paper in front of her.

"Have you talked to anyone here?"

"Not really."

"Why not?"

When I first arrived at Fairfax, Dr. Woods tried to get me to open up. But I didn't trust him. His approach was clinical and his voice was void of emotion.

I tell Dr. Rutledge the truth. "I didn't trust the doctor."

Both eyebrows lift. "Why is that?"

I shrug. "Because he doesn't care what happens to me."

This is the first time I've ever said that out loud. It feels good. Dr. Rutledge doesn't try to change my mind.

She continues to write on her notepad. "Do you think he won't believe you?"

I smile knowingly and respond quickly. "No, I know he won't believe me."

"Does anyone support you?"

I used to have one person on my side that made all the struggles bearable, but Lachlan has stopped believing in me. I wonder how much time I have before I stop believing in myself.

"No one does," I reply, my voice threatening to give out on me.

"How does that make you feel?"

"How would *anyone* feel knowing that no one is on their side?" I counter. "It feels like shit."

She nods and smiles, seeming perfectly fine with my short but honest answers. "Understandable. If it were me, I'd be angry too."

I look at her from beneath my lashes, trying to decide if she's buttering me up or if she's being truthful. I see nothing but honesty in her expression. And then the tears start to pool in my eyes. I shrug and keep my gaze on the ground. My vision starts to turn blurry and I'm seconds away from crying.

Silly. Stupid. Childish. I can call it whatever I like, but I can't keep the tears from forming. I answer her because it beats sobbing like a head case. "I'm not angry. I'm just . . . beat down."

"Why?"

"I know what happened is the truth," I say. "But it doesn't make sense. Even to me. And if I'm confused, how can I expect everyone else to believe me? I just—" Abruptly, I close my mouth.

Stop right there, I tell myself.

I'm getting carried away.

Dr. Rutledge doesn't push me. "Naomi, I've read your files." She looks me in the eyes and says slowly, "I just want to help you."

I've never seen what's inside "the files," but I imagine it's a whole clusterfuck of lies.

"That's not who I am."

Dr. Rutledge tilts her head to the side. "What isn't?"

"What's written here." I tap the manila folder sitting on her desk. "That's not me. That is someone else's take on what happened. Not mine."

"Tell me your story, then."

"You're just going to judge," I say.

"Not if you give me a chance."

I lean back in my chair and cross my arms. "No."

"Why not?"

"Call me crazy, but maybe I'm reluctant to open up about my life to a complete stranger."

"I'm not here to judge you," she says. "I just want you to tell me what you know. Tell me what brought you here so I can get you back into the world."

Overly perky or not, there's something soothing about this woman. Something inviting. As though I can tell my darkest, most fucked-up secret and she'll accept it without blinking an eye.

In opening my mouth, I'm placing my trust in her. Trust that she'll accept my words and believe that what I'm telling her is my life. She acts as if her request is the simplest thing in the world. To me it's like she's asking me to cut a vein open and bleed out for her.

"The Naomi I know would have never just given up so quickly. She would have fought to stay in the present."

Damn you, Lachlan Halstead.

I can just see him sitting next to me with his honest eyes. I could always see everything in his eyes. His frustration, laughter, happiness, anger. He never hid anything. It was the one thing that always drew me to him. Right now, it's killing me, though. I see his face and I hear his words when I just want to ignore them.

She looks down at her papers. "Tell me about Max and Lana."

I wish the sound of their names didn't affect me. In a perfect world, their names would just roll off my shoulders and I would calmly tell Dr. Rutledge that I'd never heard of them. She would look at me dubiously and I would tell her that I had no idea who those people were. She must have the wrong file.

But the world is far from perfect.

The reality is that the minute I hear their names, the air slowly leaves my lungs. My heart pounds, until it feels like it's going to burst out of my chest.

"No," I say harshly. "No. I can't."

Dr. Rutledge lifts a brow. "Why not?"

"Because." I look down at my sweats and pick at invisible lint.

Her office has been quiet the entire time I've been here. But a static noise reaches my ears. It's loud and makes me shriek. It sounds like a radio not quite in tune. And then I hear a voice behind me.

"Naomi." The hairs on my arm rise. "No one will believe you." The voice becomes louder, powerful, darker.

Paranoia makes me turn in my seat. Nothing is there, at least in the physical sense. But I feel something. The presence is so ominous, it feels like it's only a matter of seconds until the bowels of hell reach up and swallow me whole.

I remember the girl I saw in the hallway. Her eyes flash through my mind. *"How the hell am I still here?"*

I don't want to get to that point. I know I'm close. Darkness is ready to pull me under.

"Naomi? Are you okay?"

I look up at Dr. Rutledge, but I hear Lachlan's voice.

"The Naomi I know would have never just given up so quickly. She would have fought to stay in the present."

And then Max's.

"If you love me, then don't give up."

Their words mesh together. Their voices become one. And it becomes a small piece of hope for me.

I give her a blunt nod. My body is shaking.

"I'll tell you."

She sits there calmly, waiting for me to tell my story. But before I say a word, I hold her gaze. *Pay attention,* I say with my eyes. *Listen closely. Hang on to every word. But most of all, please believe me.*

3

WHITE LIGHTS

SIX MONTHS AGO, IN THE SUMMER HEAT, SURROUNDED BY laughter and people that I've known my whole life, everything changed. The sun was setting. Colors of burnt gold, orange, and blue painted the sky. Champagne flutes tapped together. A gentle breeze cooled my warm skin. Paper lanterns were strung inside the white tent. Everything felt normal and serene.

I was so sure. So confident. You see, I thought I could control my life. I thought I had the power to make my own decisions. Good or bad. It didn't matter as long as they were mine.

The reality was that all the power I thought I possessed was never mine to begin with. It was destiny's. It was all around me—walking me down the path it saw fit.

The breeze that was a reprieve from the summer heat? It caressed my skin, but it guided me forward. It encouraged me to put one foot in front of the other.

And those beautiful white lights? They were thousands of stars pulled down from the sky. They twinkled bright. They lured me in.

That beautiful sunset? It was a prelude to that night. The colors blended together, making people stop in their tracks and stare. They held their breath, watching the transition. The ending of the day was the ending of a powerful song, one that filled you up with anticipation because all the mistakes you made in the blazing light of day were erased. And the night was just beginning.

But I didn't look long enough. I skimmed over everything with approval. "This is beautiful," I said to my best friend, Lana.

She nodded and toyed with the fabric of her dress. She was the reason I was here. She was the only reason I would willingly come back home during my summer break.

"Come on." I closed my eyes and dramatically breathed in the air. "A perfect summer night. A perfect summer party."

"It's the worst, isn't it?"

"Every party is the worst for you," I said.

She didn't put up an argument. There was shy and then there was Lana. She was her own unique person, who reserved her true self to a select few.

Lana's shoulder touched mine. Her voice lowered as she looked at the people in front of us, calmly waiting to get into the tent. "It's the people here. All that matters to them is their money, their expensive clothes, their Beamers, Mercedes, and Jaguars. It's ridiculous. *They're* ridiculous. It's . . ."

"The same as it's always been," I finished for her.

We rubbed shoulders with people that we had known our entire lives. They finished every sentence with "my dear." Flashed their perfectly straight and whitened teeth. They were members of Congress, diplomats, and successful entrepreneurs. They all had exorbitant amounts of money and multiple mansions in numerous locations. Every possession they owned was a symbol of their wealth.

Welcome to McLean, Virginia.

"Thanks for coming with me," she said.

"Anytime." I looped my arm through hers and took one step. Then another. "How long do you want to stay?" I asked.

"Just fifteen minutes. That should be long enough to make my parents happy."

"I can do fifteen," I said casually. "And a business associate of your dad's is hosting this event?"

"Yes," she confirmed.

I thought back to our conversation in the car, trying to remember his name. "Maximilian?"

"Everyone calls him Max," Lana replied.

I turned to her. The line was slowly moving forward. "Have you met him before?"

"Nope."

"So he could be some fat old, bald dude that cops a feel when he hugs?"

"Or he could be some young, gorgeous guy," she suggested.

I snorted. "Definitely not."

We didn't get a chance to talk more about this Max. The line was moving at a quick pace, and when we entered the white tent, the two of us stared at the people around us. I saw smiles. Heard laughter. I felt the happiness around me. Lana saw an area jam-packed with people. She heard voices that made anxiety slowly creep up on her. She felt the beginnings of a panic attack.

"Hey." I nudged her shoulder and gave her a reassuring smile. "Just fifteen minutes. That's it."

She nodded. Her face was pale. But she took a deep breath and stepped forward with me. Our lips pulled up into friendly smiles. We made our way around the tent. We made artificial conversation. Saying "hi" to this person, and "good to see you" to that one.

Out of the corner of my eye, I saw Lana's parents, Michael and Constance. Her dad was one of the U.S. senators from Virginia. I remember the countless rallies that Lana would endure during her dad's election. She would stand there stiffly while her mom beamed at the crowd, soaking in all their attention. Even now, her mom had a brilliant smile on her face. I waved at them. They nodded our way and smiled in approval, satisfied that Lana was here.

Tonight, I represented my own family. My parents were successful in their own right, yet not on the scale of Lana's family. They were away for the summer, touring Europe. One week would be spent in Italy, the next in the Bavarian Alps, then off to Prague. I was staying with Lana for the entire summer.

I grabbed champagne from a waiter passing by and held it away from my body, knowing that within seconds, someone would accidentally bump into me and I'd spill it on my dress.

The tent was filled to capacity, yet they were still letting people in. I weaved in and out of the crowd, trying to find a single spot that would give me a few inches of space to myself. There was none. I opened my mouth to say something to Lana, but she wasn't next to me. I turned in a circle, standing on my tiptoes to find her, but it was useless. The crowd had broken us apart.

"Naomi!" someone called out.

I turned around.

The man walking toward me was Patrick, a friend of my parents. He was bald, with gray hair growing out on the sides. Like most people there he was filthy rich, which gave him power.

But he had ruddy cheeks and a big smile on his face, and that made him approachable.

"Hello."

"Have you met the host of tonight's party?" he asked.

"No, I haven't."

"We need to change that!" Patrick turned in a full circle, on the prowl for Max. Finally he gave up, cupped a hand around his mouth, and shouted out for the host. Most of the people around us stopped talking long enough to glare at him. Patrick was oblivious and sipped his drink. "That boy . . . he's something else."

Anyone younger than thirty was dubbed "that boy" by Patrick, so this Max couldn't be too old. But as curious as I was to meet this mystery host, I had to find Lana. She was the only reason I was there. "You know, I don't have to meet him," I said. "I'm looking for L—"

"Nonsense," Patrick interrupted. "It will only take a few minutes."

He continued to scan the crowd.

"He's my stockbroker now and it was the best damn decision I've made in years!" Patrick said absently. "I had my reservations . . . yes, I did. Why should I trust this boy to help me invest? But he's proved me wrong!"

Patrick laughed and finally looked at me.

I smiled politely.

I looked over my shoulder because that's all I planned on giving this Max. A passing glance, maybe a polite wave hello. That was all.

But that's not what happened.

What happened was that I looked once and never turned away. I don't even think I blinked.

There was nothing old about Max. Nothing at all.

He was tall, around six-foot-two. With that height I expected him to be lean, but his white oxford shirt molded against his shoulders. The sleeves were rolled up to his elbows, and I saw the bluish veins that traveled from his wrist up his strong forearms. His posture was relaxed, legs crossed, hands tucked into his black dress pants, as he listened to the man next to him.

I could tell you all about the features that made him textbook handsome. I could, but I hardly noticed them myself. All I noticed was the force of his confidence. It shone through his eyes, and his wide smile.

The longer I stood there, the more the room felt like it was closing in on me.

I stood on my tiptoes, peered around a shoulder, and took him in.

A pretty redhead leaned in close to him. He smiled at her and scanned the crowd. The whole time I had been staring at him he'd been completely unaware, but then he caught me. Instead of looking away, I boldly stared back.

His brow lifted and his lips curved up into a sexy smirk. He moved away from the table and took a step forward in my direction.

That's it. Come closer, I beckoned with my eyes.

That smile was for me. He looked right at me. Someone bumped into me, muttered "sorry," and I waved the person off, refusing to look away from Max. I felt possessed. I couldn't look away. Frissons of excitement flowed through me as he walked toward me. If I was feeling this way with him clear across the room, what would it be like standing only inches away from him?

"Come here, my boy," Patrick said.

I jumped and looked over at Patrick. I'd forgotten he was there. Actually, I'd forgotten about everything. Forgotten about the music and laughter and the roomful of people.

"Have you met Naomi?"

I met his gaze head-on. I knew I looked calm and in control, but past my dress, my flesh, directly behind my ribs, my heart was pounding like a drum.

Just breathe, Naomi, I told myself. *He's just like every other male.*

"No," he said. There was a playful gleam in his eyes. "I haven't."

He held out his hand. He gave me an intimate smile that made me question if we'd met before. Goose bumps broke out. But I would have remembered that smile. I would have remembered this feeling. We hadn't met before.

"Nice to meet you," he said.

That. Voice.

It was deep, almost hypnotic. He had a southern drawl. He pronounced every word slowly. Just one simple word coming from his lips sounded forbidden.

He smiled at me. It was a slow smile that tugged at his lips and traveled all the way to his eyes. I felt every inch of that smile pierce my heart.

I shook his hand.

My blood was starting to hum. His grip tightened. I went to pull away, but he held on a few seconds longer. Our gazes held. I couldn't remember a time I'd ever been looked at like that. His eyes pierced me with one thorough look. I felt it go through my body.

I finally found my voice. "Likewise," I said.

This is where he asked me for my last name. And I gave it to him. He asked more questions and I answered. A moment later I left with Lana.

Mission accomplished.

Game over.

We all go on with our lives.

Except that never happened.

"Naomi," he said, and I knew I could get used to my name coming out of his mouth. "Naomi, are you having fun tonight?"

"Am I having fun?" I mused, and looked down at my empty glass. My hands were shaking. "Well, I was." The waiter came by. I swapped my empty glass for a new drink and smiled at Max. "Never mind. Everything is better now."

He crossed his arms and gave me a devastating smile.

Everyone's always told me that my smart mouth gets me into trouble, and they're probably right. But Max didn't seem to mind. In fact, it seemed to be the one thing that kept his eyes riveted on my face.

He took another step forward and tilted his head. "What do you think of the party?"

I took a step closer. "I don't think you should be asking me that."

"No?"

I shook my head and smiled. "Look over there." I pointed toward an overweight, balding man in the corner. Max turned and his shoulder grazed mine. We both watched the man lift his glass, toasting to his friends. They drank and their laughter rang out around the tent. "I think he's having enough fun for the entire crowd."

Max smirked.

I looked over my shoulder and found my next target. Lana's mom. "Take that beautiful lady." She was directly in front of him, but he leaned in and peered closely at her. His jaw brushed against my hair. I sucked in a sharp breath and continued to talk, like I wasn't feeling a thing. "She lives for these parties where she can be the center of attention. And she'll stand there, complaining to her friends that the maid didn't pick up her dry cleaning on time and the gardener didn't prune her rosebushes." On cue, the ladies around Lana's mom leaned in and patted her arm. "And now her friends are giving their condolences because there's nothing more tragic than unhealthy roses."

He looked down and smiled at me. There was a pull between us. Talking to him came naturally. It was just so easy.

"You think that's what they're talking about?"

"I know so," I said confidently.

"But you're not like them?"

Max moved in just a bit closer. He smelled amazing. I couldn't tell if it was cologne, body wash, or his own personal scent, *Eau de Max*. Either way, I wanted to bury my face in his neck.

I blinked away the image and processed his question, but I couldn't form a coherent answer. With him standing this close to me, I could see everything. His thick black lashes, the flecks of brown in his eyes, and the tiny scar below his right eye.

I wanted to keep looking at him, finding things that most people would never notice. But he stood there, eyebrows lifted, waiting for me to answer.

I raised the glass to my lips and took a drink. I needed all the liquid courage I could get. He followed the line of my jaw, the curve of my throat, like he was transfixed. There was no champagne left. I stared down at the empty glass. "Other than my questionable drinking habits, no, I'm not like the people here."

I lifted my eyes and prayed like hell that he found my comment funny. But he was staring at me with a thoughtful look on his face. A mixture of lust and fear. I couldn't really blame him.

How many times in your life do you experience this level of attraction?

I blinked, and the white lights strung above us blurred yellow. Conversations around us died down. A curtain closed around the two of us. We were in our own world.

His eyes traveled slowly across my body. I'd taken care to make sure I was dressed conservatively for tonight's party, but Max was quickly stripping me, making me feel like my pale pink, cap-sleeved dress was nonexistent. My blood went straight to my head.

I reached out and grabbed onto the nearest chair.

And then someone cleared his throat and we both realized that Patrick was still standing next to us.

All the noises that were drowned out before were now playing on the highest volume. A wave of voices drifted around me. Music played. Waiters moved in and out of the crowd. A person bumped into me.

Our moment was over.

"I should get back to my guests," he said slowly.

"You should."

He stayed rooted in place. And so did I.

He finally took a step back. "I'll see you soon."

There he went.

I found Lana a few minutes later. She was standing close to the bar with an anxious look on her face. When she saw me, her face lit up.

"There you are," she said with relief.

"I saw him."

Lana frowned. "Who?"

"The host. Max."

"Oh yeah?"

I nodded. My heart was still pounding. My head still spinning. "So what do you think of him?" she asked.

"He's something," I muttered.

Max was standing close enough for me to point out. He was talking to a guest, completely unaware that I was staring at him. I took advantage of the situation and nudged Lana.

"There he is," I said.

Lana looked in his direction. She blinked and then looked back at me. Maybe my feelings showed in my eyes. Maybe that's what made Lana's smile fade. "What about Lachlan?" she said.

My spine stiffened and the euphoria I'd felt seconds ago faded. It felt like my ears had popped and now everything was muffled.

"What *about* Lachlan?" I replied.

Lana was my best friend. She knew everything there was to know about me and she knew how strong my feelings for Lachlan ran.

"Why did you bring him up?" I never gave her a chance to answer. "He's not here," I said firmly. "So let's not talk about him."

Lana stared at me a moment longer before she nodded. "Okay."

She didn't push to know what had passed between Max and me. But if she did, she would have understood my reaction. She would have seen my fear. No guy had ever made me feel this way except for Lachlan Halstead.

I kept all the memories I had of Lachlan at bay, hoping that I was strong enough to hold them back long enough to leave the party.

The plan was to stay for fifteen minutes, but I couldn't seem to step out of the tent and walk away. So we stayed. We talked to her parents. I pasted a smile on my face. Danced for one song. And whenever Max was close by, my body came alive, blood roaring in my ears and my heart dancing in my chest.

The evening was coming to a close. Most everyone there had a slight buzz. I was one of them. But I couldn't tell if it was from Max or the champagne.

Max stepped onto the stage, where the musicians sat. He looked over the crowd and tapped his wineglass. Conversations dwindled. Every head turned in his direction.

He lifted his glass. Everyone did the same. Everyone but me. Mine was pressed against my chest.

"I'd like to thank everyone for coming . . ." What did he say after that? I don't know. I was watching everyone around me. They were all falling under his spell. Max pulled people in with his smile, his charm. He knew it was his strength and he used it to his advantage.

I swirled my drink, watching him, wanting to know just how much power he had to slide into this secret circle so quickly.

"I hope to see everyone very soon." His eyes made contact with mine. I felt a jolt go straight through my body. My first instinct was to retreat, like a wild animal encountering something dangerous.

But he looked away and gave the crowd his charming grin. "Now enjoy the rest of the night!"

Everyone murmured their agreement and drank their wine. But Max didn't drink to them. His eyes found mine and he tipped his wineglass in my direction.

A silent toast.

Get ready, that one tilt of his glass said. His lazy smile disappeared and his eyes became feverish the longer we looked at each other.

I mimicked his actions and tipped my glass.

I had no idea what I was in for.

4

GOING UNDER

OVER THE NEXT FEW DAYS, I SPENT THE MAJORITY OF MY TIME with Lana. I didn't see Max once. That wasn't to say I didn't have the want to see him. My heart and memory teamed up to taunt me. They haunted me with visions of his face and the way I felt that day. I was slowly starting to become impatient. I wanted to see him again. I wanted that feeling back and that scared me. So I was waiting until I could put a lid on this strong desire.

But today that was all about to change.

Lana and I were supposed to be going out for lunch. But she took a quick left and the next thing I knew we were in Tysons—a large business district close to McLean.

We sat there, parallel parked, on the side of the street. Lana drummed her fingers on her thigh nervously, staring out the window.

"Are we going to sit here forever and stare at the people walking by, or are we going to go eat?" I asked.

Lana reached back to grab some documents from the backseat. "I need to drop these off for my dad."

"You want me to do it?" I said.

I knew how she felt about crowds . . . about people in general. This wouldn't be the first time that Lana had to run errands and I took over for her. Plus, I was hungry, and the quicker we got out of here and to the nearest restaurant, the better.

I expected Lana to hand them over. But her grip tightened on the papers. "I don't think that's a good idea," she said.

She looked out the window, at the looming building next to us. I looked with her. While people walked quickly to their cars or into stores to get away from the heat, this building stood tall in the humid weather. Above the revolving doors, in black letters, was the company name, and I finally understood her hesitance.

I turned to face her. "Max works here?"

She nodded slowly.

"And you're concerned why?" I smiled. "Lana, I've met the guy once. That's it. There's nothing to be worried about."

"But . . . Lachlan. You haven't talked to him in days."

I threw my hands up in the air. "Why are you suddenly bringing him up? You hardly talk about Lachlan. In fact, I don't think you ever have up until a few days ago! There's nothing wrong with not talking to him," I replied.

Lana didn't look convinced, and I'm sure I wasn't doing a good job at keeping my emotions out of my eyes. Every time Lachlan's name was mentioned, I felt a deep pain slash through me.

"Just give me the documents," I said quietly. "I'll hand them over to his secretary or one of his co-workers or whoever the hell is here and be on my way."

Lana didn't say anything.

"Or *you* can deliver them," I suggested.

Lana placed the papers into my outstretched hand. Before I got out of the car, I looked at her one last time. She was staring out the window, her lips pressed into a thin line.

"It's not a big deal, okay?" I said. "Max is just one guy. That's it."

"Okay, okay."

I waited for her to smile. No one smiled like Lana. It transformed her face. She went from being somber and quiet to someone so beautiful it made you want to do a double take.

But she didn't smile at me.

I opened my door, knowing this conversation wasn't over. Not in the least.

"His office is on the seventh floor," Lana called out.

I gave her a thumbs-up and walked out into the blistering heat. If I stayed out here longer than five minutes I was liable to start melting. The heat made everything in the far distance blurry, almost pixilated. I'm surprised steam wasn't rising from the sidewalks.

Only a few steps away were the revolving doors. I couldn't stop staring at them and I couldn't stop my mind from conjuring up the image of Max.

I heard his silent toast echo in my ears: *Get ready.*

And even in this scalding heat, I shivered.

Taking a deep breath, I followed Lana's directions and crossed the main lobby. My flip-flops sounded against the black granite floors. I signed in, grabbed a visitor card, and went right to the elevator. I was surrounded by men in suits. They spoke quietly on their cell phones or to each other. I stared at my reflection in the elevator doors and knew that I stood out in my white short shorts and green racer-back tank.

The doors finally slid open. I pressed 7. My fingers drummed against my thigh as I watched the numbers flash above me. It was crazy, but I was starting to get nervous. Maybe this wasn't the best idea. Maybe Lana was right.

2, 3, 4 . . .

I took a deep shaky breath.

5, 6 . . .

My grip tightened on the papers.

7 . . .

The doors slid open to a typical office. Plush black chairs against the wall. Black-and-white pictures of high-rise buildings. Magazines on the end tables. Green plants placed throughout the space. Right in the middle of the room was the secretary's desk, with a pretty brunette behind it.

I put one foot in front of the other.

Get this done and get out of here, I said to myself.

The brunette looked up. She gave me a friendly smile. But she took in my dress code and her smile waned. I couldn't really blame her for judging. I looked at the name on the counter. Sophie Miller.

"May I help you?" she asked.

I lifted the stack of envelopes in my hand. "I need to drop these off."

"You can just hand them to me. I'll make sure he gets them."

"Thank you," I said.

Sophie grabbed a pen and notepad. "Who should I say this is from?"

I leaned on the counter and smiled. "I'm Starlight from the local strip club. Your boss has a running tab and I was just delivering his newest bill."

The pen dropped. Sophie's head shot up. Her mouth was hanging open. This was fun. Some of my anxiety began to fade.

And right when I was starting to relax, the door behind her opened. A man walked out. He wasn't Max.

I smiled.

I wanted to sigh with relief, but right behind the man was Max. My smile faded. My body started to tingle. He had on a white dress shirt, tucked into navy-blue dress pants. A striped tie, and a tailored vest showcased his wide shoulders. He crossed his arms and I saw the silver watch on his wrist.

My body felt leaden. My movements were slow. And it was all because of him. I gripped the counter. It didn't even matter that he wasn't looking my way. His magnetism fell off him in waves, pulling me under, drowning me slowly, making my lungs constrict with every breath.

Max had a focused look on his face as he talked. I knew he was in his element. He was a shrewd businessman. One who was intelligent enough to know when to shut up and listen, and when to speak.

My resistance, the little I had built up, was starting to fade. I had to get out of there fast. I attempted to get Sophie's attention. *Attempted* was the key word. She was fixated on Max.

I tried using my manners. In a polite voice, I said Sophie's name. She didn't look at me.

I tapped the counter. Still nothing. I glanced over at Max. He was wrapping up his conversation. My heart started to race. I felt like these were the final seconds I had before a bomb went off and exploded in my face.

"Hey." I snapped my fingers. "Sophie!"

She jerked her head back to me and gave me an impatient look. "Yes?"

I quickly rushed my words. "I need to be going. Can you just say that Naomi stopped by to drop these off for—?"

Max stopped mid-sentence. So I stopped mid-sentence.

His head turned in my direction. I silently cursed myself. He had been gesturing with his hands, but now they were frozen in the air. He blinked and looked at me as if I weren't real.

I wished that were the case. I wished I could snap my fingers and disappear that second.

His silence made the man next to him stop talking and stare at me. The man looked between Max and me, then excused himself.

"Naomi?"

How did he do that? How did he make my name sound so . . . sinful?

I cleared my throat. "That's my name."

He walked over to me. "How are you?"

I shrugged and gripped the envelopes tightly in my hand. "I'm all right."

He tucked his hands into his pockets and leaned against Sophie's desk. "Having a good summer?"

I stared down at the counter as I answered, trying to appear unaffected. "I am. Just been really busy. You know how it is."

"Ah, of course. Busy," he repeated.

My eyes lifted and were caught by his gaze.

"Yeah, just visiting friends and running errands. I figured I'd make the most of my time while I'm here."

That was a lie. If Lana hadn't woken me up this morning, I would have slept until noon and sat around watching reruns of reality shows with a plate of brownies on my lap.

"How long are you home?" he asked.

"Until September."

Maybe it was my eyes, or my mind playing tricks on me, but I swear he was slowly inching closer to me. Or maybe I was inching closer to him. Either way, the space between us was slowly starting to disappear.

I looked down at my hands. I was gripping the papers so tightly that in a few minutes they would be wadded up in a ball. My mind kicked back into gear. I shoved the envelopes at him.

"I'm just dropping these off." Max looked at the envelopes and back at me. "For Michael," I said dumbly.

He said nothing. Just smirked and reached out his hand.

If this were a movie, I would press pause at this part. And I would point to my hand on the screen. I would show you how I made sure to grip the very edge of the papers. How I went out of my way to make sure we didn't touch. Then I would press play, and when I did, you would see his fingers grazing the back of my hand and me standing there frozen solid. And if you listened very carefully, you would hear the sound of a faint tear. That was just the sound of my heart unraveling like a torn ribbon.

All from one touch.

"Thank you," he said.

I took a step back. "I'm gonna go. Sorry for interrupting."

"You're not interrupting." He held up a finger. "Just wait."

He looked back at Sophie and told her she could take lunch early. She grabbed her stuff. When she passed me she looked me up and down curiously. I wanted to tell her to stay. I was even willing to go as far as to tell her I was sorry for being a smart-ass earlier. I was that desperate.

But she left. The door clicked shut.

There were no noises. Phones had stopped ringing. Printers and fax machines were silent. No voices or laughter. Not even footsteps. Nothing. Just the two of us.

This time it wasn't really in my mind. This time, we really were in our own world.

"What was that?" Max said.

"What was what?"

"The look my secretary gave you." He opened up the paperwork as he talked to me. I watched his hands. Long, tapered fingers. Bluish veins traveled up his arms. A vision of those hands wrapped around my waist, pressing into my skin, guiding me closer to his hard body, flashed through my head. It was gone in an instant. But my gut twisted and that greed I had for him intensified by a million.

"Did I miss something?" he asked.

"Oh, it was nothing," I said evasively.

He lifted a brow. I changed the subject.

"So," I drew out slowly, trying to think of a new topic.

Max leaned on the counter. "No, no, don't try to change the subject. What happened between you and my secretary?"

He was persistent. Why was I so surprised?

"I might have introduced myself in a not-so-professional way," I said.

He turned his body toward me. It was a simple shift, but it made all the difference in the world. One step forward and I would be able to smell him. One step forward and I could actually make my vision a reality. One step forward—

"Which way did you introduce yourself?"

My body jerked back.

This time I didn't dodge his question. "I may or may not have told your secretary my name was Starlight and that I was from a local strip club, here to drop off your running tab at the club."

I expected him to be pissed off. But his eyes merely widened and he laughed. A deep laugh that came from his belly. For a reason I'd never figure out, I smiled at him. I smiled and stayed in place when I should have been waving at him over my shoulder as I walked to the elevators.

Max slid closer. My smile faded. Here he was. Nothing stood in between us. I could yank him by the tie. I could kiss him. I could make my dreams a reality and have his body pressed against mine within seconds.

I did none of that.

Sunlight gleamed across the counter. It warmed my skin. Max's gaze remained steadfast. He made my skin burn like fire.

I backed away slowly. "I gotta go." I took another step before I pulled my eyes away from him. "It was nice seeing you." I was only a few steps away when I called out over my shoulder, "Tell your secretary I'm sorry about the whole Starlight thing."

"When you come back tomorrow and have lunch with me you can tell her."

I stopped. My blood roared in my ears.

He wasn't done.

"Better yet, let me take you to dinner Saturday."

My hand was inches away from the doorknob. I stared down at the metal before I squeezed my eyes shut.

I didn't want to like what he said. I wanted to feel nothing. But I felt everything. That terrified me. And rightly so. Anyone who has the power to open up your heart without you even knowing should terrify you.

"Naomi."

I turned. He leaned against the counter, looking so self-possessed that I was ready to claw my way out of the room if I needed to.

With agile ease, he pushed himself away from the counter, only to approach me slowly. "What's stopping you from saying yes?"

The electric spark between us. The one that becomes more powerful each time I see you. It makes me go from wanting to have your complete attention to wanting to be the center of your universe.

I said nothing.

Max tilted his head, staring at me, trying to figure out my answer.

"Just have dinner with me," he said.

"We'll see," I said.

"A simple yes or a no will do."

"We'll see," I repeated slowly.

Before he could say another word, I forcefully pushed the door open. And with my legs feeling like jelly, I walked toward the elevator.

Waiting for the elevator doors to part felt like years. I could see Max in the reflection of the stainless-steel doors. He was looking right at me. When the doors finally opened, I anxiously walked in and pressed L. Before the doors slid shut, I looked up, hoping he had walked away. But he was still in the same place, with the exact same focus he'd had on me minutes earlier.

The elevator started to move. My stomach dropped. I closed my eyes and sighed heavily.

The only thing I expected Max to stir in me was lust. It was a natural feeling. A chemical reaction. But he was making me go beyond that. Now I wanted to know his mind. The true Max. I wanted to know everything.

This was bad.

5

THE MARK

WEDNESDAY, THURSDAY, FRIDAY.

Sunlight reflecting off my Ray-Bans. Laughing with Lana. My hand outstretched, touching the wind, as I drove.

The days blurred together at warp speed as I played the part of a relaxed college student enjoying her summer. And I was doing a damn good job. No one knew that those three days were simply a grace period before I had to give Max an answer.

He never called. And it drove me crazy. I stared at my phone, waiting to see his number show up on my screen. I was fifteen again, pining away like a pathetic little puppy.

Saturday arrived.

I spent the morning avoiding my phone. After a shower, after I paced my bedroom for an hour, I called him.

He answered briskly.

"You wanted a yes or no answer from me . . ." I paused and stared out the window. "Do you still want that?"

"I do," he said slowly.

Hearing his voice instantly made my blood pump furiously throughout my body.

I exhaled, my breath shaky. "Then yes."

I could feel his wicked grin through the phone. "I'll pick you up at eight."

EVERYTHING I TOLD MYSELF I WOULDN'T DO WITH MAX, I DID. I said I wouldn't have dinner with him and I was sitting across from him in one of the nicest restaurants in McLean. I said I wouldn't put any effort into getting ready, but I dressed in a deep blue maxidress that had a V-cut in the front and left almost my entire back exposed. It was one of the sexiest dresses I owned. I said I wouldn't let him get a reaction out of me, but as we walked into the restaurant, goose bumps instantly prickled my skin when his hand settled on the bare skin of my lower back, making me regret this dress.

And now I was barely surviving, because of the looks that Max shot in my direction. When he looked at me, his eyes narrowed slightly, like he was trying to get a better focus on me. I leaned back in my chair. Feeling like I had been shot in the chest.

Bang.

I opened up to him in a way that seemed impossible. I told him about college, my dislike of exams and papers and the professors. And Max listened the whole time, his eyes never straying, his attention purely focused on me. It was thrilling.

Max took a drink of his water. He was leaning back with one arm draped over his chair. His gray dress shirt stretched across his chest and arms. I took a sip of my drink. I had already gone through three glasses of wine. Every time I looked over at him, my mouth suddenly became dry. I needed to find a better coping mechanism or my liver was going to shut down.

"So did you get your college experience?" he asked.

"I guess so."

"You guess so?"

I shrugged. "It was nothing like I expected."

"What did you expect?"

I thought over his question, chewed on my bottom lip. "More . . . freedom." His brows lifted and I quickly spoke up. "I don't know . . . I guess I just thought I would find myself. Sounds cliché, right?"

Max grinned, and my heart started to pound at an alarming rate. "Not at all. Everyone expects that, but hardly anyone really gets that."

"Did you change?"

"No. You see, I was good at studying but even better at having fun."

When I pictured him having fun I pictured his arm slung around a new girl each week and jealousy took root in my stomach, twisting its way up my body until I had to force away the image of College Max.

"If we had crossed paths in college . . ." I started out slowly, contemplating my words. "Would you have noticed me?"

"I would've noticed you then, just like I notice you now," he said in an intimate voice. His words slammed into me.

Max paused and braced his elbows on the table, looking like whatever he was about to say was going to take everything out of him. Right then was my cue to speak up. It was the perfect moment to tell him that I didn't need to hear anything. My lips parted, but nothing came out.

"Is there someone in your life?"

"There are a lot of people in my life." I pretended to mull over his question. "Yesterday I had lunch with a friend and after that I had to go get gas and I ended up talking to the cashier at 7-Eleven . . . I could keep going on and on," I said cheekily.

He smiled wickedly and leaned in closer. "What I meant was, are you dating someone right now?"

Lachlan barged into my mind abruptly. Without asking, without caring that I was trying so hard not to think about him. I shifted awkwardly in my seat. "Actually . . . there's someone from my childhood," I said quietly.

"Yeah?" he said. I couldn't figure out if I was seeing jealousy or intrigue in his eyes.

"It's a long story," I explained.

"I have all the time in the world," Max replied.

"Not for this story you don't."

I wasn't going to say any more. I didn't want to talk about Lachlan; I think that showed in my expression. Max asked for the check and the subject was quickly dropped. I breathed a sigh of relief.

We stood up from the table at the same time. I squeezed my clutch as he slipped on his jacket. As we walked toward the exit, I felt his palm settle against my back. His fingers spread against my bare skin. It was the exact same spot as before.

The valet parked his car in front of the restaurant. To everyone else, it was probably a warm summer night. But everyone else hadn't sat across from Max. They didn't have his eyes on them for minutes on end, making their skin feel like it was in flames.

I took a deep breath.

I slid into the passenger seat. The door shut. I was surrounded by the scent of Max's aftershave. I rubbed my hands against the goose bumps on my arms. They started to fade. When Max opened his door, they came back to life.

Before he put the car in drive, his fingers curved around the steering wheel and he thoughtfully stared at his hands with a tense expression, as if they had all the answers to his problems. When he finally turned to me, his eyes raked from my blond hair down to my legs.

"I can take you back to your house."

I waited for him to continue.

"Or . . ." he drew out.

Never had I ever been more relieved to hear that word.

"You can come home with me."

When he said those words, his voice lowered.

Max stayed silent. I stayed silent. The engine hummed. Car doors slammed. Conversations and laughter were heard. Everyone and everything in the world continued around us, completely oblivious that whatever I said next had the potential to change everything.

I could have lied and made up some bullshit story about having to be up early tomorrow. I could have told him that I didn't feel well. Or that I was really tired. But I didn't. I went with what felt right.

"Your house," I confirmed.

The entire drive to his house was tense. My heel tapped against the floorboard. I clutched my seat belt like it was a lifeline. Max asked questions and I gave him one-word answers. I didn't want to talk. All I could think about was what would happen when we arrived.

I wanted time to stop. I wanted to take a deep breath and calm my heart. But we were all too quickly turning into his driveway. Max cut the engine and glanced over at me. I was achingly aware of the heat coming from his body, of what he could give me.

He got out of the car. I stayed put. Seconds later he opened my door and ducked his head to look at me. The interior light slanted across his face, brightening his hazel eyes. I watched his gaze flick between my lips and eyes.

Lips. Eyes.

Lips. Eyes.

Finally, he settled on my lips.

"It's okay to get out," Max said slowly.

Was it really? Even when the words slipped out of his mouth he seemed unconvinced. What were we walking into?

My lips curled into a tense smile and I let him lead the way up the sidewalk. I'd barely given his house a passing glance the last time I was here. But tonight I took it all in. His house was a decent size. Not too big. Not too little. The exterior was nothing but brick. Spotlights placed behind the shrubs cast a yellow glow onto the windows. It was nothing like the exorbitant mansions around here. It surprised me, in a good way. We walked through the front door. The foyer was spacious, with minimal decor. It was so quiet. The sounds of our footsteps echoed loudly. It sounded unnatural. Every single click of my heels reminded me that I was alone with him.

"Home sweet home," I murmured underneath my breath.

Max was close enough to hear me, though. He looked over his shoulder at me and smiled. "You want a tour?"

"Sure." A tour was harmless.

His first stop was to the right. He turned on the lights. "This is my office."

Max walked over to his desk as if it were his first instinct. He took off his black blazer, dropped it onto his chair, and glanced down at the papers on the desk.

I leaned against the wall. "Not too shabby."

He smiled. "Glad it meets your approval."

I watched him as he moved papers around, his sharp brows knitted in concentration. His arms were braced on the desk and I wanted to walk closer, until I was caged in between him and the desk. I wanted all his focus on me.

On cue, Max glanced up at me and smirked. There was nothing playful in his gaze. His eyes pinned me to the wall and left me immobile. They dared me to walk forward and act out my thoughts.

It took me a second to gather my breath. My heart pounded in my ribs almost to the point of being painful. Finally, when I could move without shaking, I walked around the room, looking it over. A large mahogany desk stood in the middle of the room. The walls were painted a coffee brown. Two leather chairs faced the desk and the wall to the left was nothing but a floor-to-ceiling bookshelf. Opposite the bookshelf was a couch that looked like it was there more for show than anything else.

Max walked around the desk, only a few steps away from me. I tried not to fidget and take a step back.

"You ready to see the rest?" he asked.

The image of seeing his bedroom flashed through my head. I took a step back. Suddenly, a tour of the house didn't seem so harmless. "It's getting late. I should be getting home."

He advanced slowly. "It's only eleven. But if you want to go home, I can take you home."

I kept moving until my legs bumped into the couch. When no words came out of my mouth, he stepped closer, with one foot in between my legs, effectively caging me in.

"Do you want to go home?" he asked in that slow drawl.

I was short of breath.

"Naomi?"

My eyes were level with his chest. I had to tilt my head. Back, back, back it went until I connected with his eyes.

"What?"

"You never answered my question."

"I can't think," I mumbled. "You're invading my personal space."

Most people would have backed away, but Max leaned forward. His lips were so close. It was torture. Like dangling forbidden fruit in front of my face—I just wanted a single bite.

"Are you sure?" he said.

More than anything I wanted to close my eyes right that second and lean into him. In the back of my mind I knew that he had asked a question, but I couldn't think. His large frame loomed over me and made it impossible for me to see anything but him. His scent was wrapped around me, and all I could do was inhale.

"Still invading your personal space?"

My breasts were pressed against his chest. I felt his arousal against my thigh. His eyes became hooded and my breath escaped in short gasps.

When you're this close to another person, it's crazy what your eyes see first. I could have noticed the way his nose brushed against mine or how his lips were inches away. But all I saw was how the tendons in his neck were strained the longer we stayed apart. I watched as his pupils dilated. The black slowly spread, taking over his hazel irises. He was stopping this kiss from happening and that made me want it more.

Then his head tilted to the left, and his lips moved gently against my own. Like he was memorizing the curve of my lips, the way they tasted. He was going slowly. He was building me up.

I didn't have his patience. I pushed my tongue into his mouth. I raised my hands, intending to link them around his neck and pull him closer. But he intercepted my fingers and linked them with his own. Our palms touched. His grip tightened about the same time he increased the pressure of his lips. I sucked in a sharp breath.

And then Max pulled back. He blinked repeatedly. Our hands were still connected. That was all that kept us from completely touching. The silence was deafening. But it was the quiet that happens before a storm, before a strong gust of wind or a powerful lightning strike.

My mind pulled up the memory of the first time I saw him and the silent toast he gave me. *Get ready* echoed in my ears before Max pulled me to him with our linked hands. Everything after that turned ferocious. I came at him with an intensity that had been building up inside of me since the day I met him. My hands clawed at his shirt, trying to get him out of his clothes. He licked and sucked on my lips like I was the best thing he had ever tasted. I moaned into his mouth. I felt his knee wedged between my legs. It was then that I realized I was on the couch and he was looming above me. I was past the point of caring. Logic had disappeared the minute I stepped into that room. I was just desperate to keep his lips on mine.

I arched my back, trying to get closer.

Max's hands drifted from my waist to grip my arms tightly. Seconds later, he pushed me away. His chest heaved as he stared down at me with a frown. I panted and licked my lips.

He held my jaw in his hand and stared at me with panic. "Son of a *bitch*," he growled.

I wasn't alone. I knew that everything I felt, so did he.

So I pressed my palms against his shoulders and pushed him onto the couch. I kicked my heels off. I hiked my dress up. I climbed over him like I owned him. He didn't stop me. His eyes widened like he knew the balance of control was shifting out of his territory.

Just one more kiss. *One more touch and I'll be finished,* I thought to myself. And in my mind it made perfect sense to keep going—to curb my craving of Max.

One quick jerk was all it took and his shirt was out of his slacks. I didn't have enough patience to unbutton it. My fingers crept under the material with a mind of their own. I rose on my knees and with my lips still on his, I dragged my fingers up his stomach, memorizing every hard ridge.

"Shit," he hissed.

I smiled against his neck and pressed myself into him, completely aware of how tense his body was beneath me. He was ready to break. Ready to take me right here. The craziest thing out of all of this was that I wanted him to.

One more kiss? Was I delusional?

One kiss from Max and I became voracious.

Lip biting.

Bare skin touching.

Hands all over.

I wanted it all.

My tongue dragged down his throat and flicked against the skittering of his pulse. I pulled my hands from underneath his shirt and went straight for the buttons. I was ready to see what I was touching. He helped me. I anxiously parted his shirt and pushed him deeper into the sofa.

For a second, I looked down at him, taking in his impressive body. Without realizing it, I started to rub myself against him. Both of his hands wrapped around my hips. His fingers pressed deeper into my skin and his breathing increased as my hands traced every muscle.

I was ready to lick every single line and curve of his stomach. I lowered my head and lightly bit down on his pec. A groan tore from Max's throat.

"Naomi."

I closed my eyes as my name came from his mouth, making his chest vibrate against my ear.

"Do you want me to fuck you right here?" His voice was a deep rasp. Almost like he was in pain. "Because I'm seconds away from doing just that."

I lifted my head. Instead of answering him, my fingers grabbed his silk tie and used it to tug him closer. There were a billion ways to tell him no. I whispered into his mouth, "Yes."

A harsh sound tore from the back of his throat. All control was stolen from me in seconds. Max crushed our mouths together before he licked my lower lip, bit down and sucked it strongly enough to make my fingers dig into his shoulders in pain and pleasure. My fingers raked through his hair and I tugged on the strands, making him tilt his head back.

He responded by tugging down the straps of my dress with hard jerks, exposing my breasts. There was a pause. The two of us panting. My nipples tightened. The way I was sitting made them inches away from his face.

I watched in silent torture as his eyes stayed rooted on my chest. His nostrils flared before he cupped my breasts in both hands. "Fucking perfect," he growled.

I whimpered when he massaged them, pressed them together. Kissed the curve of one swell. He was killing me. Every noise I made seemed to spur him on.

He looked up at me. Our eyes locked. I saw the wild look in his eyes. Slowly, Max leaned forward and repeatedly flicked his tongue against my nipple. For a few minutes it was torture and complete pleasure as he went back and forth. And then his hands were everywhere at once. Pushing my dress down my stomach, brushing against my lace underwear with teasing strokes. He was hitting pleasure points at a rapid pace. I couldn't keep up, and not once did he give me a break to catch my breath.

Over and over he built me up with his hands, his lips. And I knew I was right there. So close to breaking apart.

And then his hands curled around my arms. He pushed me away, breathing harshly. I almost cried out. He flipped me over, looming above me.

Out of nowhere I heard Lachlan's voice in my head. I heard the words he said to me almost a year ago.

"I'm going to be here, waiting."

Suddenly, I felt like a traitor. A traitor against my heart. A traitor for kissing and feeling things for someone who wasn't Lachlan.

"Stop," I panted.

Max leaned back, frowning at me. I instantly jumped off the couch. I quickly fixed the straps of my dress. My hands wouldn't stop shaking. It took me three tries to cover myself and even then, I still felt naked.

Disbelief made my heart thunder in my chest.

How did it get out of control so quickly?

I turned back around. My answer was right in front of me. Max. He looked sexy, disheveled, and so completely tempting I almost took a step forward.

He was standing up now. His shirt was still unbuttoned and his tie was skewed, trailing down his naked chest. Every time he panted, his stomach muscles would clench, making my body react. His hair was in every direction.

"Why did you stop?" he panted.

I stumbled from the couch, toward the other side of the room. I didn't know how to answer him. Everything I said right now would be fueled by lust, my desire for him and what we almost did and what I still wanted to do.

"I-I just—" I fumbled through my words.

"Is everything okay?"

No, everything wasn't okay. The shadow of my first love wouldn't leave me alone. I didn't say the truth, though. Instead, I smiled and said, "Everything's fine. We were just . . . moving too fast."

"Moving too fast," he repeated.

I nodded and watched as he slipped off his tie and blindly tossed it at his desk. He buttoned his shirt back up and I wanted to tell him to stop.

He caught me staring. "You can't look at me like that."

"Like what?" I breathed.

"Like you want us to keep going."

I looked away and never answered him.

Max stopped in front of me. "You'll be here for the rest of the summer?" he asked.

I nodded and watched him with confusion.

Letting out a deep breath, Max dragged both hands through his hair and leveled me with a determined look. "I'm not letting you out of my sight."

"Because of what just happened?" I asked.

"Does that," he gestured toward the couch, "happen to you often?"

If *that* happened to me often, I would need a pacemaker. What just happened was almost soul-shaking.

"No," I finally admitted.

It was the answer he wanted. He nodded and swiped his keys from the desk before he stalked toward me. He stood in front of me and cupped my face. His eyes were still hard, with the same wild look that had been there when he kissed me.

"Give me the summer." His voice lowered into a sexy whisper. "While you're here, be with me."

"And that's it?" I challenged. "I'm free to do whatever after that?"

His jaw flexed. "Give me right now."

Both of us were avoiding what needed to be asked: would either of us be free after this summer?

I couldn't deny this raw hunger between us any more than he could, and I knew, deep down, that if I skipped this chance, I would regret it.

Maybe forever.

My answer was a simple nod. His head lowered. His lips touched mine gently. My body shook.

Fuck the truth. It was the heart that was my worst enemy. It was the one that was going to cut me. Bleed me. It would be the one to kill me.

6

IN THE DARK

MAX DROVE ME BACK TO LANA'S HOUSE. I WAS ON AUTOPILOT the entire ride. My mind kept rewinding back to the two of us on his couch.

When he dropped me off, I sat outside. For minutes? Hours? Beats me. I just stared at the clear black sky, hoping that I would forget about our kiss. That's the thing, though—logic made that impossible. Logic seemed to disappear in the moment I needed it the most, but reared its practical head when everything was said and done. And right now, it was showing me everything I did wrong.

What did you think, Naomi? That you could be alone with him and nothing would happen?

I rested my elbows on my knees and looked down at the brick steps.

Why did you tell him to take you to his house? Why?

Good question. Why hadn't I told him to just take me home?

I didn't have an answer. Nothing valid, at least. The only thing I had was excuses. It was those looks he gave me during dinner. Or when he put his hand on my lower back. It was an act of protectiveness and chivalry. Maybe it was when we changed positions and his body was beneath me? The power I felt in that moment made my skin tingle. I could get drunk from that much power. When my head was pressed against his chest, I heard the solid beat of his heart; his scent had engulfed me. I had stayed perfectly still, hoping that maybe if I pressed deep enough, his scent would sink underneath my skin.

It was all of those things wrapped into one. It built, and gathered speed, and catapulted us to that one kiss.

A kiss that changed everything.

I brushed my finger against my lower lip. I couldn't even call it a kiss. A kiss to me was two people's lips touching. Sometimes it's awkward. Sometimes it's sweet and innocent. Sometimes lust takes over.

But never does a kiss combust into something so powerful that even your heart feels it. Every touch, every moan, every breath becomes electrified.

Max felt it too. I was sure of it. He wasn't ready to admit the truth out loud. I couldn't blame him; we were both out of our league.

I closed my eyes, expecting Max to be the first thing I saw. But he wasn't. It was Lachlan. I groaned in anguish and rubbed my temples, trying to erase the image of him. *Not here. Not right now.* He wasn't supposed to ruin this for me.

Get out of my head. Get out. Get out. Get out.

My mind wanted to revert. It wanted to go back to all the memories of Lachlan and stay there. I couldn't let that happen.

The edges of my vision started to become hazy. I pushed away those memories as hard as I could.

I stood up. Talking to Lana would make things better. I would tell her everything that happened with Max. She would listen to me, like a good friend should, and would give me sound advice. I would ask her what she did tonight. She would tell me. Minutes later we would be on a totally different topic, far away from the realities of our worlds.

It was pitch black outside but there were spotlights hidden behind the trimmed shrubs, shining onto the house. Lana's family's home was an antebellum mansion that had been in the family for centuries. Lana came from old money and it showed. Behind their house was a large red barn where the family's horses were. When Lana wanted to escape and get away from everything, she would go for a ride and clear her mind.

It made absolutely no sense to see her horse walking free. His hooves crunched on the gravel. He walked right past me. His ears were moving back and forth at a rapid pace. His nostrils were flared. Normally, he was a calm horse. One that took after his master. But his fear and restlessness were apparent.

Alarm bells started to ring in my head. Something wasn't right.

I looked over my shoulder at the barn. The door was cracked open. I didn't hear any noise. Everything appeared fine. But unease made the hairs on my arm stand up. Fear trickled through my body and I should have turned around and gone back to the safety of my home, but I walked forward.

Only a few steps away from the barn, I heard the noises. Something tipped over and crashed. I heard someone gasp or wheeze, and then a grunt. It was one of those moments where my mind was screaming for me to stop and not go any farther. But I couldn't *not* look. I peeked my head inside the barn and I saw Lana pinned against the wooden beam. A large forearm was pressed against her throat, cutting her off from speaking, crying out, or even breathing. Her pants and underwear were around her knees. Her blue jean jacket was open. I saw her shirt was torn at the collar.

All of my own problems disappeared and were replaced with terror. Complete, mind-numbing terror. This wasn't two people acting on lust—that complete obsession to be with each other.

There was nothing consensual about what I was seeing.

Lana's eyes were squeezed shut as the man grunted like an animal as he moved in and out of her. His free hand gripped her hip and it wasn't out of love. It was to keep her in place.

I was detached from my body. Watching myself frozen in place. What was I doing? MOVE! One foot in front of the other. How hard was that? But I couldn't. It was as if I were in quicksand and stuck in place, and slowly sinking as I watched the scene unfold.

I'd always assumed that in a moment of panic, I would react swiftly and rationally. I would use my brain. My emotions would shut down and I would draw from the adrenaline coursing through my body to get through it all.

I couldn't have been more wrong.

I glanced around frantically at the house. *I need to get my phone,* I thought to myself. No. I needed to run to the back door and get help. I couldn't settle on a single thing to do.

I closed my eyes. Tears streamed down my face. I went to cover my ears, to block out all the noises, but the sounds had stopped.

The silence was deafening. I was afraid to open my eyes. When I did, the man turned to face me.

It was her dad.

I couldn't breathe. My legs swayed as if the ground beneath me were giving away.

He didn't look my way. His shirt was loose. His pants were unzipped, showing his flaccid dick. I recoiled from that visual. God, I wished I knew how to use a gun. I would have aimed it right between his legs.

Lana was slumped against that wooden beam. Her pants were still around her ankles. He was breathing heavily while Lana kept her gaze on the ground. He leaned down and his knees made a popping noise. Out of everything I saw that night, I flinched at that action.

He laughed, and it was filled with so much hate and rage. "You know I'm the only fucking person that truly loves you, right?" he said.

Lana stayed silent. He jerked her hair tightly by the root, until she was looking at him. She stared at him with rigid composure. Her eyes were void and I realized, in that moment, that she was used to this treatment.

His voice rose as he stared down at her. "Right?" He tugged, and her skull hit the beam.

"You're right," Lana croaked. She cleared her throat and started over. "You're right. You're right. I know. I'll be good," she whispered like a little girl.

He nodded once before he zipped his pants up and walked toward the open door.

I panicked. Fear made me turn and move on shaky legs. Fear made my heart speed up until I was panting for breath. I ran around the corner of the barn. My back rested against the wood. My hands were placed on my bent knees. I felt like I was seconds away from losing my dinner.

Gravel crunched loudly, and I held my breath, straining to hear his movements. Finally, I heard the screen door shut. I waited until it finally felt safe to move before I ran back to the barn. Lana was still sitting, but now her jeans were buttoned up.

She clutched her jacket together with one hand and rested her forehead against her knee. Her entire body shook violently before she leaned sideways and threw up. The sounds coming from her made me cringe. When there was nothing left in her stomach, she sat up and wiped her mouth with the back of her hand.

I stepped into the entryway. "Lana?"

Her head shot up and the pole light right outside the door brought light inside the dark barn, enough that I could see the wet streaks on her cheeks.

I walked closer and she stood, albeit on shaky legs, and turned to stare at an empty horse stall.

"Are you okay?" I whispered.

The look on her face and the hunch of her shoulders made me want to run forward and hold on to her as tightly as I could.

She wiped her cheeks and gave me a shaky smile. "Yeah. I'm fine."

Like a dummy, I stood there, staring at her blankly. Were we going to pretend that everything was okay? I turned back toward the house, making sure no one was watching us. I kneeled beside her.

"Lana, I saw everything," I whispered.

A loud hiccup was her only reaction.

I repeated myself. This time, with heavy emphasis.

A painful groan tore from her throat, and it seemed like years went by before she slowly nodded. It was her only acknowledgment of the situation.

"We need to get you to the hospital," I said.

"No!" she rushed out.

"What do you mean, no?"

Stubbornly, she shook her head. "I'm not going."

"Why not?"

"It's not going to change a thing."

"Yes, it will! It will never happen again."

"But it will," she said very quietly.

She finally looked at me. I saw her fear and I saw the humiliation.

I had so many questions. *How long has this been going on? Does your mom know? Why didn't you tell me?*

And I had to keep them all to myself; Lana could barely breathe, let alone talk.

I stood up. I dragged all ten fingers through my hair in frustration and paced back and forth.

Processing everything was like swallowing glass. Painful. So painful.

I turned, and my words burst from my chest like a bullet releasing from the chamber. "He's your dad," I said brokenly.

My knees gave out. I sat next to Lana. My shoulder touched hers. I could feel her pain as if it were my own. And it was so heavy and so consuming that a sob tore from my throat. Lana was crying into her hands. I felt useless, like I couldn't do a damn thing to ease her pain.

She continued to cry and I turned my head to stare at her family's beautiful house. My teeth were grinding together and my eyes narrowed. *Not a damn thing?* logic whispered. *Fight for her. Fight, since no one else will.*

7

SHUT YOUR EYES

MY SESSION WITH DR. RUTLEDGE BACKFIRED. IT WAS ALL MY fault. I knew better than to give her a small piece of the story; she can walk away from everything I tell her, but I live with it every day.

I'm sitting on my bed. My shoulder blades graze the wall. My fingers wrap around my legs. My toes curl into the sheets. I rock back and forth, trying to breathe calmly, but it comes out convulsive.

I need to sleep, but I can't.

Light faded hours ago. The moon is barely out, but there's enough light to cast a purple hue into my room. I see the shadow of the naked tree limbs on my floor. They sway in the sky, back and forth. I see that frozen icicle. Still solid. Still hanging on. And I try to remind myself that I can hang on too.

But my resolve slips. My eyes drift to the corner of the room.

And I see the man sitting there, watching me with cold, unblinking eyes. It's Lana's dad. He looks like he wants to tear me apart.

I hear his voice. It's gritty. It's harsh. It makes my blood freeze in my veins.

"Are you afraid of me?" he asks.

Sweat beads on my upper lip as I stare down at my legs.

Don't you speak to him. Don't you dare, I tell myself.

I look up.

He crouches down. I hear his joints pop from the movement. It sounds like thunder. It ricochets in my skull until I grip the sides of my head in pain to make it stop.

He's the one that speaks to me. He's the one that terrifies me. He's the very core of my nightmares.

"You're nothing. You know that, right? That bitch of a doctor sees through your lies. When she gives up on you, who will be with you after that?" His voice rises. "No one! No one but me!"

His words are like acid. They burn my soul. Dissolve my hope. They open up old wounds and make them bleed. I scream in agony. I scream at the top of my lungs to block out his voice. But he rises to my challenge, and now he's screaming too.

Fingernails dig into my scalp. I smell the metallic scent of my blood and keep pressing harder and harder.

Mary runs into my room. I keep screaming, but I watch as she looks at me and turns in a circle, looking around the room. She won't see him. And I knew she wouldn't. He won't reveal himself to her.

He stops yelling. I stop yelling. His lips kick up in a grin. He holds a finger to his lips and shakes his head.

I drop my head onto my knees and start to whimper.

"Naomi," Mary huffs. She yanks my hands away from my ears. "What's wrong?"

She bends down with an expectant look on her face. I blink once. Twice.

"I-I need something to make me sleep," I stutter.

Mary drops my wrists like they're poison. "I've already given you your medication."

She encourages me to lie down, but I stay upright.

"It's not working," I say impatiently. "I need more."

"I can't give you more."

She gently tries to lay me back down on the bed, but I resist.

"Why not? I need it." Tiny pricks of pain start to form behind my eyes the longer I stare at Mary. My hand shoots out. I hold onto her arm tightly. "I need to sleep. I need to—"

I need to forget. I need one minute of the day where I don't feel mind-numbing terror.

She wrenches her arm free and walks backwards to the door. "Naomi, I can't go above Dr. Rutledge's head. She prescribes your medication and dosages."

"That's a fucking joke!" I yell.

"Talk to Dr. Rutledge about it tomorrow."

"I can't wait until tomorrow!" Mary looks away and I plead. "Please, Mary."

For a second, I see a glimmer of sympathy in her eyes. Only a second.

"You'll sleep just fine," she says before she walks to the door. It shuts with a firm click.

Mary thinks she's keeping me safe by shutting the door, that exhaustion will take over and I'll go to sleep. But she just locked me inside with the devil.

I'm in hell.

I'm in hell.

AFTER MARY LEAVES, I TURN INTO THE HEAD CASE SHE THINKS I am. I pound on the door. I kick. I shout. I go to my desk and pick up the chair and throw it at the door.

And the whole time, he watches me in the corner with a knowing smile. He picks up on my fear. That's what attracts him. I'm giving him everything he wants: control and power. Every time I whimper, or lurch back in fear, he feeds off of it. His body becomes stronger, his voice becomes louder, and this mental hold he has on me becomes more painful. Gut-wrenching, drop-to-the-ground-in-agony painful.

If I had more strength in me I would do the controlling. I would tell him to stay the hell away from me. I would tell him that he doesn't scare me.

I know that will never happen.

My fingers curve around the edges of the desk. The door slams open. I look up and watch Mary's reflection in the window. She turns on the light and my eyes squint, trying to adjust. My gaze moves to the figure still in the corner, still watching. Two nurses follow Mary into the room. They try to hold me down. Every muscle in my body strains against the hands holding me down on the bed. I bend and contort my body in every angle. I bite the male nurse's forearm for holding my shoulders against the mattress. I kick at the female holding my legs down. I don't want them touching me.

Then the on-call doctor comes in. I see the syringe in his hand and stop straining. There it is. My relief. My lungs expand and I suck up all the air I can. Soon, it's all going to be okay. I'll be able to rest without seeing *him*.

"Naomi, Naomi," Lana's dad tsks in the corner. "That's only temporary safety. I'll always be here waiting."

I ignore him and focus on the syringe. My sleeve is shoved up all the way to my biceps. I feel the doctor search for a vein and try not to jerk away from him. He finds a vein and that sharp prick of pain is worth it. I'm on the road to relief. Just a few more minutes and I'll be there.

Keep your eyes closed. He's not there if you can't see him, says the voice in my head.

"I'll still be here watching you," he says in a cold voice that borders on sadistic.

None of the people hovering around me react to his evil voice. Only I do. I'm starting to care less and less. The drug is doing its job. Very, very slowly. But I think it slowly pulls you under on purpose. So you, and only you, can remember the feeling.

I look at the light on the ceiling. It morphs into a kaleidoscope of white fragments. They turn into orbs that separate and break open into a million pieces. I watch them multiply and it's a beautiful sight. Somehow, I pull my eyes away from the display and look at the faces around me. The female nurse that held my legs is now standing by my side. Her face is blurring in and out. She strokes my hair and says in a gentle voice, "Just relax."

I nod. Or try to.

Just relax, just relax, I repeat to myself.

After the doctor and nurses leave, there is nothing but the sound of my own breathing. I place a hand over my racing heart and roll over on my side. The drug is swimming through my veins, taking me over. My muscles relax. My bones start to feel weightless.

I'm light as a feather.

I let go and leave my body.

I'm an apparition.

My skin is translucent. I feel clean. My mind is at peace. I stand up from the bed and look around at the small room. I feel like I'm on a stage. I look down at my surroundings before I look down at the ugly truth—my broken self.

I can't believe this is me. Dull hair. Pale skin. Legs tucked close to my chest. Arms wrapped around my knees.

I start to ache. It starts out slow, but it gradually spreads. I look at my translucent skin and a body starts to take shape. I start to feel heavy. I panic.

I step away from the bed. I keep moving until I'm off the stage. Until I'm on the opposite side of the room, hoping that I can stay in this escape a little while longer.

It's too late, though.

When I open my eyes, I'm staring at the white wall. I'm back in my body. This broken, weak body.

A feeling of security surrounds me. And then I smell the scent of pine. Seconds later, an arm wraps around my stomach. Lachlan.

"Shut your eyes," he whispers against my neck. "You can control your mind."

My heart beats in a staccato manner before it slows down. *Lach-lan. Lach-lan,* it beats.

His arm tightens against me as if he can hear the tune.

"I'll tell you a story." His hand reaches up and moves my hair to the side. "You want me to tell you a story, kid?" he asks.

Not once do I turn around. I don't want to look over my shoulder and see nothing but wrinkled sheets. I don't want this to all be in my mind. So I nod and listen to the deep timbre of his voice. So sure. So calm. Every word feels like a caress—a gentle reassurance that I just might be okay.

Before the blackness pulls me under I hear Lachlan whisper, "Ten years ago you were brave. Ten years ago you took what you wanted. Ten years ago started the beginning of us . . ."

8

IDENTITY

10 YEARS AGO

Tonight my dad yelled about fireworks.

He slammed his hand on the table as we ate dinner and yelled, "That damn Halstead boy was shooting rockets, sparklers, fireworks, and God knows what else, till four in the fucking morning! I should've called the police."

They were beautiful. But I would never say that out loud. I sat there quietly and watched my dad rage for an hour before I asked if I could be excused.

I went to my room, turned off my lights, and stared out the window. I was trying to get a better view of my neighbors' house. The neighbors I was taught to hate.

The Halsteads moved next door four years ago. And throughout the last four years, my dad would rant about them every chance he got. *"Damn the Halstead family. I could have bought the land their house is on . . ."* And on and on it went. It would always start out as a grumble, but his voice would become louder, stronger. His eyes became darker.

It scared me. I didn't understand his hate. They seemed okay to me. I had met only Mr. Halstead, and that was with my body hiding behind my nanny as she talked to him and their gardener. Mr. Halstead was this large man who seemed to be as tall as the sky. He wore a hat that covered his head, but I could see his eyes. They were kind eyes. He smiled at me. Told me to call him Jeremiah. I was too nervous to answer.

That was also the first time I saw Lachlan. He was directly behind his dad, playing with his friends in a tree house. They were being silly, climbing and dangling on branches. I watched Lachlan walk across a tree limb with a mixture of jealousy and awe.

I knew I was supposed to obey the rules. I knew I was supposed to dislike the Halsteads because my dad disliked them. But I couldn't.

Last year, on the Fourth of July, they set off fireworks. They woke me up. Scared me. But when I ran to the window and saw all the pretty colors and lights, I couldn't erase the smile on my face. Even with the large field between us, I swear I heard cheers and hollers from their house.

Later on the next day, I told my mom I'd seen the fireworks. She nodded and turned the page of her magazine. "That's nice, Naomi."

"I wish my birthday was on the Fourth of July," I admitted. "Then those fireworks would be for me. It would be Naomi Day. A national holiday."

My honesty earned a sharp look from her. She pursed her red lips. "Don't be ridiculous. Your birthday is your birthday."

I realized that she was right. July 19 was my birthday.

No national holiday.

No Naomi Day.

Just my birthday. I celebrated my ninth birthday with no fireworks.

But turning ten was a big deal. And instead of presents and a birthday cake with candles to blow out, the only thing I wanted was bright lights. I wanted to see them light up the sky and make everything seem brilliant. I wanted to hear more cheers and hollers, and I would pretend that they were for me.

Tonight, I wanted to be as bright and brilliant as those fireworks. I wanted to be alive. I was going to do something I had thought about for the last few months.

I was waiting until my parents went to bed and then I would escape from my room. The wait was torture. I stayed up past my bedtime and kept myself busy by watching the clock every five minutes. When the time finally came, I quietly opened my door and tiptoed downstairs. Adrenaline coursed through my veins. Fear was there too. But excitement trumped my fears and made my hands shake with anticipation.

I shut the patio doors behind me and ran across the gravel, toward the barn, and quickly led my horse out of its stall. Rumor was a beautiful Arabian with a shiny chestnut coat and a calm temperament that made the two of us bond.

I stroked his neck and casually talked to him. "We're going on an adventure tonight, Rumor." His ears pricked. I smiled. "It's only to the neighbors'. I'm going up to this tree house that no one else uses. Someone should use it, right?" I asked.

We stopped next to a broken tree stump. I used it as a boost and quickly jumped onto my saddle.

A sigh escaped me as I looked around at the dark landscape. I felt like I was the only person that existed. The world was mine and mine only. I could go anywhere I wanted. The dark sky, with a smattering of stars, was my map.

I felt like an adventurer.

A thrill seeker.

I pushed down my excitement for a second and focused on quietly escaping the boundaries of my family's property. When I was a good distance away, I pressed my heels into Rumor's side. A second later we took off.

It was exhilarating. Strands escaped my braid and blocked my view, but that only made me laugh. Rumor's hooves thundered on the cold ground. *Ba da bum. Ba da bum. Ba da bum.* It was a beautiful sound.

Freedom.

All too quickly, I was on Halstead property. The house in front of me was similar to my own. Impossibly large, with enough space to fit a village inside.

I barely gave it a passing glance.

Easily, I jumped over the fence, and instead of cutting through the immaculate yard, I took the long route. My eyes were focused on that tree house the whole time.

I stopped at a tree a few steps away from the tree house and dropped down from the saddle, tying the reins around a sturdy branch. Before I stepped away I looked all around me, making sure the coast was clear.

All the lights were off in the house except for a television flashing in a second-floor room. It made me pause for a second before I accepted that I was still in the clear.

Hurrying across the damp grass, I stopped in front of the large oak tree and stared at the wood slats nailed to its trunk. Nothing could take away the happiness I felt right at that moment. I was here. I was actually here, standing in front of his tree house.

"What are you doing?"

Something close to a gasp and wheeze came out of my mouth.
I turned around and flattened myself against the tree. My heart
thundered as I stared at Lachlan.

He was taller than I remembered. He needed a haircut. I
couldn't see his eyes. I could only make out the slope of his nose
and the outline of his lips, which were in a thin line as he stared
at me solemnly.

I was scared out of my mind. All my determination had been
for nothing, and now I was caught. I would never get the chance
to go up into that tree.

And Lachlan was quiet because . . . well, I had no idea why
he was quiet. But every second something wasn't said, the more
terrified I became.

I cleared my throat. "Y-you don't still use this, do you?" I
croaked.

Frowning, he looked at the tree house and back at me. "No.
Not really." He took a step forward and I dug my fingers into
the tree bark. He stopped, only a few steps away, and gave me a
curious look before he stuck out his hand.

"I'm Lachlan Halstead. Who are you?"

He could tell my parents I was trespassing. He could get me
into huge trouble. That was enough to send me running back to
Rumor. But my feet stayed rooted in place. I forgot that I had a
voice or that I even had a name. I struggled to breathe for a second and just stared at him.

I forced my tongue to move and with my hand shaking, I
reached out and shook his hand. "N-Naomi Carradine. I'm
your neighbor," I said with a squeaky voice.

Lachlan looked over his shoulder, in the direction of my
house.

Please don't tell on me. Please don't tell on me, I chanted in
my mind.

"So what are you doing here?"

"I just wanted to see the tree house."

"In the middle of the night?"

"Please don't tell my parents!" I said frantically. "I only wanted to climb up there. That's it. I promise!"

He laughed with ease. "Relax, kid. I won't rat you out." He tucked his hands into the pocket of his hoodie and looked up at the tree. "Why do you want to go up there, anyway? It hasn't been used in years. I'm surprised it hasn't collapsed."

I squirmed and looked down at the ground. "Since you weren't using it, I thought I could," I mumbled.

He kept his gaze on the tree and nodded. "Good enough answer." Slapping the base of the tree, he looked at me expectantly. "You going up?"

That's what I'd come here for. But now that he was next to me, I was nervous and still scared that he would tell on me.

I looked away from Lachlan and tilted my head back as far as it would go. I nodded slowly.

"I'm going up."

I gripped the wooden steps with shaky hands. When I peeked through the opening to the house, I smiled and hefted myself up. Lachlan was behind me. He immediately walked to the corner, looking bored. I was anything but. I was only a few feet up from the ground, but I felt like I was in the clouds.

"How are you doing over there?" Lachlan asked.

"I love it," I breathed.

"You don't get out much," he murmured.

My shoulders tensed. "I do too."

"I'm just kidding." He walked around. The wood creaked underneath his feet. Finally, he rested his elbows on the ledge next to me and stared out into the sky. "So all you want to do is come up here and sit?"

"Yes."

He said nothing.

"I was right," I finally said. "It's beautiful up here."

The two of us sat in silence, but I was okay with it.

"If that's all you want to do, then you can come up here whenever," he said.

My eyes widened before I anxiously turned toward him. "You mean it?"

Lachlan shrugged. "Sure. But I don't know if sneaking out in the middle of the night is a good idea for an eight-year-old."

My chin went up in defense. "I'm ten."

He didn't look impressed.

"You're outside too," I said. "And you're not that much older than me. Aren't you thirteen?"

Lachlan's eyes narrowed. "Fifteen."

I'd ticked him off, but this was the most fun I'd had in so long.

"Well, have fun up here," he said. "I'm going inside. And to bed. Like normal humans."

"Hey, wait!" I said urgently. Lachlan stopped and looked at me expectantly. "What did you used to do when you came up here?"

"A lot of pointless games, really."

"Like what?"

He sighed loudly and sat down. "Stupid games. I'd shoot invisible guns, and then climb down to make runs to the house for more ammo. Sometimes this would be my spaceship. A few times this was my secret agency headquarters. Most of the time, I'd make this place my secret hideout. Or a stranded island."

I saw all the games he described perfectly. My imagination ran wild, seeking and grabbing everything he was saying with greedy hands. If I looked to the left, I could see mountains with plush green grass and flowers sprinkled throughout. Directly in front of me were palm trees and clean blue waters that touched the sand. To the right were ruins of a castle that once stood tall in Germany. I could see it all.

"That's why I always came up here," he explained. "I could dream up anything in this tree house."

I nodded and tried to keep the huge grin off my face.

"Dream up anything," I repeated in awe. "I want to do that."

"You don't do that stuff? You're ten! All ten-year-olds do that."

Not all.

There were limits that I never crossed. I played board games, played with Barbies, and rode horses. I rarely used my imagination. It never ran wild like Lachlan's did.

"No." I looked down at the wooden floor with shame.

"Not once?" he asked.

I said no again.

He persisted. "You're lying."

I cleared my throat and looked at the sky.

"I'll create a story for you. But you have to keep it going." He stretched his legs and crossed them at the ankles. I couldn't tell if he was staying solely because he felt bad for his strange ten-year-old neighbor or because he might actually enjoy my presence. I'd accept either option.

"Okay. The world has been invaded by aliens. And now the CIA is relying on you to protect the human race." He continued on with his storytelling, painting the perfect picture for me to imagine.

I watched him with fascination.

"What's your name?" he quizzed.

My eyebrows drew together tightly. "Naomi."

"No. What is your name?" He emphasized slowly. "Just imagine and you can be anything."

I smiled, grasping onto the meaning of his words. The possibilities were endless. "Claire . . . no, I like Julia. Oh! No!" I excitedly sat up onto my knees. I couldn't keep up with my brain. It was exhilarating. "I want to change it to Elliot Kid! I like that!"

"Nice," he said, and then he smiled. It was true and honest. Nothing deceitful about it. I'd earned that smile, and I'd do just about anything to earn another smile from Lachlan Halstead.

He talked to me for hours. Until the sun was up. Until my eyes were threatening to quit on me. Until I absolutely had to leave.

That night, Lachlan Halstead woke me up and pulled my mind into a whole new world. I was way too young to know that at the fresh age of ten, I had willingly handed my heart over to Lachlan Halstead.

9

ROOM 62

"Did you get any sleep?"

I glance at Mary. "I got some."

She tilts her head, a sympathetic look on her face, and I can tell that she knows I'm lying.

We're close to Dr. Rutledge's door when a nurse stops in front of Mary and pulls her away. I've seen this nurse around. She's the same age as Mary, but she has a permanent frown on her face and wears scrubs in dark, solid colors to match her rigid personality.

My eyes narrow and I watch the nurse's lips move rapidly. I can make out only bits and pieces, but I watch her form the words *suggests* and *group therapy*.

It suddenly becomes hard for me to breathe.

Group therapy.

No way, no how. I'd rather have a lobotomy than sit in a circle and talk about all my problems.

Mary looks at me over her shoulder. You know it's going to be bad when your nurse, the sane one, doesn't look happy. I should have run from that look alone.

The uptight nurse walks away, leaving Mary and me in an awkward silence.

"Change of plans," Mary announces.

"What do you mean?"

She gently grabs my elbows and we do a quick U-turn. "Dr. Rutledge wants you to try group therapy."

I stop walking and face her.

"I don't want to do that."

She tugs on my arm. "Why not?"

"I just . . . I just don't want to do that."

"Group therapy is very effective," she reasons.

"Maybe for someone else, but not for me."

Mary doesn't answer.

"I saw the way you looked at me when the nurse told you! You think it's a bad idea too."

"Give it a shot. You have nothing to lose."

Translation: *Your options are becoming really limited. If you don't start improving, there's nothing left for you.*

I move one foot in front of the other, feeling like I'm walking toward my demise.

"How long is it?" I ask.

"Just an hour."

We arrive at Room 62. A large, open room where most group therapy sessions are held. Blue plastic chairs are in the center of the room. It looks like a cozy little circle, like we're in kindergarten, getting ready for show-and-tell.

I stand in the doorway and watch everyone. One girl stares down at the carpet, whispering to herself. Next to her is a middle-aged woman. I've seen her a few times during dinner or in the rec room. I call her Pretend Mommy. I think her real name is Victoria. In a place where no one is put together, this woman is. Her face is exquisite. She has porcelain skin and a small, snow-sloped nose that makes her almond-shaped blue eyes even larger. Not a day goes by when she doesn't look put together. Her brown hair is always brushed and around her shoulders. She wears red silk pajamas, with a fur coat wrapped around her, almost every day. She smells like lilac. In her arms she rocks a plastic baby back and forth. She stops rocking the baby and sings it a lullaby as if it's crying.

Clearly she's crazy.

And clearly I'm on the fast track to following her down that road because her presence is comforting to me. She appears so motherly to me. If I close my eyes and forget, I'm no longer in a mental hospital. Pretend Mommy is a real mom, who's holding a real baby.

On the opposite side of Pretend Mommy is a skinny girl named Amber. She is the resident anorexic. She sits there, staring at everyone with resentment.

I go to turn around. Mary grips my shoulders and says in a gentle voice, "You will be fine."

"I wish I had your confidence," I say weakly.

She squeezes my shoulders. "Everything will be okay. I'll pick you up in an hour."

Mary's not going to leave until I sit down. I walk into the room. It feels like everyone is looking at me. They have their own problems and issues, but I swear they're whispering to each other, "Do you see her? Look how fucked up she is. She'll never be able to leave Fairfax."

I choose the seat closest to the door. If shit gets weird, I'll be ready to bolt. But that seat happens to be next to Amber. Her lip curls in disgust.

Fuck you too, skinny bitch.

I cross my arms. My legs bounce up and down. I wait for that nervous feeling in my gut to fade, but it gets stronger the longer I sit there.

More people come into the room. The chairs are filled up.

A male doctor and two female nurses walk in. I watch them carefully as they talk quietly near the door.

Get this over with! I want to scream.

I bite down on my lip.

The doctor clears his throat and the room grows quiet. He introduces himself as Dr. Cooper before he goes into this whole spiel on group therapy and its benefits. He says that this is a safe place. An outlet for us to really open up and let everything out.

I stare at him doubtfully.

He continues to talk, and that's when I start to hear another voice.

It's distant at first, but it comes closer and closer until the voice is right next to me, and I hear, "You're a filthy bitch."

My skin breaks out into hives. My fingers grip the blue plastic chair I'm sitting in as I look around the room frantically. Did they hear Lana's dad? Could they see him behind me?

But everyone is staring at Dr. Cooper with boredom.

So I try to follow their lead, thinking it will distract me. I focus on the doctor's lips. He's talking about cognitive behavior . . . I think.

"I really want you all to focus on positive traits you possess." He looks in my direction. "Amber. Would you like to say what positive traits you have?"

She stops picking at the dead ends of her hair and glares. "None. I have no positive traits."

My fingers drum anxiously and I keep looking all around the room. The doctor clears his throat. "That's not true. I'm *positive*"—See what he did there?—"that you do."

I look behind my seat. I tilt my head to the side and glance at the chairs stacked in the corner. He could be hiding over there.

Amber looks at me. "What the fuck is your problem?" she snaps.

"Now, Amber," Dr. Cooper says. He stands up and walks over to us. Before he opens his mouth, he kneels down to look Amber in the eye. His bones pop loudly.

The sound echoes in my ears.

I know Dr. Cooper is talking. I see his mouth moving. But I hear no words.

Radio silence.

My eardrums start to ache.

The silence gets stronger and more powerful. I rub my ears, trying to ease the intense pressure. It feels like my head is about to explode.

And that's when I see him.

Lana's dad peeks out from behind Dr. Cooper. He's kneeling down. Elbows resting on his thighs, in the exact same position as Dr. Cooper.

But he gives me a sadistic smile. That's the same smile he makes before he attacks. My breath is stuck in my throat.

I react instantly.

I lean back in my chair. It tips over. I fall to the ground. I scramble away from him. I don't stop moving until my back touches the wall. He stands up and slowly makes his way toward me. He's dressed in a navy suit, a white dress shirt, and a navy striped tie to match. He looks harmless, but it's those cold eyes that stand out. They're eyes that don't feel. They reveal that he has no heart and has never had one.

"You're a little bitch," he says.

A choked sound escapes me. I squeeze my eyes and try to focus on my breathing. He's closer. I can feel his steps vibrating the ground beneath me.

"Go away. Go away." My voice becomes stronger. "Go away!"

He grabs onto my ankle and I kick him off. My hands curl around my head.

"Leave me alone!" I scream.

He keeps saying my name and grabbing at my ankles. I fight back but my muscles ache. I'm getting weaker and that makes him stronger. That makes his grip more painful.

Distantly I hear a feminine voice.

Dr. Rutledge.

"What happened?" she demands.

Someone answers, but I can't understand what's being said. Everything has become muted.

"Naomi."

I open my eyes. Her face is blurry. All I can make out is the outline of her body. But right next to her I see Lana's dad.

I shove my head back. It slams into the wall painfully.

"Can you hear me?" Dr. Rutledge asks.

He doesn't care that Dr. Rutledge is next to me. He keeps touching. He grips my jaw until it feels like it will snap in half.

"You've ruined everything!" he shouts. "Your fucking life is mine!"

Dr. Rutledge says my name loudly this time. "Breathe," she commands. "You need to breathe."

I focus on her words, and the pressure on my jaw lets up before his hands disappear altogether.

I open my eyes and it's just Dr. Rutledge in front of me. Mary stands behind her with a panicked look.

"Take a deep breath," Dr. Rutledge urges.

Everyone else in the room stares at me as if I've lost my mind. I can't really blame them.

"Get me out of here," I pant. "Get me out of here!"

She holds her hand out and I latch onto her like a lifeline.

"Don't make me come back here!" I plead.

Dr. Rutledge wraps an arm around my shoulder. Mary moves to my left, gently holding my forearm. We walk out of the room. My balance is off. My legs feel numb. I move carefully, as if I'm walking on a tightrope.

"I'll do anything but come back here," I plead. I can still hear the pop of his bones. It makes my body twitch. I keep talking. "I'm trying to get better. I promise I am but I can't stop seeing *him*. He's everywhere I look!"

"Naomi, calm down," Dr. Rutledge says soothingly. She hurries us down the hall. "Just focus on breathing right now."

I'm still gasping for breath as we walk into her office. Mary closes the door behind us, giving us privacy.

And for once, the silence feels good. He isn't here. I'm safe. I can breathe.

Tremors still rack my body as I sit down. My skin is clammy. The aftershocks of his attack were almost worse than the real thing. I still feel his grip on my legs, squeezing tighter and tighter until it feels like my bones will break.

"Naomi," Dr. Rutledge says. "Keep taking deep breaths."

I listen to her and make myself slowly breathe in and out.

In and out.

In and out.

I suck up all the air I can get and the pain slowly fades.

When I look up at Dr. Rutledge she nudges her head toward her desk. There's a glass of water sitting there. I grab it and gulp it all down.

I cradle the glass between both hands. Her chair creaks as she leans close.

Please, don't make this worse than it already is, I think to myself.

"Can you tell me what happened back in group therapy?"

"No."

My grip tightens on the glass.

"Can't or won't?"

"Won't," I say, my voice hard.

And for the first time since I've met Dr. Rutledge, she doesn't say a word. She just sits there patiently, spinning a paper clip on her desk.

"I saw Lana's dad," I finally admit.

His face flashes through my mind.

"Did he say anything?"

I nod. "He was screaming at me. He kept calling me a bitch. Told me that my life was his . . ." My voice breaks.

"You are safe here. You know that, right? And Lana's safe too. Her dad can't hurt her anymore."

Lana's name makes me sit up straight and I start to tremble. "How do you know that?"

Dr. Rutledge shifts in her chair. "I've spoken to her," she admits.

"When?" My voice rises. "Where is she?"

She skips over my question as if she never heard it.

"What happened to you today was just—"

"Where is she?" I interrupt.

"She's in a safe place; that's all I can tell you."

"Why won't you tell me?"

"Because you need to heal. You can't fix her, Naomi, if you're broken."

Her words hit me hard. I'm supposed to be the pillar of strength for Lana and without that, who am I really?

I want to cry, but I hold myself together. One breakdown is enough for today.

"Everything you saw during group therapy was just your mind playing tricks on you."

"He was there." My voice shakes with conviction. "I saw him. I felt him grabbing me."

"He wasn't there," she says, enunciating each word carefully.

I use the same tone. "He was."

I know we can keep going back and forth. But what it all boils down to is that Dr. Rutledge is the sane one.

Not me. I'm the one locked away.

It's my word against hers, and I know everyone will believe her.

"Why don't you go lie down, okay?" she suggests slowly. "I'll see you tomorrow morning and we'll pick up where we left off."

I can barely think about right now, let alone tomorrow.

So I nod and stand back up. "Okay."

Dr. Rutledge opens the door for me. Mary steps forward and escorts me back to my room.

The rest of the night I'm in a complete daze.

10

DON'T DREAM

"It's time to go, Naomi."

I turn away from my window and stare at Mary. She stands in the doorway, tapping her foot impatiently. But there is no way in hell I'm going back to Dr. Rutledge.

I cross my arms and give her a level look. "No."

Mary tilts her head to the side, a stern expression on her face. One that says, "Do we have to do this the hard way?"

For the past week this has become our routine. Mary tells me I need to go see Dr. Rutledge. I tell her no. Mary calls for assistance and another nurse helps drag me down the hallway. I struggle, trying to break out of their hold, but in the end I always find myself sitting across from Dr. Rutledge. After group therapy, I put a wall up, afraid that any other methods Dr. Rutledge had in mind would destroy me.

So she sits there, behind her desk, asking her typical questions:
"How are you?"
"Did you sleep well last night?"
"What are you thinking about right now?"

I never respond. I watch the clock tick the time away and it becomes a standoff. Me saying nothing, refusing to back down, and Dr. Rutledge persistently talking, trying to get me to open up. In the end, I outlast Dr. Rutledge and she lets me leave. But I never leave her office feeling victorious, because the truth is that my nightmares have gotten worse. No matter where I go, I see him. Dr. Rutledge has upped my Ambien. It helps some, but not enough.

I'm scared that soon the medicine will stop being my hiding place. I'm afraid that he'll find me and rip me to pieces.

I walk around in a complete daze. The line between sane and insane is starting to become blurred. Everything is starting to confuse me. And the most terrifying thing of all is that I'm starting to become one of the patients that sit in the rec room, staring blankly at the television for hours on end.

I sigh and move away from the window. Today, I'm too tired to put up a fight.

Mary gives me an approving nod. She's proud. She thinks this is a step in the right direction.

We walk slowly down the hallway, treating this like a stroll through the park. If you think about it, this stale air and the sterile walls really are my park.

Mary knocks once on Dr. Rutledge's door before she opens it. She looks at me and nudges her head for me to go in. Reluctantly, I go inside. Rutledge looks up and smiles. She sits in her chair, looking so prim and composed, as though she has the answers to all my problems.

I stare at her with rebellion.

She gestures toward the chair in front of her desk. "Will you sit down?"

I cross my arms.

Dr. Rutledge sighs. Just sighs. And I'm struck by the sweet, soothing sound of it. I want to sit back and sigh like that and pretend that there are no problems weighing me down.

"Are you still giving me the silent treatment?"

"I'm not giving you the silent treatment."

She looks at me dubiously. "That's where you're wrong. You're still angry about group therapy, and ignoring me is the only way for you to handle the situation."

I flinch, as if she has thrown a knife at me, missing me by inches.

"Can you blame me?" I say.

"Of course not. I've already admitted that group therapy was the wrong choice." She pauses and says in a gentle voice, "But I'm not against you, Naomi. When I ask my questions it's for a reason."

I walk forward. The whole time I stare at Dr. Rutledge with cautious eyes. "What's the reason?"

"You've had no proper diagnosis," she explains. "And I want that for you. You've been here almost two months, and that is two months too long."

I sit down slowly. It seems we finally have something we can agree on. But I'm not going to open up instantly. Why should I make this easy for her?

"How has your day been so far?"

"Okay," I say reluctantly.

"What activities do you do during the day?"

"Stay in my room for a little bit. Go to the rec room . . ." My voice drifts. She lifts a brow. "I'm locked up in a crazy hospital. What do you expect?"

"So you do nothing?"

"Nothing," I confirm.

"Do you like to read?" she asks quickly.

"No," I respond instantly.

"How about movies?"

"No." Another lie.

She continues to ask questions. I answer, my responses coming out in rapid succession. I wait for her to give up, but she never does.

"Do you have any friends here?" she asks, her eyes never leaving my face.

"A few." Still lying.

"How has your appetite been?"

I frown. What a dumb-ass question. It's so pointless and stupid that I answer honestly. "Fine."

"And how are you sleeping?"

"I'm not," I respond instantly.

Dr. Rutledge sits back in her chair with satisfaction. I fell into her trap. It was only a matter of time until one of us slipped up. I look away, angry at myself. But in a way, it feels good to have the truth out there.

Seconds tick by with neither one of us saying a word. I pick at the loose thread on my sleeve. The whole time I feel her eyes on me.

She's the first one to speak.

"Why can't you sleep?"

I grit my teeth together and say nothing. The minutes tick by.

"You look upset," she says. "What are you thinking?"

I shift uncomfortably in my chair. "Lana."

"What about Lana?"

My head tilts. "Did you just ask that? 'What about Lana?'"
I mimic her voice. "My friend needs me and I'm stuck here in a

mental institution with no way out. Of course I'm going to be thinking about her."

"And how do you feel when you think about her?"

"I just told you," I say impatiently.

"No, you told me that you're thinking about her. That she needs you. And you're stuck in a mental institution. I asked how you *feel*."

I agonize over her words.

"Guilt," I answer, slowly. "I *feel* guilt."

My fingers curl around my elbows. And something ominous starts to cover my shoulders. My muscles tense up instantly.

"Why guilt?" she asks.

I start to answer but stop. There's a blissful moment of silence. I hear no voices in the hallway. No birds chirping outside or wind blowing against the window.

And then my ears pop.

Suddenly, there's an echo of voices. They come up on me slowly before they're in my head all at once. There's so much noise. Distorted voices speaking at once. There are shrieks, shouts, laughter, crying, and moans. It becomes impossible to think straight. I'm being pushed out of my own head.

My hands shake.

I really am starting to lose it and it's all Dr. Rutledge's fault. Before our sessions and group therapy things weren't perfect, but they definitely weren't as bad as they are now.

Everything starts to build up inside me. I feel like I'm slowly fading from my own body. It's terrifying to lose mental control. Even though I'm sitting down, I feel off balance. My body pitches forward.

I go into full-out panic mode.

I jump out of my chair. I stumble away from her desk until I touch the wall.

"I know what you're doing." My voice shakes. Dr. Rutledge looks at me with alarm. "You tell me that you want to see me get out of here, but you don't. You're like every other doctor here. You ask your questions so you can go through your checklist of symptoms. And, if I have a few of them, then, Oh! I must have this disorder or that disorder. But I don't want or need your help!" I yell over the voices. "I'm the only sane fucking person in this place, but now you're starting to make me into the other patients!"

Dr. Rutledge is sitting up straight. "Calm down, Naomi," she says cautiously.

"No!" I point at her. "Try having your own family admit you into a mental institution. Try having everyone that you need and love disappear on you when you need them the most!"

My hands curl into fists; I bang them against my head.

If I hit hard enough maybe I'll knock out all of the voices.

"Stop." She stands from her chair. She looks frantic, almost scared. "Stop it!" she shouts.

I close my eyes and keep slamming my fists.

"Naomi! Stop!"

Her voice is closer. It makes the voices in my head panic. Their volume increases; the voices shriek and my ears start to ring. It hurts so much tears start to stream down my face.

And then I feel her grab my hands.

I freeze. It's like a balloon has just been popped.

I raise my eyes. I don't try to hide my fear and pain. I let Dr. Rutledge see it all.

I watch her pupils dilate as she takes it all in.

My darkness.

My frustration.

My pain.

My humiliation.

She drops my hands. They fall to my side like heavy weights. She walks around her desk and lays her palms on its surface. Her body hunches over the same time her eyes slam shut.

We stay quiet. Me rocking back and forth against the wall and her staring down at her desk helplessly. Until she lifts her head and glances at me. The title of M.D. disappears. She's a person. One with flaws. One with scars.

"You know why I became a psychiatrist?"

I stare at her blankly and wipe my cheeks with the back of my hands.

"Why?" I say reluctantly.

"I've always been fascinated with the human mind. How we process things. How we feel. What emotions we project," she admits.

So far, I'm not impressed.

"During my residency, I realized that maybe there could be something more behind my decision in pursuing this field."

I don't understand where this conversation is going. But I know these conversations between doctor and patient never happen. The doctors ask the questions and expect answers. They never open up and tell you something personal about themselves.

I slowly stand up. "What do you mean?"

"I have family members that have struggled with mental illness. My fascination stems from them. I wanted to figure out where all their pain came from. Why it seemed like they couldn't shake the darkness constantly looming around them." Dr. Rutledge sighs.

I don't think it's so light and sweet as before. This time I see the pain and sorrow behind it. She has darkness in her past.

I look down and trace the veins running across the back of my hand. "Have you found an answer?"

"Sometimes I think that I have," she says carefully. "But then I read something new, or start meeting with a new patient, and I realize that I'm trying to solve the impossible. We'll never have a sound answer. Everyone is different with the way they feel, think, love, and express themselves. I guess that's what makes the world go round."

I think of Lana. She's in the bathroom, staring at her reflection. She's given up. She's tired of all the pain. I'm standing in the doorway, telling her not to give up, but she won't listen.

Goose bumps cover my skin. And I try my best to shake the image away.

Dr. Rutledge laces her fingers together and takes a deep breath. I know confession time is over and she's back in her normal role. "I'm not Dr. Woods. When you talk, I listen to you. I believe you. But I need you to trust and open up to me. Okay?"

I know why she went back to the doctor mode, but I already miss the other side of Dr. Rutledge. When she talked to me, my humiliation lessened. I didn't feel like a failure who doesn't have control over my own mind. Somewhere, during our talk, a small fragment of trust started to appear. It was hardly noticeable, but at least it was something.

"Okay," I say.

"I know this isn't easy for you. Just remember that even the purest of souls have darkness in them. It might be hard to spot. Perhaps they've perfected the art of covering it from the world. Or maybe it's hidden in a dark corner of their mind. But it's there. No one in this world is scar free."

My shoulders relax. I nod, and that seems good enough for me.

"All I want is for you to tell your story the best way you know how."

I take a deep, cleansing breath. To say I had just begun with my story was an understatement. I wasn't even close to scratching the surface.

"I told Lana that maybe we should stay at my house. That she would be safe there . . ."

11

NO EASY WAY OUT

"WE HAVE TO GET YOU OUT OF HERE," I WHISPERED.

Even though it was just Lana and me out in the barn, I was still too afraid to speak up. Too afraid that her dad would hear me and come back outside. I wanted to make use of the time we had and leave this place as soon as we could.

But Lana wouldn't move. She stared at the ground with a vacant look in her eyes and rubbed her fingers across the red marks on her neck. I don't even think she realized what she was doing.

I gently laid a hand on her shoulder and nudged my head toward the open doors. "Did you hear me? We have to go."

Lana jerked away from my touch. "No."

My mouth hung open. "You can't be serious."

She stood up shakily and brushed away the dirt and hay from her legs. "I can't go," she muttered.

I wanted to grab onto her shoulders to get her attention, but she was a wounded animal. Ready to run away from me at any second.

I treaded lightly and took a small step forward. "I know you're scared, but you have to get out of here. I'll help you. Where do you want to go? You can go anywhere."

"I want to go to my room. And I want to go to bed."

"You can't go in there."

She brushed past me and I watched in amazement as she started to clean up the area. Ropes that had been hanging on the wall were in a tangled mess on the ground. One looked close to slipping off the wall; it was swinging back and forth like a pendulum. A saddle had fallen into a large bucket of water. Pails lined against the wall were tipped over and horse feed was scattered across the floor.

Lana got to work. She moved from one side of the barn to the next, her pace brisk and sure. When she bent down to right the pails, I rushed over to her.

"Stop." I grabbed the handle. "Lana, what are you doing?"

Her back straightened. She let go of the handle and moved on to the next pail. "I can't go to bed knowing the barn is left like this."

Was I an accomplice to a crime for letting her clean up? I felt like it. But it wasn't as if I had experience in this type of situation. It was as though I had a blindfold across my eyes. I was moving forward, but very slowly, hoping that whichever direction I took was the right one. The worst part of it all was that the more she straightened things up, the more color slowly crept into her cheeks. Her breathing became normal and the tears stopped falling.

My gut was churning. I realized, with a sick sense of dread, that this made her feel good. Hiding the evidence felt right.

She didn't stop moving until everything was back in its rightful place. And then she dusted her hands off and looked around the barn.

"I'm tired," she announced.

Was I dreaming right now? I had to be. What I was experiencing couldn't be real. I blinked, my lashes fluttering against my skin, but Lana was still in front of me. Still had a blank look on her face.

"Don't go in there," I whispered.

She held my gaze and said, "You're still going to stay here, aren't you?"

I tilted my head to the side. "What other choice do I have?"

"You have plenty of choices."

"And none of them involve leaving you here," I replied. "I can't undo what I saw."

She walked out of the barn, but not before I heard her say, "For your sake, I wish you could."

I was too shocked to move. To breathe. To speak.

Technically, I was supposed to be staying there for the rest of the summer. But how could I step back into that house, knowing what I knew? And how could I *not* stay there, knowing that my friend needed me? I closed my eyes for a second and trailed behind Lana. I finally caught up to her and together we walked to the back door. She opened the door and the hinges squeaked. I swear it was a warning for me to stop right there.

I hesitated. For years this house had felt like my own. I would walk in and out of it with ease. But now it just felt wrong.

I stepped inside, bracing myself for Lana's dad to jump out and attack, but like most homes at this time of night, it was completely quiet. The only difference was that this quiet was eerie. The refrigerator hummed and the air conditioner blew cold air through the vents. I was close to jumping out of my skin.

Neither of us said a word as we walked down the hallway, toward the stairs. Next to the stairs was the formal living room. A single lamp was on. The room was one solid color: ivory. On the fireplace mantel were family pictures. One was of Lana when she was eleven. She looked directly at the camera, with a small smirk on her face. It was a smirk that I had seen time and time again. I'd chalked it up to her shy personality. But now I saw that the small smirk wasn't because she was shy, it was because she was cautious. Scared.

I tried to carefully walk up the stairs, but no matter how hard I tried, the steps creaked underneath me. I couldn't say the same for Lana. She moved so silently, it was as if she were walking on air.

Her parents' room was at the very end of the hall. The door was closed. Only a few steps away was her dad. I had to pull my eyes away from the door, because if I stared at that smooth surface one more second it would turn into a screen and project what I'd seen Lana's dad doing. I squeezed my eyes shut and walked into Lana's room.

I shut the door behind me. I couldn't believe I was actually going to stay here.

Lana turned on the lamp on the nightstand. I crossed my arms and stared at her room with a critical eye, trying to find anything that would stand out to me. Something that would be evidence that something wasn't right.

But everything was the same.

There was a dresser in the corner. An off-white, full-length mirror was next to her closet. Her bed was made, the comforter a light shade of gray.

Now that I was really looking at her room with clear eyes, I could see it wasn't a bedroom. This was a staged bedroom. De-signed in such a way that anyone who came into their house and saw her room would think Lana had a put-together life.

She could grab her toothbrush and purse, and no one would know that she had even lived here.

I wondered how many times she had cleaned up her room like she had the barn. I trembled at the thought.

Lana moved around the room, opening and closing drawers. She held her pajamas to her chest and quietly walked into the bathroom that was connected to her room and shut the door. A few seconds later I heard the shower turn on.

I closed my eyes and leaned my head back against the door. Blindly, I reached for the lock. I couldn't find one.

I bent down and inspected the doorknob.

There was no lock.

"Son of a bitch," I whispered.

I stood back up. I wrapped my arms around my midsection. I felt sick to my stomach. The urge to leave was powerful, but I couldn't leave Lana.

As Lana walked out of the bathroom, a trail of mist followed behind her. Her sleep pants had pink sheep on them. She wore a white T-shirt that was three sizes too big. She looked too small and fragile for the things that had happened to her. How had she not broken apart?

I bit my cheek to keep from crying.

Lana took the decorative pillows off her bed, tossing them in the corner. I moved away from the door. My fingers trailed across her computer desk.

She got into bed and reached over to turn off the lamp. She looked over at me. "Good night."

She turned off the lights. The sheets rustled as she got comfortable.

"'Night," I whispered.

This was how she was going to end the night.

No tears.

No emotions.

No anything.

I lay flat on my back. Every muscle in my body was tense. I was afraid to relax. I was afraid to move. Or even breathe. So I watched the ceiling fan blades move slowly above me. I tried to focus on happy things. Good things. The fan blades reminded me of a Ferris wheel. I pictured a state fair and how out of three months of summer, the fair always landed on the hottest day. I envisioned the greasy food, the shrieks of laughter, and the buzz of conversations.

I narrowed my eyes and did my best to keep the scene going. But the memory of Lana and me when we were thirteen popped into my head. We were waiting in line for the Ferris wheel. She was staring up at the ride, pupils dilated. The line started to move. I urged her to walk forward. She turned and looked at me with frantic eyes. "I'm not going on that." She got out of the line and stood to the side. My turn came. When I reached the very top I looked down at her. She was still there, by herself, with a vacant expression.

"How was it?" she asked when I got off.

It was nothing. I had been too busy looking at her, making sure she was okay. I shrugged and told her it was okay. We moved on to a different activity, and I had brushed away the moment.

But now I understood that Lana didn't need to be in control of her life. She just needed to be ready for whatever came her way. I could still hear the water dripping in the bathroom and the normal creaks that houses make. I tried my best to ignore the noises. My eyes involuntarily drifted back to the door. I quickly looked away, my fingers gripping the sheets.

Lana's breathing was starting to even out. I turned and stared at the back of her head.

Did I even know the person I called my best friend?

I used to think so.

I knew that she couldn't dance. She loved movies because in two hours or less, you were normally guaranteed a happy ending. Sky blue was her favorite color, and she loved waking up early to watch the sunrise and hated rainy days.

I thought those facts were part of her story. But they weren't. They were just a simple punctuation mark—the beginning of who she really is.

"Lana?" I whispered.

I didn't count on her answering. I just had to keep my mind busy.

For a few minutes there was nothing but silence. The sheets rustled and she said in a hoarse voice, "Yeah?"

I knew that she didn't want to talk about it. But there was this ache in my chest that was deep and powerful. It wouldn't leave until I talked to her.

"How long has it been going on?" I whispered.

I heard her swallow. "Since I was ten."

Her words echoed around the room, taking up the air around me, making it impossible for me to breathe.

"Does anyone know?"

"Just my mom." She said the words so casually, as if we were shooting the breeze and talking about what we ate for dinner.

"A-and she's done nothing?" I whispered.

"It would bring shame on the family," Lana whispered back.

"So she sweeps it under the rug and pretends nothing's happened."

I was stunned speechless.

When you look at Lana's mom you see heels, pearls, and lipstick. She's always so put together. She's a throwback to the era of Susie Homemaker.

Quickly, I was realizing that her image was just smoke and mirrors. That mist was starting to fade and I saw the truth.

I had no words. At least nothing that could erase what had happened to her.

"I'm so sorry," I said brokenly.

They were just three simple words. But said in the right way, said with truth and compassion, they could put a soul back together.

A choked sound came from Lana. It sounded like an animal dying, and it was gut-wrenching. Tears instantly pooled in my eyes; my vision blurred.

I didn't hug her and I didn't bother her with any more questions. I just lay there next to her and let her cry.

After a few minutes, her sobs turned into hiccups and then sniffles. She turned her face and was staring up at the ceiling with me.

"I'm not going back to school," she announced.

I looked over at her sadly. I wanted to be shocked and ask why, but I couldn't. My heart was stuck in my throat.

"I couldn't hack it," she continued. "It was torture. I tried to make friends, but I didn't know how. I didn't know how to allow those small conversations to snowball into a friendship. I tried to study, but I could never focus. I would have panic attacks during my classes, and pretty soon I stopped going to class altogether."

Lana brushed away her tears with the back of her hand. "I

stayed at school, trying to tell myself that each day would get better. I locked myself in my apartment and . . ." Her voice broke. "It felt like I was going crazy. It felt like there were no other options for me. I had planned on getting away from this house my whole life. Going to college, where I could finally start my life. But knowing that would never happen, that I couldn't hack it . . . it killed me more than anything else."

My brain was maxed out with everything she was telling me.

"I thought school was going well for you. I . . . I talked to you every day and you seemed fine."

"I made you think it was okay," Lana replied.

I shook my head, my hair rustling against my pillow. I didn't know what to say, or where to go from here.

For the first time in my life, I was at a complete loss.

EVENTUALLY, LANA DRIFTED OFF TO SLEEP.

It was sometime in the early morning before I did. I think I could have stayed up the entire time, but the birds started to chirp outside the window. As crazy as it sounds, their chirps were soothing. It was a comfort to know that some other being was up.

And now a blinding light was slanted across my face.

I cracked open one eye and immediately winced. That blinding light was the stupid sun pouring in from the window.

I wasn't in the mood for clear skies and anything associated with happy days. I wanted to go home, draw the shades in my room, and hibernate until this entire memory became a distant thought.

I wanted to take the easy way out.

I sat up and stretched my neck. I looked down at my body. I guess sometime during the night I had changed into some pajamas. My hair was tangled around my face and my eyes were still heavy with sleep. I didn't need a mirror to know I looked like complete shit.

How I looked was the least of my problems, though.

I glanced over at Lana.

She was perched on the windowsill. The brilliant light didn't seem to bother her. I could just see her thinking to herself that if she soaked in enough light, maybe, just maybe, all the darkness in her life would fade.

I cleared my throat.

Her head whipped in my direction. She gave me that small smile of hers. "'Morning."

I grumbled a reply.

"What time is it?" I asked.

"Eight."

I rubbed my eyes. How I was even functioning right now, I'd never know.

"I was going to let you sleep in."

"No, it's all right. I needed to get up."

She crossed her arms, digging her feet into the carpet.

"Do you want some breakfast?" she offered.

I peered at her carefully. "No, I'm not hungry."

"Are you sure? Because I smell eggs and bacon, and I know how much you love that. Or we could make something else," she rambled. "How about French toast? Do you like French toast?"

She was out of her mind if she thought I would go downstairs to eat breakfast and take the chance of seeing her parents.

"Lana."

"Yep?" she asked brightly.

Before I fell asleep this morning I had planned everything out. I was going to talk to her about getting away from her dad, no matter how terrified she was. But the look on her face was desperate.

I swallowed and put a fake smile on my face and said, "Let's go lay out by the pool."

"That sounds good," she said, looking visibly relieved.

I could pretend for a few hours.

Maybe for a day.

I would do that for her.

12

RIPPLE EFFECT

After an hour, I was done pretending.

I tiptoed around the house, trying to avoid her parents. Her dad had already left for work and her mom was walking out the door by the time I walked downstairs.

I was in the clear . . . for now. I couldn't avoid them for the whole summer. If I was going to stay here, I had to figure out how to rein in my anger. I would have to figure out how to be around Lana's dad. I just didn't know how that was possible, though.

The pool was steps away from us, with water as clear as the sky. The smell of freshly cut grass was in the air. The radio was on, playing a song that made Lana's foot tap against the chair.

We lay there, the sun shining down on us. Beads of sweat started to form on my neck. I was pretty sure that if I held my hand out in front of me it would waver in the heat before it slowly started to melt.

I was starting to get restless. Too much silence between us and too many thoughts in my head.

"We should do something," I said.

"We *are* doing something," Lana said tiredly.

"No. I mean something fun, like a road trip."

I knew Lana was controlled by her fear, but maybe if I turned the leaving part into a fun vacation, she would agree. It was a long shot, but it was the only thing I could think of right now.

She gave the sun her cheek and looked at me. "What?"

"Yeah!" I said anxiously. "We could go to California. Instead of laying out by a pool, we could have the ocean in front of us and the sand beneath us!"

The more I thought about it, the more it made sense. But Lana shot my idea down in a heartbeat.

"Why not? This is summertime. This is what people our age do."

She stared solemnly at me, never answering. We were the same age. Our eyes should reflect that. But hers showed she had lived a lifetime filled with more darkness than light, more tears than smiles, and more brutality than happiness.

"You promised you wouldn't bring it up."

My shoulders stiffened. "I'm not."

Lana lowered her sunglasses. "How long have we known each other?"

"Ten years."

"Yeah. Ten years. And in that ten years I've kept this a secret. Do you know why?" She leaned in, never giving me the chance to answer. "Because I wanted to protect you."

Lana was the one that needed protecting, not me. I was fine. I stared at her, unable to say a damn thing.

"Naomi," she said slowly. "I knew you couldn't handle it. You can barely handle it now."

"But you can?"

Lana shrugged. "It's all I know."

She accepted her pain fiercely. So much so that it was almost crippling. Her thoughts and dreams and fears were woven and created by her past.

"So that's it?" I asked. "You're just going to live with this pain for the rest of your life?"

Lana shifted in her seat. "Can we drop this, please?"

If I kept persisting she would bolt, and I might make things worse than they already were.

"Yes," I finally said. "For now."

She gave me a smile and straightened out her towel. Before she lay back down, she looked at me, the smile gone. "You're going to keep this a secret, right?"

I looked away.

"Naomi," she said my name softly. "Please tell no one."

LATER IN THE DAY, LANA FELL ASLEEP IN HER ROOM. I LEFT HER and went downstairs. I should have been the one tired, but I had adrenaline coursing through my body. Sooner or later, I would crash, but not right now.

I had just gotten off the phone with Max. He would be coming over soon. I'd seen him mere hours ago, but our date and kiss felt like it had happened weeks ago. I was so caught up in Lana that I really hadn't had the chance to think about him . . . or us.

Did I want the summer with him? When I'd said yes, I meant it. Even now I wanted it. Yet the situation with Lana changed everything. I didn't see how I could have both in my life without the two of them interconnecting. Lana was my best friend—a sister more than anything else. Max . . . he was something. I could feel it in the way my heart tightened and flipped whenever I thought about him. And being something meant that sooner rather than later he would find out about Lana. It was too big to keep hidden.

I sat at the computer desk. I had swiped Lana's laptop before I left the room. I clicked on the Internet icon and waited for the Google home screen to appear. I nibbled on my fingernail, impatiently waiting. When it did show up, my heart went into overdrive. I felt scared and nervous, questioning why I was doing this.

I typed in *US Senator Virginia* before I could talk myself out of it. Instantly Lana's dad appeared, highlighted in black and directly beneath the search bar. I clicked the option and waited for the page to load. I knew I was safe. No one was here besides Lana, but I still looked over my shoulder in paranoia.

There were pages of sites that came up. A campaign website. His own personal website and a Wikipedia page. He even had a fucking Facebook page.

But I ignored the websites. I clicked on the photos first. Most of them were pictures of her dad shot at different angles, speaking to a crowd, with dozens of mics in front of him. There was one of him walking down the street of McLean with a nameless man beside him. Her dad was pointing to something off in the distance, the nameless man looking impressed.

There was nothing damaging connected to his name. His record was squeaky clean.

What did I really expect, though—one quick Internet search and I would have the answer to all my problems? My Nancy Drew skills were pathetic.

I opened a separate page and typed in the word *rape*. My

stomach started to churn. I wasn't an idiot. I knew the meaning behind the word. I just didn't know how to handle what came *after* the word. I was clueless, and after this afternoon, I was deflated and more confused than ever. I rested my chin on my palm. My fingers drummed against my lower lip as I quickly scrolled down the page.

"What are you looking at?"

I turned, falling halfway out of the chair. My back painfully hit the desk.

Max was standing behind me. His arms were crossed, brows knitted in concentration as he stared at the screen.

"You scared the shit out of me!" I breathed.

"Sorry," Max said, and he helped me up. But he didn't sound sorry. His voice was tight and in control. "What are you looking at?"

"How the hell did you get in?"

"I knocked on the door. No one answered."

"So you just walked on in?"

"I knew you were here and I saw your car in the driveway." Max frowned. "I told you on the phone I was coming over after a meeting. Remember?"

"I remember." I had completely forgotten.

Max stared at me carefully before he said, "I didn't think I'd be interrupting anything." He looked over my shoulder at the screen. "Clearly I was wrong."

I reached behind my back and slammed the laptop shut. "It was nothing."

"Nothing?"

"Yeah."

"What you were Googling doesn't seem like nothing."

I stood up and brushed past him. "I don't know what to tell you."

"Naomi," Max said behind me. His voice cut through the air, making my shoulders stiffen.

I swallowed and looked up at the ceiling. I'd promised Lana not to tell. Max stood there, his eyes boring straight into me. And I knew he wasn't going to leave until he found out the truth.

"How was your day?" I asked brightly. Max didn't say anything, and I continued talking as if nothing were wrong. "Did you have a good day at work? I had a good day," I said nervously. "Just sat by the pool, and now L—"

"Naomi," he interrupted, his voice hard. "Tell me what's going on."

I licked my lips and exhaled. My mouth opened and closed. Nothing would come out. The words were on the tip of my tongue, but Lana's face as she pleaded with me not to tell anyone flashed in my mind. I saw her pain and humiliation.

Max crossed his arms and stared at the counter thoughtfully. "Since you won't say anything, I'm gonna make a guess of my own. All right?"

I nodded.

"I saw what you were Googling. Both times. And maybe I really am reading into it. Maybe it's nothing. Or maybe—"

His voice faded away when he saw me staring at him bleakly. I wanted to tell him that his guess was wrong, but I couldn't.

"Michael?" His mouth opened and then shut. I kept waiting for him to say more, but he never did.

I nodded. That was my only answer to his open-ended question.

He closed his eyes. "Fuck," he whispered.

A dull ache planted itself in my chest as I stared at him.

He stepped forward, his arms outstretched, ready to embrace me, but I flinched. It wasn't that I didn't want to be held by him.

It was the fact that I was so angry with myself for being so careless and allowing him to find out. I had failed Lana.

A hurt expression crossed Max's face. I wanted to step forward into his arms just to take away his hurt.

He started to pace. Hands on his hips and his eyes focused on the floor. His jaw was clenched so tight it looked like it was going to break. I didn't say a word.

The longer we stood there, saying nothing, the quicker Max changed. His brows were furrowed, forming a tight V, and his eyes were so cold. He was starting to get angry and I understood that, but I didn't expect it to reach this level. His rage was so powerful and so immense that it drifted from him and surrounded the two of us.

He rested his hands on the kitchen counter and hunched his body for a second. He stood back up. His hands combed through his hair, gripping the strands tightly.

"Fuck!" he exploded.

I flinched. His head snapped in my direction. He repeatedly blinked and tilted his head to stare. It was as if he had forgotten I was here.

I waited for his questions. Because they were there. I saw them all in his eyes. But he didn't say a word. All he did was walk over to me. My body started to shake as he combed his fingers through my hair. My head dropped to his chest. Tears slipped down my cheeks as I listened to the strong pounding of his heart.

We stood there, silently, both lost in our own thoughts. He was trying to absorb what I had told him and I was scared out of my mind. Now that he knew, what would he do?

Max gently moved away. He looked composed, but I could see so much anger in his eyes.

I watched as he grabbed his car keys from his pocket.

"You stay here," he said very quietly before he turned and walked away.

Things were going from bad to worse in only a few seconds. I followed him. "Where are you going?" I asked, my voice alarmed.

"Just have something to do."

It felt like my heart had dropped all the way to my stomach. "Stop!"

Max grabbed the handle. The door opened. I came up behind him and pushed it shut. There was nothing but the sound of our heavy breathing.

"I'm just going to go talk to him." He tapped the door.

I was pretty sure he wanted to punch the hard oak until all his anger was gone and the door was hanging off its hinges. I would actually prefer that than have him leave right now.

"No, you're not."

He closed his eyes. He laughed, but it sounded like a moan. "Why aren't you letting me do this?"

"Because you can't."

"Someone needs to do something!"

"You don't need to be involved." He stared at me with shock. I grabbed his arm. "Please think about this," I pleaded. "You're going to go out there and do something you'll regret."

"I can promise you I won't regret a single thing."

"You're not in control right now and you know that."

Max looked away. He knew I was right.

I leaned against the wall. "I think," I started out slowly, "that you should just take a deep breath and think."

"You're afraid."

He had no idea how afraid I was. I looked past Max, a faraway look in my eyes, and I saw Lana hugging her knees to her chest and sobbing in the barn. I nodded.

"I am."

His eyes closed, and when they opened, some of that anger was gone. "Come here."

I pushed myself away from the wall. He enveloped me into his arms and held me tightly and kissed the top of my head. I closed my eyes. "I won't talk to Michael today," he said into my hair. "But I *will* talk to him."

That was what I was afraid of.

I sighed before I pulled away. Some of his anger had faded, but there was a spark of determination in his eyes. I may have stopped him today, but tomorrow was a whole other story.

"Will you be able to come with me tomorrow night?"

He stared at me blankly, totally caught off guard by my question.

"It's a party," I elaborated. "I want you to come with me. I told my parents I'd go months ago."

"I'll be there," Max said.

"Good," I said with relief. I chewed on my bottom lip, knowing I had to tell him the rest. "But . . . *he*'ll be there."

All that anger from earlier reappeared in his eyes within seconds. We both knew who *he* was.

"He's going?" Max asked.

"Yes," I confirmed.

"And you're going," he said grimly.

I nodded.

"Can I trust you not to . . . do anything?" I asked cautiously.

"Yes," Max bit out. His lips were pulled into a grimace, as if saying yes was causing him physical pain.

"I don't know if I believe you."

I knew I couldn't avoid Lana's dad forever. And a large part of me wanted to see him. I was dying to look him straight in the eye and tell him that I knew everything he had done. And that other part was terrified. But Max was a whole different subject.

"You're making me nervous," I said.

"Relax," Max replied. He gave me a smile that never reached his eyes. "I'll be a fucking boy scout. I won't do a damn thing," he said, and walked to the door.

This time, I didn't try to stop him.

His hand gripped the knob as he looked back at me. Our eyes connected at the same time. And maybe my eyes showed my pain, my worries, and my fear, because he walked back to me and cupped my face in his hands. I tilted my head back to look at him.

"Everything's going to be okay," he whispered.

I nodded. It was all I could do.

Max kissed my forehead and walked out the door.

The door shut with a click. I slumped against it and closed my eyes.

13

STAIRWAY

THERE WAS A GROUP OF MEN AROUND MAX. ONE OF THOSE MEN was incredibly drunk, incredibly loud, and incredibly annoying. He wouldn't stop talking.

". . . And you know what I said? I said, 'Ridiculous!'" The drunk man's hand landed firmly on Max's shoulder. "My stock-broker here wouldn't steer me the wrong way! He has a sharp eye. Goes in for the kill and makes the buy when the market's right! He has a sense for these kinds of things. And my bank account thanks him for it!" The man laughed, and his whiskey breath drifted my way.

I kept smiling but turned away and made a face over my shoulder, then took a sip of my drink. It was my third glass of wine. And all my worries and fears over seeing Lana's dad started to weaken. We had been here over an hour and hadn't seen Lana's parents yet.

This party was in sharp contrast to the one Max hosted. This one was inside a ballroom, with crystal chandeliers hanging above us and polished granite floors below us. Men in tuxes with black bow ties. Women in haute couture gowns in bold colors. I'd missed the grandiose memo, though, and went with a white cashmere top with a keyhole in the front, paired with a fitted black skirt that grazed the floor.

The drunk man's laughter died down. Max smoothly disengaged himself from the group of men. "If you fellas will excuse me, I need to go back to this beautiful creature," he said, his hand curving around my hip, "before someone steals her from me."

As we walked away, I leaned close and said, "Are you real?"

Max winked at me. "I'm as real as it gets."

"I swear everyone in this room loves you."

"They love the money I can make them," he replied.

"No. I think you've cast a spell on them. All I've heard are praises of you. And the women are looking at me like I'm public enemy number one and must be executed instantly."

Max raised his brows.

"Don't believe me? Let me show you how your night would be if I weren't here," I said.

I walked away and turned back in Max's direction. He looked at me with amusement. My smile was wicked. Naomi who? I was in character. I was a determined woman on the prowl. I walked forward—my steps confident—and bumped into his shoulder.

I covered my mouth and curled a hand around his arm. "I'm so sorry." I stared at him with wide doe eyes. "Oh! I know who you are. I've heard so much about you."

He started to play my game. Lips curved up in a come-hither smile. My blood roared in my veins.

"What have you heard?" Max asked, his voice a low, sexy whisper.

I lowered my voice and pointed a finger at him. "I've heard that you're the best thing to ever come to McLean." Another wicked smile. "I've heard that you could rock my world."

His eyes widened. He looked embarrassed. "Are you done?"

I wiggled a brow. "Oh, I've just begun."

We shared a smile that made the invisible cord wrapped around us tug, pulling us closer. My skin tingled.

Max looked over my shoulder. His eyes widened. An expletive slipped from his lips. When is that reaction ever good?

Even though I didn't want to, I turned around. My smile faded as I saw Lana's parents.

"Do you want to go?" Max said into my ear.

I discreetly pressed my body into his. "No . . . no, let's stay."

"Is that really a good idea?"

"I'll be fine," I assured him.

Max held my gaze. He didn't believe me. I didn't even believe myself. I was stunned to see her father walk so confidently into the room. Lana's dad met my eyes as if he knew I had been looking at him. He held my gaze for a second too long. Goose bumps covered my skin as he walked over, hand in hand with his wife.

"Ah, hell," Max muttered.

Her parents stood in front of us. We all stood there, poised like chess pieces, waiting to see who would make the next move.

Lana's dad smiled. He stretched his hand out to Max. "It's good to see you."

And then her dad looked in my direction. "Naomi."

I forced myself to say hi. He didn't know I knew and I reminded myself that, for now, it needed to stay that way. So I played the role of a guest having a great time. Smiled at this and nodded at that. It didn't mean it was easy, though. My fingers were so tightly laced behind my back, my circulation was close to being cut off.

I pictured a parallel universe where I could just leave my body. I would move throughout the crowd and no one would notice me. When I was a safe distance from Lana's dad, I'd watch as he pretended to be the perfect husband. And in this parallel universe, I would raise my hand. Index finger pointed, thumb lifted. Here was my gun.

I'd aim at his onyx heart.

Pull the trigger.

Bang.

Wouldn't it be lovely if everything in our imagination were real?

Lana's dad would disappear off the face of the earth. Her pain would evaporate and a fresh new start would be before her. We'd all live happily ever after.

I kept picturing that parallel universe. Until Max looked down at me.

Whoosh.

Slam.

I was pushed back into reality.

"Dance with me," Max said, and before I could answer him he put his hands on my shoulders, gently guiding me to the dance floor.

"I know what you're doing," I said out of the corner of my mouth.

"Then just go along with me."

He wrapped his arm around my waist, guiding me closer, until we were only a hair's breadth apart. I moved at the right time, and smiled at the people around us, but my heart wasn't in it. I could feel Lana's dad's cold eyes following us around the room. Max squeezed my hip. I looked up.

"Don't let him ruin tonight," he said.

"It's kind of hard not to."

"Where's the Naomi from earlier? The one with the sparkle in her eye?"

"Hiding," I mumbled. "Like any sane person."

Max bent close and said for my ears only, "Fuck him. Pretend he's not here."

That was impossible to do. Just then I heard Lana's dad laugh. My shoulders tensed. Anger started to build inside of me. The song finished. The drunk man was back at Max's side, starting up a whole new conversation. Max's hand curved around my waist. As they talked, I looked over my shoulder. I spotted Lana's dad instantly. He had a drink in his hand and was taking small sips as another guest talked to him. But then that guest patted Lana's dad on the shoulder and walked away. Her dad was alone.

Here was my chance. Max was distracted enough that I could slip away.

"I'm gonna go get a drink real quick."

Max nodded and I walked toward the bar before I made a beeline for Lana's dad. His wife's back was turned. She was talking to a group of ladies, waving her hands dramatically as she told a story.

I walked right past her and moved closer to Lana's dad. I saw nothing but red. My anger overpowered common sense and I went in for the kill.

I stopped next to him. He turned as if in slow motion. His lips curved up into a smile and the longer I stood there, staring into his eyes, the angrier I became. I had so much I wanted to say. So much pent-up rage inside of me that I didn't know where to start.

The longer I stood there, saying nothing to him, the quicker his smile faded. I opened my mouth and took a deep breath, ready to tell Lana's dad everything I really thought about him. I wanted him to know that I knew. That I'd seen it all and that I would never let it happen again.

"Naomi." Max laid his hand on my shoulder, stealing my one chance to tell Lana's dad off. "It's getting late. We should be going."

My throat was closing. Lungs were constricting. Max tugged on my arm. I wanted to push him away. I wanted to say so much, but I didn't. It felt like I was seconds away from passing out. It was almost as if my anger for Lana's dad was so powerful and all-consuming, my body couldn't handle it.

Max smoothly maneuvered us through the crowd, all the while saying good-bye to a few guests. I remained tight-lipped the entire time. I looked over my shoulder. Lana's dad was staring at us with calculating eyes. Something was brewing inside that fucked-up head of his. A plan was sliding into place, and I would be lying if I said I wasn't a little scared.

Okay, a lot scared.

When we exited the room, I jerked my arm out of Max's grasp. He breathed through his nose and made no attempt to hold me again. We said nothing on the way to his car. And when I did get into the car, I slammed the door behind me.

He started the car and the radio blasted. It was some upbeat song and it was the last thing I wanted to hear. Max instantly turned off the radio, as if he could read my mind. I stared out the window, watching the many silhouettes coming from the ballroom windows. I had been so, so close.

Max turned in his seat. I knew he was staring at me, waiting for me to speak. But I could wait him out. I could wait all fucking night if I had to. Finally he gave up and pulled out of the parking space.

There was pent-up anger in both of us. It swirled around us, making the air thick and heavy. We should have said something, anything, to release it. I couldn't, though. I had too many thoughts ricocheting in my head. My mind refused to hold onto a single one.

Max's eyes remained on the road. He took one hand away from the wheel and loosened his tie with impatient jerks. Streetlights were lined along the road, slanting dull yellow light across his face, letting me see his grim expression. His grip tightened on the steering wheel.

He broke the silence first.

"When I saw him, I had to control myself from wrapping my hands around his neck and choking him," he confessed. Max looked over at me. "I didn't think I'd have to worry about *you*."

I stared straight ahead. The road seemed to go on forever. Headlights illuminated our faces for a millisecond before we were washed in darkness. I looked out the window and saw nothing but a black landscape.

Neither one of us said a word the rest of the ride.

He pulled into his driveway and parked. The engine ticked slowly. "So this is how we're going to end tonight?" he said.

I didn't want tonight to end like this. This was the time when people relaxed and settled in for the evening. But the two of us were anything but relaxed. We were two ticking time bombs, only seconds away from exploding. I had to get out.

I grabbed the door handle, taking one good look at Max before I slammed the door. My heels clicked against the ground. Not even a second later, another door slammed and I heard footsteps behind me. I walked up the porch steps.

Max gripped my arm. "Wait."

I stopped in my tracks. He let go of my arm.

I paced the length of the porch, just listening to the sound of cicadas in the distance. I finally stopped and rested my palms on the railing. "I just can't do it," I said. "I can't be around him."

"Then don't."

"You make it sound so simple!" I whirled around, my anger finally getting the best of me. Max stared at me. In the depths of his eyes, I saw just how much this ate him up. "Tell me how to deal with this," I said quietly.

I crossed my arms, rubbing my goose bumps away. Max was silent. He stared at me thoughtfully and walked up the steps.

"I've talked to him," he said.

I slowly straightened. Before he spoke, my heart had finally slowed down. But now it had picked back up, pounding wildly.

"What?" I asked.

He leaned against the railing and crossed his arms, staring at the floor. "He came to my office today and I told him that I knew everything."

"What?" That seemed to be the only word I could say.

"I told you I wouldn't do anything yesterday," he reminded me. "And I didn't."

My fingertips dug into my skin as I stared at him.

"It makes me fucking sick to know this and not do anything about it. So I reacted," Max explained. "He had an appointment with me this morning. He talked about stocks and money, and the whole time I pictured myself reaching across the desk and choking the fucking life out of him."

I swallowed. I'd had the same kind of thoughts. More than I'd like to admit.

"What did he say?" I finally asked.

His lips thinned. "He denied the whole thing."

"He's lying!" I shouted.

"You don't think I know that?"

"Did he say anything else?"

Max stared at me, an inscrutable look on his face.

"I have to know," I said slowly.

"He said nothing happened. Told me that he would never touch his daughter." Max's eyes darkened. "He smiled and told me he hoped these accusations wouldn't affect our business relationship."

My heart sank at his words. "Why didn't you tell me this earlier?"

He cleared his throat and looked away. When he glanced back at me, his eyes had softened. "I didn't want to ruin tonight."

"You think he's going to do anything to you?" I asked.

"No," he said confidently, "I don't. And I don't want you to worry about him."

"How can I not, though?"

Max pushed himself away from the railing and stood in the middle of the porch. "I don't want him to ruin our night." He moved in. I walked toward him. "Please, ignore him."

I sighed and gave him a blunt nod.

"We were having fun before they arrived, right?" he said coaxingly.

It was the deep timbre of his voice and the intense look in his eyes that made my aggression break apart. What took its place was hunger. Blood roared underneath my skin. My hands started to shake from the urgency building up inside me.

He lifted a single brow and moved closer.

My body tensed with physical awareness. It was a slow tingle that spread through my body and had my breath coming out shaky and unsteady.

The last word that came out of my mouth was, "Yes."

And then he took a step forward, gripped my face, and kissed me.

There was no soft meeting of the lips. It was a kiss meant to steal the breath away from me. A kiss that stole my fate within seconds.

Everything around us became hazy. Sounds became muted. We were locked in our own world. I couldn't escape. And I didn't want to escape.

I stood on my tiptoes and wrapped my hands around his neck. My fingers curled into his hair. We stumbled backwards. He pressed me into the door. His hands outlined my curves, thumbs pressing into my flesh. As his fingers moved up, he gripped my neck, holding me in place. Our lips and hands worked in tandem.

I tilted my head to the side, opened my mouth farther, and I felt his tongue move against mine.

I took his jacket off. It fell to his feet. He hiked up my skirt until it was bunched around my waist. He lifted me, and instinctively my legs locked around his waist.

I was working on the buttons of his shirt when he opened the front door. He pushed us inside. I held onto him tight and made sure my feet didn't touch the floor.

The door slammed shut.

I lifted my head away from his for a quick second. A lamp was on in his office, casting us in a soft, warm glow. The two of us were panting, and I jerked his tie up and over his head and tossed it on the ground.

I grabbed his jaw with my palm, my fingers curling over his bottom lip. He looked at me. The hunger I had for him was like an addiction. It controlled me. It took away the power I thought I had and controlled every single action I made. I pressed my lips against his open mouth, still gripping his jaw with my fingers. He was caught off guard and I loved that. I licked the seam of his soft lips before I sunk my teeth into the lower one.

He hummed his response and walked forward. I pushed his shirt down his arms. My hands were frantic. Touching his shoulders. Gliding down his back. We bumped into a table. I heard a vase shatter. That didn't stop us.

He walked us up the stairs as we were still grabbing, still touching each other everywhere. This all-consuming need was thrilling. There were no reservations. No boundaries. Nothing was stopping us from fucking each other right here.

My fingers blindly reached for his belt buckle. It jangled loudly as I jerked the strap free. I moved on to his zipper, slipped a hand inside his boxers, and touched his cock. And in the middle of the stairs, Max dropped to his knees.

I was perched on the step above him. This new position didn't stop me from reaching farther into his pants and touching him with feather-light touches. He started to breathe heavily, so I wrapped my hand around him. The soft skin was so warm, silky. I increased the pressure and moved my hand from base to tip. A dazed expression crossed his face within seconds.

One of his arms wrapped beneath my back. His hand cupped my ass, pressing me closer to him. The other hand curved around my thigh before it slipped underneath my skirt. His palms touched my thighs. Fingertips drifted upward. My breath came out in shallow gasps. He looked up at me. Air crackled around us. His eyes stayed on mine as he slowly pulled my underwear down. The material grazed my skin. It moved over my knees. Trailed down my legs and caught on my heels.

Cool air touched my skin. I should have covered myself, but I didn't. Because in front of me I had a man who stared at me like he lived to do anything and everything for me.

I felt powerful and I never wanted the feeling to leave.

"I want to touch you right here." His finger brushed against my clit.

My legs jerked.

He grabbed a condom from his wallet and put it on quickly.

"But I want to be in you even more." His hands settled on the step above me and suddenly we were eye level. My thighs started to shake. "So I'm going to fuck you. And I'm going to watch your face as you scream my name." His voice was so steady and deep, I could have come right then and there.

One pause. One look into my eyes. One moment to brace myself. I wrapped my fingers around one of the stairway rails.

He bent closer and said against my lips, "And you're going to scream, love."

Then, with one quick thrust, he completely filled me. I closed my eyes and saw nothing but fragments of blinding white light. Sex with Max was just like his kisses, fast and all-consuming. Do or die. Now or never.

We found a rhythm that had me closing my eyes and groaning. I wanted more, though. So I lifted my hips obediently, meeting his thrusts. But this time, I pressed my heels into his ass, holding him so tightly inside me that my eyes rolled in the back of my head. I watched as Max's eyes closed. His mouth opened. Not a sound came out.

His hand covered mine over the railing. With every surge he squeezed his hold around me.

He started to gain speed. Each thrust became stronger and more powerful than the last.

My toes curled. My feet lifted. High heels fell off and tumbled down the stairs.

My orgasm was right there. It brewed in my body. It formed enough power for my back to arch and my hips to lift. I felt like I was moving higher and higher until I was levitating. I was weightless. No bones. Nothing holding me to the ground.

It was peace. It was mind-blowing. All too quickly, though, I was falling back to Earth.

My hands dropped heavily to my sides. My heart was close to beating out of my chest.

Max's release followed right behind mine. I touched his back as his body strained. His chest heaved. Fingertips dug into my skin. Muscles flexed. He shuddered; an anguished groan tore from his throat.

His movements slowed before he collapsed onto me, breathing heavily.

A moment later he lifted his head.

Neither of us said a word.

14

TRANSCEND

I STOP TALKING.

The memory becomes distant. I'm standing still, but it's moving away slowly. Farther, farther, farther. It becomes a small speck in my mind before it disappears altogether.

A shaky breath escapes me and I meet Dr. Rutledge's gaze. Every time I tell her more of my story, I'm sucked back to those moments. It's painful to come back to reality. I want to stay in my past where Max was waiting, where I still had Lana with me.

Dr. Rutledge looks at me with understanding before she looks down at her watch. "It's already five p.m. We'll resume tomorrow."

God, yes. I can't take much more. I need to get out of her office and make sure all my memories of Lachlan, Max, and Lana stay here. I picture myself locking the door and tossing the key behind me and running far away.

I stand and walk to the door.

"Naomi?"

I wince and turn. *Don't tell me there is more.*

"You did well today," Dr. Rutledge says gently, with a hint of pride.

I shouldn't bask in her words, but I do. She's listening to me. She's giving me a chance, and that shows me that maybe not every doctor in Fairfax is a total dumb-ass.

Mary is waiting for me in the hallway. We walk toward the dining room for dinner. Neither of us says a word. I'm trying to leave Max and Lana behind in Dr. Rutledge's office, but it's impossible. They follow me everywhere.

I can't escape them.

We stop outside of the dining room. "I'll pick you back up in forty-five minutes," Mary says before she walks away.

I'm twenty going on six. Hell, everyone here is. Everything I do here requires supervision. It was annoying the first time, but now I'm used to it.

The irony of this room is the layout. It looks like a classy restaurant. White pillars, a fireplace between two sets of French doors. Dark blue carpet. Pale yellow walls, and of course, two large paintings of flowers hanging on the wall. I make sure to look at them once during every meal. I consider it my art therapy for the day.

I grab my food, which consists of runny mac and cheese, a generous scoop of green beans, and a slice of dry chocolate cake. Plastic utensils and water.

There are tables scattered throughout the room. Some people sit together and talk. Some don't. Some are like me and sit with no one. My only habit is sitting close to Pretend Mommy. She's at her usual table, with her baby cradled in her arms.

I chew my food slowly and people-watch. Sitting at a table

behind Pretend Mommy is Amber. She picks at her macaroni, sifting through the noodles until she finds one that meets her standards. She finally chooses one, sucks the cheese. She goes to discreetly wipe her face, but I watch as she spits the noodle into the napkin.

She repeats this routine. A nurse sees the same thing I do. She walks over to Amber and talks quietly in her ear.

Amber grinds her teeth and holds another noodle to her mouth and stares for a few seconds. And then she snaps.

"I want to go back to my fucking room!" She picks up her tray and throws it at the wall.

Havoc breaks out everywhere. Patients start to shriek. A few giggle. One cries and hides under the table. Pretend Mommy cradles her baby to her chest and sings a nursery rhyme.

There's a guy sitting at a table next to mine. His name is Xander. He looks to be around my age. His dark brown hair is always mussed. He's lean, probably a little too skinny. That makes his high cheekbones even more prominent. He is unfazed. He leans back in his chair and grins. I want to think he's a lifer. That would explain his joy over all this chaos. But his haunted, mud-brown eyes make contact with mine and I see a brief understanding there, one that only someone with a torn-up past could understand.

Xander might be used to his chaos, but I don't think I ever will be.

I abandon my food and walk over to a nurse talking to Amber. "Can I go outside?" I ask above the noise.

She gives me an impatient look. I can already tell that she's going to say no.

"I'm not going to escape or go all crazy," I say quickly. "I just want a few minutes of peace."

She looks me up and down. I must pass her inspection. Or

maybe she's tired of the chaos going on and she couldn't care less what I do. Either way, she briskly says yes and turns back to Amber.

I shove open the door. The cold air slams into me so painfully I almost wheeze. But the door shuts behind me, and as the noises from inside fade, I realize I would take this freezing air any day over sitting in that dining room.

I walk across the snow and make my way to the railing. In front of me is a stretch of land with grass covered by snowflakes and naked trees standing bravely in the freezing temperatures. You know, if I want, I can make a run for it. I'll have thirty minutes, an hour at the most, where no one will even notice I'm gone. As tempting as the thought is, I'm terrified. I keep looking over my shoulder, afraid someone is watching me from the inside and can read my thoughts.

I shove my hands into the sleeves of my hoodie and walk over to the flight of steps. I sit on the top step. This is as close as I'll get to freedom.

The balcony doors creak open behind me. I keep my face forward as the doors clicks shut.

"Naomi."

Goose bumps spread across my skin just from the sound of his voice. *Lachlan.*

He sits down next to me and takes a deep breath. It forms into the air like a mist of smoke. I try to grab it before it disappears, but I'm too late.

"I've been looking for you," he says.

I stare straight ahead. "Who told you where I was?"

His shoulder touches mine and he makes no effort to move away. I close my eyes and just take this in. His warmth, the feel of him. My hands curve around the underside of my thighs. I continue to stare out into the trees.

"No one," he says. "When I walked into the dining room you were walking outside, and . . . here you are."

"Here I am," I say, testing his words, trying to make sense of them.

Am I really here? Sure, in the physical sense I am, but that means nothing. It's my soul, the very core of me, that feels split up. And Max, Lachlan, and Lana hold those pieces.

Finally, I look over at Lachlan. I want to reach into him and grab the part of myself that he stole.

My heart is stuck in my throat as I look him over. I love him so much. I love him too much to be considered healthy. I know that. And yet, I love Max with almost the same intensity. Does that make me a terrible person? Loving two men at the same time? I suppose. But I crave both of them more than air.

If I had to choose between the two of them right here, right now, I couldn't. I don't know how to live without either one.

Lachlan has slightly changed. I know that's impossible. It hasn't been that long since I've seen him. His hair looks longer. Usually he's clean-shaven, but there's stubble on his face. His eyes look weary and so sad. I want to ask what's keeping him up at night, but I'm pretty sure I already know.

"You told me you weren't coming back." I feel too much right now, so my eyes start to well up with tears. The emotions have to get out somehow. "You can't just keep coming in and out of my life. It will kill me," I say brokenly.

He drags his fingers through his thick hair. "I don't know if I should even be here right now," he admits. "I just miss you so fucking much."

I let his words sink in and instantly feel a surge of energy that I haven't felt since the last time I saw him.

"I miss you too," I whisper.

Lachlan's sharp hazel eyes focus on me with determination.

"They allow you out of here on passes or something like that. You know that, right?"

I didn't. "How do you know?"

"I asked. If you can get away from here for the weekend . . . do you want me to take you away?"

I want it more than my next breath. I find my voice and whisper, "I'd love that."

"Good. It will happen," he says with confidence.

Lachlan has enough optimism for both of us. I really don't believe that they'll ever give me a weekend pass. I'm starting to believe that I'll never get out of here.

I look away. "Have I always been crazy?" I ask absently.

"Don't say that about yourself."

I nudge my head toward the building. "They think I'm crazy. Keep trying to diagnose me." I toy with the material of my sweatpants. "Even my new doctor . . . she can't seem to figure me out."

"Do you like her?"

"Better than my old doctor. For some reason, I trust her." I shrug awkwardly.

"That's good, though," Lachlan says.

I glance at him. "I saw you a few nights ago."

Lachlan frowns.

"You laid with me," I continue. He sucks in a sharp breath and links his hands behind his neck. His eyes slam shut, like he's in pain. "Crazy, right? You weren't there, but you were. I swear you were. You talked to me. You told me a story to help me fall asleep. Even now, I can't tell if you're sitting next to me or if I'm imagining this."

Abruptly, he stands up and kneels on the step below me. His knees are buried in the cold snow, but he doesn't seem to care.

"I'm here right now."

Both of his hands wrap around my knees. His fingers rub my skin softly. I stay perfectly still and watch his hand travel from my knees, up the sides of my thighs, and to my waist. He grips me tightly, as if I will flee any second.

"Someday, you're gonna get out of here." He utters the last of his words slowly. "And everything's going to be okay."

I believe his words only because they're all I have left. Bending close, I wrap myself around him and tuck my face into his neck. I breathe him in like it's the last thing I'll ever be able to do.

"Tell me what you're fighting and I'll fight with you," he whispers into my hair.

My hand curls around his neck, holding him in place. A painful moan tears from my mouth. If I could reach inside myself to find the words, I'd tell Lachlan I miss him every day. That every day apart makes me feel like I'm slowly being drained of life. But I don't have to speak. Lachlan hears the truth without a sound escaping my mouth.

"I know," he whispers. He pushes himself closer and our faces are inches apart, our breath mingling together. "I'm going to get you out of here."

Hope has all but disappeared from my spirit. But I feel it now. I hold on tight to it. Who knows how long this feeling will last.

He pulls away reluctantly. His fingers brush against my cheeks, making slow circles. "I have to leave."

"No," I protest. My hands tighten around his neck. "Stay."

"I didn't sign in at the front desk. Mary will find me, and you know she's not afraid to kick me out of here."

"Stay," I whisper against his lips.

"I . . ." He starts to say something, but it fades into the air.

His lips move against mine. Slowly at first. But then the kiss picks up speed and the two of us become almost desperate. My fingers curl into his hair. He breathes through his nose. His body leans into mine, and the feel of his weight makes warmth spread throughout me.

Then Lachlan rips himself away. The two of us are breathing heavily. His hands grip the railing. "I have to go." I don't know whether he's saying that for himself or me. "But I'm not going to stay away, okay? I love you," he says fiercely.

"I love you too."

He stands and walks up the stairs. I hear snow crunching underneath his feet.

I drop my face into my hands. I reach into my memory and go through the years until I find one that makes the blow of Lachlan leaving soften.

I find a memory that makes my lips softly curl into a smile. I find a memory that makes me numb to the cold, and to the feeling of loneliness.

15

NAOMI DAY

8 YEARS AGO

"I CAN'T BELIEVE I'M LETTING A CHILD LIGHT A MATCH."

I concentrated on the rocket. "I'm twelve years old, Lachlan. I'm not a child."

He snorted. "Just hurry up before you catch something on fire."

At that, I blew out the match in his hand and grinned.

"Don't do that." He dug inside his pocket and pulled out another matchstick. "I only have a few left."

Today was July 19. My birthday. It took me two years, but I was finally going to have fireworks. I couldn't stop moving around. I was so excited. I reached out and tried to catch a lightning bug for the eighth time and failed. Lachlan sighed and within seconds, caught one. Cupping it between his hands, he transferred it to my waiting palms. He handed it over the way a big brother would. In a brisk gesture that said, *"Here. I just did it for you so you would stop trying."*

"Where is all this energy coming from?" he asked.

"I'm just excited to see all the bright colors!" I smiled. "I think this is the best birthday present ever," I confessed.

"How did your family celebrate your big day?"

"We had cake and presents."

"That's it?" Lachlan frowned. "No birthday party? No sleepovers? Don't girls do all that crap?"

"Not all girls do that crap," I said, and changed the subject. "Can we light the fireworks now?"

"Man, you're impatient," he teased, and handed me the match.

It took me three times to light the match. My fingers shook as I put the flame against the fuse. Seconds later there was a hissing sound and sparks. We sprinted away and turned in time to watch the sky light up.

For the next fifteen minutes we set off as many fireworks as we could. I stared in awe the whole time.

I wanted to light up more, but Lachlan said no. "We'd better stop before we get in trouble." He slid the matches back into his pocket. "Happy birthday, kid," he said, before he turned and walked away.

"Hey, come back!" I shouted.

"Kiiiid," he drew out. But he came back to me. "What?"

"You can't leave."

He looked down at his watch. "I got a date in fifteen minutes."

A year ago Lachlan got his driver's license. His parents had a shiny black car waiting for him in the driveway. He had the freedom to come and go as he pleased. I hated it.

And here he was, getting ready to leave again. Anger flared inside of me.

"With who?" I asked.

"With a senior."

I crossed my arms. "With who?"

"Laura Kline. Do you know her? Yeah. Didn't think so."

I didn't know Laura Kline, but I already knew I disliked her.

"Well, you can't leave," I said, matter-of-fact.

He frowned, but there was still that mischievous gleam in his eyes. "I'm waiting for the reason why. Why can't I leave?"

"I have no one else to celebrate my birthday with!" I exclaimed. It came out like a whine.

"What about Lana?"

Lana was my best friend. Her dad worked with my dad. One day, a week after my tenth birthday, she came along with her dad. Instead of coming inside, she sat on the porch steps, staring at the ground. I sat next to her and happily introduced myself. She stared at me in a mixture of shock and curiosity. I talked her ear off and she sat and listened the whole time. By the end of the day, she slowly started to thaw. I saw her kind spirit and knew she would be my friend.

That was two years ago. We've been best friends ever since.

"She's not here," I said.

"Okay . . . don't you have any other friends?"

"No."

He frowned. "No one else?"

I looked away. "Just you."

"You need more than just me, kid."

"Or I could just have you and Lana. That's way better than a lot of friends. It's simple math, really."

"How do you figure?"

"My grandma always told me that she would rather have

four quarters worth of friends than a hundred pennies worth of friends."

"You're still missing the two other quarters."

"Nah. You two are enough."

Lachlan grinned. "Who can argue with that?"

He looked back down at his watch, then at his car sitting in the driveway, and let free a heavy sigh. "We have one more rocket left. Wanna light up the sky?"

My eyes widened and I nodded anxiously.

We kneeled back on the ground. I scratched at a mosquito bite on my leg as Lachlan prepared the last rocket. He lit a match. When it shot up into the sky, I craned my neck and watched the show. He stood next to me. Not once did he take his phone out and look at the time. We were both too caught up in the grand display. It wasn't bigger or brighter than any of the other fireworks. But it felt like it.

"Happy birthday," Lachlan said. "Make a wish."

I made a wish that every July 19 would be like this. With bright lights and smiles and laughter.

I wished for Lachlan to be by my side for the rest of my life.

16

BLACK HOLE

SOMEONE TOUCHES MY SHOULDER.

I gasp and whirl around. Mary is standing beside me.

I'm back at Fairfax. Still outside. Snowflakes cling to my hair and my hands feel like icicles. Remnants of my memory are still there. If I close my eyes and really focus, I can hear the distant echo of fireworks and cheers from a small, twelve-year-old girl.

"Are you ready to go in?" Mary asks.

I stand on shaky legs. "How long have I been outside?"

"For about an hour. You looked deep in thought."

She has no idea.

We walk inside the dining room. Everything's cleaned up. There are only a few patients quietly eating. It's as though Amber's outburst never happened.

I'm still in a daze as we walk back to my room. Fluorescent lights above us cast my skin in an unhealthy shade of yellow. I walk inside my room. The lights are already on. I stop short and look around.

I just came back from a memory so innocent and wonderful. My reality, living at Fairfax, is the complete opposite. I don't want to be in here.

I go through my nightly routine: Bathroom. Wash my face. Change clothes. And when I'm done, Mary's in my room with medication in one hand and a small cup of water in the other. Except tonight I go through the routine feeling numb. My mind won't pull away from Lachlan and twelve-year-old Naomi.

"Get some sleep," Mary urges. She turns off the light and shuts the door.

Not even a second later I see Lana's dad in the corner.

He's seething with rage. He's crouched down, ready to attack at any moment. My heart skips a beat but I don't react. The medicine is doing its job. It's making me not care. But Lachlan's visit is even more powerful than the medicine.

And he, Lana's dad, knows that. His voice gets louder. On another night, it could terrify me . . . but not right now. Right now it drifts past me and all his vicious words start to fade until they become a distant echo. My skull feels like it's sinking into the pillow. I'm drifting farther, until I'm being pressed down into the mattress. It's as if I'm free-falling, pushing past the floor and the frozen ground. I keep moving, watching years of my life pass in front of me.

I want one more memory. Maybe I'm greedy and asking for too much, but I want to see Lachlan again.

My body stops moving. I close my eyes, and I dream.

17

SILVER LINING

"'Lachlan. Good to see you. Is it summer break already?'

"No," I groaned, and laid my palm against my forehead. "I sound like an idiot."

I took a deep breath and tried again.

"'Oh. Hey, Lachlan. How are you? I totally forgot you were coming home.'"

I'd been practicing my reaction and what I would say to Lachlan for the past hour. I was lying down in the tree house, staring up at the clear, dark sky. There was freedom here to say my words without embarrassing myself.

Lana had told me to practice what I would say to Lachlan. Yesterday, she sat with me up in my room, telling me that she does this anytime she's nervous about meeting someone new.

She swears by it. But the technique wasn't working for me. I was no closer to controlling my shaky voice than I had been hours ago.

It was that time. Summer. When Lachlan would come home from college and everything in my life would slide back into place.

He left for college last year. I remember the night before he left, sitting up in that tree house, knowing that things were going to change. Big time. He was going to outgrow me. Of course he was. What eighteen-year-old would want to keep talking to a thirteen-year-old girl?

I told him that I wanted to go with him. Lachlan just sighed and tugged on my braid and said, "You can't, kid. You gotta stay here and get older, wiser, and smarter."

"I'm thirteen," I said. "I'm already older, wiser, and smarter."

He laughed. "Okay. Well, you have to graduate high school. Then you can go wherever you want."

I ducked my head and stared down at my shoes. "I want to go wherever you are."

"Don't say that. If you could go anywhere . . . anywhere in the world, where would it be?"

I hadn't thought that far. I'd dreamed up places, but I never thought those dreams would come true. "I-I don't know."

"Don't know? What do you mean you don't know?" He held his hands out in front of him. "Be adventurous, kid! When you get out here, you can do anything you want!"

Lachlan made it sound simple. Easy. Like it was one foot in front of the other.

"I will," I promised. "You're gonna tell me everything about college, right?"

His hands lowered. He smirked, as if what I said was funny. I wanted to ask him what was so funny. I wanted to lean forward and say, "Tell me what makes you laugh. I want to know the inside joke."

But I didn't.

"Not everything, but most," he said.

"I'll miss you," I whispered.

Lachlan smiled at me before he stood up and walked away. "Miss you too, kid."

I looked away.

"Cheer up. I'll still see you in the summer. Okay?"

He was my happiness. And my happiness was leaving me to travel 2,100 miles away to find his own happiness. How could I be okay?

The next day he left, and I had to figure out what to do with this big, gaping hole he'd left in my life. He would keep in contact with short, friendly e-mails. Each time I saw a new message from him, my heart would hammer wildly in my chest and I would click on the message, not expecting much. Lachlan was my source for living, and those messages kept me going.

I would read the messages enough times that I had the words memorized. I would read them to Lana and she would sit on my bed, smiling but shaking her head at me as if I'd lost my mind. Her visits to my house were becoming more and more frequent. We started to forge a bond that was unbreakable. We became close enough that we would fight like sisters and seconds later move to a different subject as if nothing had happened.

And that's how I survived the first year of his absence.

He's kept busy during the summer, traveling with friends. But now it was August. He was home. I didn't know how long he'd stay, but all that mattered was that he was *here*.

Finally.

I took a deep breath and tried to focus on my words. " 'I'll be really busy this summer, Lachlan. I won't be able to see you that much.'

"No, no, no," I said, and rubbed my hands down my face. "That's all wrong. He'll know I'm lying."

The wood creaked loudly and seconds later I heard, "Are you talking to someone?"

I scrambled to a sitting position and watched Lachlan climb into the tree house. My embarrassment disappeared and was replaced by happiness at the sight of him. He had grown so much that he had to duck to avoid the branches as he walked over to me.

Every year I noticed more things about him. At ten, I thought he was cute. I would write his name on pages. Over and over. Sometimes our names would be in hearts. Sometimes it was just his name alone. At eleven, I wanted to kiss him. Didn't know why; I just had this urge to press my lips against his head. At twelve it was his hair. It always looked so messy and I wanted to touch it to see if it was soft or not. At thirteen, I memorized the way he smiled. And now, at fourteen, I noticed everything about him. Shoulders. Arms. Hands.

Everything.

I shook away my thoughts. "I was just . . . talking to myself."

"That sounds healthy."

My cheeks turned beet red.

"I leave for school and you go crazy on me?" Lachlan teased.

"Ha, ha."

He sat across from me and sighed. "Can't believe you still come up here."

I patted the wooden boards beneath me. "I told you I'd use it."

"Yeah. You weren't lying."

We sat in companionable silence. He was looking at the sky and I was looking at him. His head started to turn and I looked away before he caught me.

"How has your summer been?" he asked.

I shrugged and reminded myself to answer casually. "It's been good."

"Hanging out with Lana?"

"Yep."

"Am I ever going to meet her?"

"Sure." I leaned back against the railing, making myself comfortable. "Whenever she gets the courage to come over here with me."

"And that will be?" His question hung in the air.

"Never," I said bluntly.

"She's that shy?"

"She's that shy," I confirmed.

"Have you said terrible stuff about me?" Lachlan said teasingly.

"The worst," I said without missing a beat. "I tell her about all the times I've come up here to see you and you weren't here."

I couldn't keep the bitterness inside anymore.

Lachlan looked at me with surprise. Even I was shocked over my outburst.

"Are you sure you're okay?" he said with concern.

"Yes."

Lachlan's eyes narrowed as he tilted his head to the side. "Something isn't right."

"Everything is fine," I vowed.

Lachlan refused to let it go. "You're not your usual, happy self."

"I promise," I uttered slowly, "I'm fine."

Lachlan exhaled loudly and looked around. It was awkward.

I wasn't fine, or good, or great. I was . . . nothing. But how could I tell that to Lachlan? I could barely figure out what was wrong myself. Lana said it was just the age. She said all teenagers go through it. I asked her why she wasn't going through it and she shrugged, asked what I was feeling. I told her that one minute I would be so happy, feeling like I could take on everything in the world, and that the next, out of nowhere, I would be in a complete daze. Then I would turn moody and so sad it felt like I couldn't breathe. She stared at me, blankly. I asked her if she'd ever felt that way. She looked down at the ground and said, "I have the sadness, but never the happiness."

"So . . ." Lachlan drew out. I quickly shook my head, brushing away the memory. "Any new stories to tell? There has to be something brewing in that mind of yours."

I smiled, relieved that he'd changed the subject. There were new stories every day. When my imagination wasn't running wild, I would sit down at my desk and write until my hand became sore.

"I'm still writing stories. But I don't think it's going to go anywhere."

"Are you going to let me read one?"

I blushed. "No."

I knew what my stories were. Love letters to Lachlan. In every single story, he was my muse for the hero. When I wrote, when I imagined, my heart bled out a piece of the truth.

"Why not?" he asked.

I shrugged, brushing away the dirt that was scattered across the floorboards. "They're just stories."

"Just stories," he repeated.

"I'd tell you," I said in a rush. "But you're probably too old for them."

"Me? Old? Get real. I'll never outgrow your stories."

My pulse was pounding as I replayed his words. I hoped he meant what he said. "Are you sure?" I asked. "Because—"

"I'm serious. I want to hear one."

I relaxed, looked up at the endless sky, and closed my eyes. Once again, Lachlan drew me into a little world of dreams. I could live there forever. And who could blame me? The imagination is the best place to be.

My shoulders loosened and all those jittery nerves seemed to disappear as I talked.

I told him my story. It was the end of days and only five people were left on Earth. But they weren't alone. There was another group of people called the Eights. They looked human but were monsters, sent to destroy mankind. The five survivors had to band together to live.

I talked until my voice was scratchy, until my pulse was pounding from excitement. Until the story was told from start to finish.

Lachlan let out a whistle. "That's a good one."

Anxiously, I leaned closer. "You think so?"

"I think you know it's good."

I smiled so hard my cheeks started to hurt. I could bask in his praise for hours, but I wanted to know what he had been up to.

"How have you been?"

Lachlan leaned against the wood railing and crossed his arms. My eyes veered to his hands. Compared to my small hands, his long fingers were massive. Butterflies fluttered in my stomach. I pulled my eyes back to his face.

"It's summer break and I don't have to study for hours, so I'm doing really well."

I frowned. "You don't like college?"

"I like college."

"It doesn't sound like you do."

"I do," he started out slowly. "There are just some parts I like *a lot* more." He gave me a shit-eating grin.

I was old enough to know that he was talking about girls, and it was a physical blow. Like someone had punched me in my chest.

I chewed on my bottom lip and stared at my tennis shoes. There was one question I was dying to ask. I nervously looked at him.

"Do you have a girlfriend?"

I was proud of myself. My voice didn't waver and my cheeks hadn't turned red . . . yet.

"Right now? No. But I've had a few."

"I remember . . . Laura Kline." I made a face and a gagging noise.

He smirked. "Why are you so curious? Are you getting into all that boyfriend-and-girlfriend teenager shit?"

I tilted my head. "Teenager shit?"

"You know . . ." He waved a hand in the air. "Holding hands and all that *stuff*."

"I don't know . . . I guess so."

"Who's the dude?"

I'm looking at him, I thought to myself.

"Some guy," I said evasively.

"Ah . . . he's a *guy*. Not a boy. Must be older . . . what, fifteen?" he teased.

I narrowed my eyes. "Much older than fifteen."

He frowned. "Kid, anything that's older than fifteen is too old for you."

"No, it's not."

"It really is," he argued.

I picked up a leaf lying next to me and twirled it around. He didn't know what was best for me. No one did but me.

"Can I give you some advice?"

I lifted my eyes to his and said reluctantly, "I guess so."

"Every guy your age is an asshole. Don't trust them."

"What about *your* age?"

He gave me a grin that made me suck in a sharp breath. "We're still assholes. Basically, you can trust none of us. And all that kissing stuff?" He shook his head. "Don't do that either."

My eyes narrowed. "So what can I do?"

"Write letters or shake hands."

"Shake hands?" I said skeptically.

"Yeah. That's all you need."

I frowned and didn't say a word. I didn't know what I wanted, but I knew one thing: I didn't want to shake his hand. I looked at Lachlan and caught him staring at me. His brows were knitted together, and I was too afraid to ask him what he was thinking about, too afraid that he would give me more "boy advice."

I quickly spoke up. "What time is it?"

He looked at me a second longer and grabbed his phone. "It's two fifteen."

"In the morning?"

"No. In the afternoon. The sun just didn't feel like rising today."

I lightly kicked his foot. I stood up and brushed the dirt off the back of my shorts. "I need to get home."

I didn't want to leave. It felt as if Lachlan had just climbed up that ladder seconds ago, and now our time was up.

"How long are you home?" I asked.

"For a week, and then I gotta head back to school."

I stared at the floorboards. A week wasn't even close to the amount of time I wanted with him. But I would take what I could get.

Lachlan stood up. "What's wrong?"

"Nothing."

Lachlan stood and walked over to me. He patted me on the head. My jaw was clenched tight over the brotherly gesture.

"All that stuff I said about boys . . . you know I'm just looking out for you, right?"

"I know. Thanks," I mumbled before I ducked out from under his hand.

I didn't want him warning me. I wasn't his little sister. If I could see that, why couldn't he?

"I'm here for a week," he called out. I stopped walking. "I brought home some fireworks for you. I know I missed your birthday, but I thought we could still light them up."

It was a peace offering.

Before I climbed down the ladder, I smiled at him. "That sounds good."

"Are you sure you're okay?" Lachlan said.

Before I jumped onto my saddle, I glanced back at him. He was looking at me with concern written all over his face. For a moment I just basked in that concern. Even though he had been gone for so long, nothing had really changed. He was still there for me, and I hoped to God that he would always be there for me. That time, age, and experience would never change that.

"I'm fine," I said, and rode back to my house.

And I was . . . for now.

I WAKE UP WITH A GASP.

My hands are gripping the sheets tightly. Sweat trickles down my spine and my heart is racing.

It takes me a minute to realize where I am and when I do, I drop my face into my hands. I want to go back to that memory and live there, when everything was so simple.

After I take a deep, cleansing breath, I lift my head and look around. I expect to find him bent down in the corner, staring me down, snickering, screaming expletives in my face. But there's no one looking back at me with hate.

It's just me here. All alone.

I wrap my arms around my waist, turn my head, and watch the sun slowly rise.

I think of Lachlan the whole time.

18

THE BRINK

"How are you, Naomi?"

I glance at Dr. Rutledge as I take a seat. "I'm good."

"Did you sleep well?"

"All right, I guess."

"Excellent." She takes a sip of her coffee before she grabs her pen. "How about we get started, then. Can you tell me—?"

"Miss me?" Max whispers.

Suddenly, he's right next to me. My heart does somersaults in my chest.

His presence is powerful enough to suspend reality. My head stays forward, but my eyes turn at the sound of his voice. I soak in his features. The slant of his dark brows. His bright hazel eyes. The curve of his lips. My fingers grip the armrests so I don't reach out and touch him. I miss him so much.

His hands curve around the armrests, inches away from my

elbows. A few seconds later, I feel the hard wall of his chest press against my shoulder. It's tantalizing. His hair brushes against my jaw as he leans close and the scent of his aftershave reaches my nose. His lips brush against my ear and I jump.

"Keep talking to her. It's your only chance of getting out of here."

I swallow and look at Dr. Rutledge. Her lips are moving, but I can't hear her. I can only hear Max.

I know what he's saying is the truth. Dr. Rutledge is my only ticket to getting out of here. And when I get out of here, I can help Max and Lana, and everything will be better. Not perfect, just better.

"I miss you," Max whispers into my ear. His voice is like sharp talons around my heart. Each word that comes out of his mouth pierces me, making my breath hitch. My face remains forward but I can just see his lips curving up into that sexy smile of his. "I need you to come back."

And just like that, he's gone. His scent. His voice. His presence. All gone. I hang my head, wanting so bad to scream in frustration.

I had him. Just for a minute Max was with me, but that is almost worse than not seeing him.

When I look at Dr. Rutledge, she's staring at me with a confused look on her face. She doesn't know that I was just given the highlight of my day. Maybe my whole week.

"Did you hear me?" she asks.

I shake my head. "I'm sorry . . . what?"

"I asked if we could pick up where we left off last session."

I nod. "Yeah . . ." I say slowly. "Yeah, that sounds good."

Words start to spill from my mouth and the whole time, Max's voice echoes in my head.

"Keep talking to her. It's your only chance of getting out of here."

19

THE PLAN

"I DROPPED HIM AS A CLIENT."

My window was down, letting the warm breeze whip my hair around my face. I didn't bother pushing the strands away. It just felt good to have a moment of freedom. Where I had no worries. But there was Max, ripping me out of this peaceful moment.

I turned in my seat and gaped at him. "What?"

Max shifted gears and kept his eyes on the road. He was dressed down today, in a simple pair of jeans and a dark blue T-shirt. The sun slipped in through the open sunroof, slashing across his forearm.

It was a hot summer day. The kind where you just want to tilt your head back, close your eyes, and do nothing but dream. We drove down a twisted country road with nothing but green grass around us. We had no destination; we just drove to get away from McLean.

A week had passed since I discovered the truth about Lana. I wish I could say that everything was starting to smooth itself out, but nothing had changed.

Lana's dad was still free. Lana was still staying at her family's house. So was I. I wasn't leaving until she left. So I pleaded for her to get out of there, but she wouldn't budge. She would always say the same thing: nothing happened. Sure, for the time being he was leaving Lana alone, but for how long? There was an expiration date. I didn't know when it would arrive, but I could feel it creeping up on the two of us.

It was inevitable that I would see Lana's dad. After the party, I expected him to say something to me, but he didn't. He just stared at me carefully. Sometimes he would smile, and it was as if he knew how badly I wanted to tell someone but couldn't. When I did encounter him, I would always react the same way. My chest would tighten and I would feel panic sweep through me, leaving me paralyzed. He would leave the room or the house, and it was only then that I would be able to breathe evenly.

And sometimes, he didn't even have to be around for me to feel that way. I would be with Lana, out in public, laughing at something she said, or walking innocently down the street, and I would suddenly be slammed with pain. It would start at my hips and spread throughout my body like tree limbs.

There were times I would wake up in the middle of the night and suddenly sit up in bed, panting and frantically looking around the room. I would feel disoriented, as though I had blacked out and lost hours of my life. But reality would always catch up to me and I would be reminded that everything in my life was a mess, slowly unraveling before my eyes.

The way I was reacting scared the shit out of me. I could only chalk it up to panic attacks, but I knew they had to get better soon; I didn't know how long I could last.

When I wasn't with Lana, I was with Max. I took his request to spend the summer with me seriously. I spent almost every day with him, but I never stayed the night. It was starting to become a point of contention between us.

He just couldn't wrap his brain around the fact that I was staying, willingly, with Lana, knowing that Lana's dad lived under the same roof.

I wanted to stay with him more than anything. I wanted to wake up in the morning draped over his body. I wanted to be able to lean in and kiss him, and have him respond by rolling me over, pressing me into the mattress, holding me so tightly that all my problems would drift away.

"I said I dropped him as a client," Max repeated.

My eyelashes fluttered against my skin rapidly. I sat up straight in my seat. "When?"

"As of yesterday."

I swallowed and ignored the feeling of dread creeping up on me.

"What did he do?"

Max shifted in his seat. Instinctively, his hands tightened around the steering wheel. "My secretary was right outside the door, so he did what he always does in front of an audience. He kept his composure and just walked away."

I nodded. It made sense. Lana's dad was a very smart man. He wouldn't seethe with rage and make a scene. He would do that behind closed doors, while he plotted his revenge.

I looked at Max with alarm. "You don't think he's going to do anything, do you?"

"No." Max looked over at me. "You think he will?"

I drummed my fingers on the armrest. "I think we're all trying to be a winner in a losing game."

"That's the thing, though, Naomi. This isn't a game. It's the difference between black and white. Right and wrong. This is no game. He's fucked with someone's life and he's not going to get away with it."

Anger seeped into his words. I knew he was barely keeping himself together.

"I know that," I said gently. "But it's not that simple. If it was, he'd be locked away right now."

"I promise you he won't get away with it," Max said heatedly.

I looked out the window. I didn't want to start talking about Lana's dad. The main reason for this drive was to de-stress and *not* think about anything.

"I've been thinking about something," I said carefully.

"And that is?"

"Getting away from all this . . . bullshit. Somewhere not too far." I shrugged underneath his gaze. "Maybe to D.C.?"

Max let off the gas and pulled over on the side of the road. He put the car in park and turned to look at me. I rotated in my seat. My shin brushed his thigh. I didn't pull away. Even when the moment wasn't sexually charged, my body still sought him out. He was a comfort for me. I think he would always make me feel that way.

I told him my idea to convince Lana to move to D.C.

It suddenly occurred to me, a few days ago, that I needed to compromise with her. She couldn't take college, couldn't take being away from everything she knew. But what if I told her she could move out and still remain close to her hometown? What if she was surrounded by a place she'd known all her life and was safe at the same time?

My plan wasn't foolproof, but it was taking shape. It was starting to make more sense as time went on.

"You sure that's a good idea?" Max asked.

"It's the best idea," I said confidently. "And it's the only idea that makes sense."

He nodded and stared at the road. I knew he agreed with my plan, but he was thinking over every option, trying to think of everything that could go wrong. "When is this apartment hunting going to happen?"

"As soon as possible."

"How long have you been thinking about this?"

"Not very long." I looked at him out of the corner of my eye.

He had taken off his sunglasses. His eyes bore straight through me.

"I've been bouncing the idea back and forth for a few days," I said.

He raised both brows. "That's it?"

"What more do you want me to say?"

"I figured if you've been thinking about this you'd have places lined up, a whole plan set in place. Think about this long and carefully so it all sticks in the end."

"You don't think I haven't been thinking about this carefully? That's all I've been doing the last week. Carefully tiptoeing around everyone and everything . . ." I looked away. "There's no other option."

"Hey," he said gently. He tipped my chin up so I was looking at him. "You know that I, out of all people, want this to happen, right?"

"Yes," I whispered.

He held my gaze. "Do it and I'll be right behind you the whole time," he said, his voice steady and sure.

It gave me a small boost of confidence. I smiled gratefully and kissed him.

"Thank you," I said.

He pulled back onto the road.

One hurdle had been crossed. The only thing I needed to do now was talk Lana into it.

20

ON THE HUNT

"IF YOU NOTICE, IT HAS A PATIO THAT HAS AN AMAZING VIEW OF the city," the realtor said.

It took me a solid week of talking Lana into apartment hunting before she agreed. I had instantly made an appointment to look at a few apartments. Lana canceled that appointment, coming up with a lame excuse as to why she couldn't make it.

It wasn't that easy this time around. Max was here. He'd left work early to apartment hunt with us. He was still dressed in his work clothes: black dress pants, oxford shirt. His tie was loosened and his sleeves were rolled up to his elbows. He scanned everything with a critical eye. His eyebrows were creased. His jaw was set. My heart stuttered and stopped, creating its own new rhythm as I watched him. It wasn't the way he looked that made me react this way; it was his concern. His determination to make sure that Lana was safe. It was a huge turn-on. I had to stop myself from reaching out, grabbing him by his tie, and dragging him close to me.

Lana scanned the empty living room. Her eyes took in everything. I could see her picturing how she would decorate this place, if it were hers. And there was no reason why this apartment couldn't be hers.

It was cozy, with just two bedrooms, a small kitchen with new appliances, and an attached island. The living room was a good size. The walls were painted a shade of ivory and the floors were hardwood.

Yet the one thing that was most important to Lana was the location.

Location, location, location. She needed safety and a sense of security. This apartment had just that.

"What do you think?" the realtor asked Max. It didn't take her long to figure out he would be the one to pass everything through.

Max didn't answer. He looked at Lana, waiting for her to answer.

She trailed her finger across the wall. "Can I think about it for a moment?"

I frowned and moved away from the wall. What was she doing? I wanted to say something right then, but I didn't.

The realtor smiled politely and said, "Of course," before she stepped out of the apartment.

Max looked at Lana, his impatience showing, and followed the realtor. I wanted to come to Lana's rescue and tell him that it was already a lot for her to come here today. In fact, I was stunned that I'd got her to go.

When I'd brought the subject up, she told me to go look around for her, but I stayed firm. I told her that she needed to see the apartment with her own eyes. This wasn't something that I could do for her. It had to be her decision. I could see the small note of optimism in her eyes, and I knew she was picturing what it would be like to actually thrive. Away from her parents and her dark past.

I told her that I would make sure to be with her. I told her that Max would be there too. That, out of everything, made her hesitate.

"Still with him?" she had asked.

I frowned. "Yeah. Why?"

She never answered me, but I could see the unanswered question in her eyes: *Lachlan*.

We hadn't talked about him in weeks, but he still hovered around me, following me wherever I went. I tried my best to pretend he wasn't there, but lately he was getting harder and harder to ignore.

This was the fourth apartment we'd seen today. Lana would find something wrong each time. The first one didn't have a quality lock. The second one had a questionable stench in the stairwell. The third one was in a dangerous neighborhood.

She was trying to find something wrong with this one. I could see her mind frantically trying to think of something.

She walked out onto the deck and stared at the view. I followed her. We were surrounded by high-rise buildings. There was a small park across the street that still gave this part of town a family vibe. The streets weren't busy. This area was safe and quiet.

In other words, it was perfect for Lana.

"Do you really think it's nice?" I asked.

"I do."

I spread my hands out in front of me. "This view will be all yours, then!"

Lana snorted. "Yeah. Right. Do they take Monopoly money as payment?" she asked wearily.

"The rent isn't too much."

Lana just looked at me.

"Okay," I drew out. "It's expensive. But Max will help out."

"No. That's not happening," Lana said firmly. "I don't have 'charity case' written across my forehead."

I crossed my arms and leaned against the railing. I settled into the role I knew best: the friend who was supportive no matter what. "You're not a charity case," I said. "You could pay him back later on."

"I'd rather get a loan."

"Then get a loan!" I said anxiously. "Whatever makes you feel comfortable is what you need to do." I paused and looked at her carefully. "What is your gut telling you?"

She chewed on her bottom lip, staring at the street below us. "That this place is perfect."

"Then listen to your gut. Your gut is totally right!" I smiled.

"I don't even know where to start or what to do."

"You can get a job lined up," I said. "I'll find you one. Or maybe you could try college again. You could start out slowly. One or two classes, and if it goes all right, you can move up from there."

I saw the hope in her eyes. She wanted to believe that every word I said was the truth.

I looked at the kids playing on the swings. Their squeals of delight could be heard all the way from up here. Lana watched them too, with a sad, wistful expression.

"This can become a reality, you know," I said quietly.

"I know. That's what I'm afraid of. What if I screw this up?"

I frowned.

She exhaled loudly and looked away. "I mean, right now I'm okay. But what happens at night, when I'm all alone? All I know is miles away." She leaned close. "I don't know what freedom is."

I swallowed and looked her straight in the eye. "I will do everything to make sure this works out for you," I vowed. "Lana, you're so much stronger than you think."

Her lips quivered.

"Nothing can stand in your way," I said.

She glanced at me. Doubt was written across her face.

"Nothing," I uttered slowly.

The front door opened. Lana and I both turned as Max walked inside. He tucked his hands into his pants. Both eyebrows were raised as he looked at us. "So?"

I gave her a pointed look, wordlessly encouraging her to tell him the truth. I knew she wanted to take this step forward, but she was so scared. Her hands were shaking as she glanced over at the park, and I could see her imagining her life here.

Say yes, say yes, say yes, I pleaded in my head.

She finally looked at me and nodded before she turned to Max. "It's perfect."

I breathed a sigh of relief.

His lips parted into a devastating smile. "Really?"

"Really," she said.

The realtor smoothly walked back into the room and smiled brightly. She knew a sale when she saw one. "Well, what do you think?" she asked Max.

He tapped the wall once and turned his charming smile on to her. "Where do we sign?"

The realtor blushed and walked over to her briefcase. I think if he flashed that smile one more time, Lana could get a few months of rent for free.

While they went into details about the contract and when

would be a good day to sign, I walked over to Lana, mouthing the word *yay,* and lifted both hands up in victory.

That hope in her eyes, the one that was barely noticeable earlier, was starting to spread, making them shine brightly.

I stopped worrying about the big stuff and just enjoyed right now.

Everything was starting to look up.

21

TICK, TICK

LANA WAS MOVING INTO HER APARTMENT TODAY.

It was an exciting time for me. For Lana, her fear overrode her excitement. She hadn't told her parents she was moving out. She was too afraid that they would change her mind. And she was even more afraid that if she did attempt to pack up her stuff, her parents would stop her. She would drive over there with me, but I would do all the packing. I had it all planned out. I would drive to her house while her dad was at work and her mom would be in town, shopping or gossiping over lunch with her friends.

I had a stack of boxes in my trunk and garbage bags just in case I ran out of boxes.

I pulled up to her parents' house. Six windows on the second floor. Four on the bottom. Each one was spotless and sparkled in the sun. And all of them were flanked with black shutters. The double, front doors were large and imposing. The color of espresso, with wrought-iron detailing and frosted glass. Surrounding the house were trimmed shrubs, and running the length of the sidewalk were flowers, the colors ranging from red and yellow to orange.

It was a picture-perfect house. The kind of house you would drive by at night, see the yellow hue of lights inside, and think, "I bet that family has it all."

I got out of my car. As I went to open the trunk, Lana got out of the car and sat on the porch steps. That was how she was sitting the first time I met her. Just ten years ago, she and I had been small girls with two completely different personalities.

"Hey," I said, as I grabbed a stack of collapsed boxes. "You ready for this?"

She looked at me. "Not even close to ready."

I walked up the sidewalk and finally saw the white pallor of her skin and the beads of sweat forming on her forehead.

"Just sit here," I said with a reassuring smile. "I'll be back down as soon as I can."

"Okay." Her voice was hollow.

I walked inside, my hands piled with moving gear, and hurried up the staircase. There was nothing but the sounds of a grandfather clock ticking softly and my quiet footsteps. It was just me and Lana's ancestors. Their pictures were framed, nailed to the wall. They had somber faces, and maybe it was just paranoia kicking in, but I swear their eyes followed me as I walked down the hallway.

The hairs on my arms rose when I walked into Lana's room. I quickly got to work. I grabbed all the clothes in her closet. Packed up her books, her journal sitting on the nightstand. Her laptop was on the desk. I grabbed it, too, along with the laptop and phone chargers. Quickly, I went through her desk drawers, making sure I wasn't leaving behind anything important. I left the pictures on the wall and every piece of furniture there. I took only the things that were personal and had good memories for Lana. Those personal items filled up only three boxes.

I looked back at her room. Anyone passing by wouldn't notice that she'd moved out. But someone who stepped into the room would notice.

As I carried the boxes down the stairs, I wondered who would be the first of Lana's parents to realize she was gone.

"Done," I announced.

Lana was still sitting on the steps. She jumped at the sound of my voice. "That was quick."

"What can I say? I'm a quick packer."

We loaded the boxes up. I slammed the trunk and looked over at her.

Lana turned back to her house, her expression forlorn. I couldn't imagine what she was thinking about and I didn't want to know. What happened in that house should stay there, locked up and never to be experienced again.

I spun my key chain. "Ready?"

"The fifth step from the top is loose."

The keys hit my knuckles. My eyebrows knitted together. "What?"

"On the staircase. The step's been loose for six years and I still sometimes trip on it coming up the stairs." Lana drifted across the grass as if she were in a trance. She stood in front of her bedroom window and pointed. "On the windowsill, in the very right corner, I carved in my initials."

"Lana—"

"This is all I know and I'm leaving it all behind."

I walked over to her and stared up at the window with her. "You're right. You're leaving it all behind."

I could feel her eyes on me.

"But you have something so amazing ahead of you. A life where you can make your own decisions. There's nothing better than that."

She continued to look at the window. I could clearly see the indecision in her eyes. She was at war with herself.

"You sure you want to go?"

"Yeah." She took two steps back. "I'm sure," she said firmly.

We left her house a few minutes later. The farther we drove from her parents' house, the more relaxed she became. A small half-smile appeared on her face.

"What are you going to do for furniture?"

She shrugged. "I don't know. Thrift store? I'm not exactly swimming in cash right now."

"Thrift store sounds good," I said agreeably.

She didn't respond. Just watched the endless row of houses fly past us.

"Am I crazy for doing this?" she said quietly.

My fingers tightened on the steering wheel. "Not at all."

"Sometimes I'm afraid it will all bite me in the ass," she admitted.

"None of it will. Everything you're doing right now is a step in the right direction."

That seemed to be my go-to saying for Lana. I had repeated those words over the past week so many times I'd lost count.

"I know my dad will try anything to get me to go back home."

"Lana . . ." I chose my words carefully.

Her phone interrupted me. She looked down the same time I did.

Her dad was calling.

I knew there was only one reason he would be calling her

right now. It figured he would be the first one to know she was gone.

I stayed perfectly quiet and tried to keep my eyes on the road, but they kept straying to the right. Lana's finger hovered over the answer button for a long second before she pressed ignore.

It might seem inconsequential for most people, but for Lana it was huge.

"Who was that?" I asked innocently.

She dropped her phone into her purse and pulled the clasp. The snap sounded loudly in the car. "No one."

I wanted to celebrate this moment. I made a quick left.

"Where are we going?" she said. "Apartment's up ahead."

I grinned. "We, my friend, are going furniture shopping."

22

REVOLUTION

"STAY," MAX SAID IN A THROATY WHISPER.

I shivered. My eyes closed. My head sank deeper into the pillow and Max's scent was all around me. It made saying no twice as hard.

"I can't," I said weakly. "I gotta . . ."

I had to do something. I just didn't know what that something was. Everything that was important in my life seemed to fade in Max's arms.

His head was bent as his lips traveled down my neck. Pieces of his hair brushed against my skin, making me shiver. The minute we stepped inside his house we came at each other with this frantic, all-consuming need to touch.

"I really gotta go," I groaned with frustration.

Max's lips stopped moving. He looked up. His lips were

damp and slightly parted. I wanted nothing more than to stay right there, curl my hands into his hair, and drag his lips to mine.

He rolled over and lay on his back, staring up at the ceiling. He was breathing heavily, his abs becoming defined with each breath.

I jumped out of his bed before I changed my mind and turned back around and jumped him.

Max rolled onto his side. "Why do you have to go?"

"I just need to," I said absently.

I walked around the room, searching for my shoes. Pieces of clothing were scattered across the floor. Max's jacket. My cardigan was tossed in the corner.

"Everything *is* okay now."

Lana moved into her new apartment a week ago. And while it was a huge relief that she wasn't underneath her dad's thumb anymore, I couldn't just shut her out; I carried her with me wherever I went.

I continued to stay with her. I would hear her crying herself to sleep, or sometimes screaming out. I asked her if everything was okay. She would never answer me, even though I knew she could hear me.

"Everything is okay. Right?"

I found one heel next to the door. "Yes . . . but . . ."

"But what?" Max said.

I looked at him. The other heel was partially underneath the bed. I put both on and walked over to him.

Max sat up and slid to the edge of the bed. His hands were on the bed, shirt still unbuttoned. He opened his legs and I walked in between them, staring down at him.

"Things have just been . . . difficult," I said carefully.

Max stared at me. "How difficult?"

"Pretty difficult."

I was being generous. There were some days when it seemed like everything was going to be all right. But then there were those days when it felt like I was in hell with Lana. It felt like the world was crumbling down around her, around me. That feeling sucks the will to live out of you. Leaves your energy depleted and steals your happiness.

And then the next day would be okay. Lana would have to start over, rebuilding her happiness. All I could do was watch.

His hands curled around my hips. I stood frozen in place. "Just stay," Max said. "Stay here. I'll take away all those worries for a few hours."

His eyes were heavy-lidded and the right side of his lips curved up in a half-smile that should have been innocent. It was anything but. My defenses instantly crumbled.

With one tug, I was on top of him. His hands held me tightly against his warm body. His kiss was slow on purpose. Meant to drive me insane. Meant to coax me into staying the night with him. He did these slow little licks that made me moan. My mouth opened. My body relaxed deeper into his. He sucked on my lower lip and tugged gently. I barely noticed the sting. Not when his hands moved up and down my thighs.

I gasped into his mouth.

His fingers found the zipper of my dress and slowly dragged it down.

My dress parted, allowing him to slip his hands inside. Fingers grazed my spine. I sucked on his tongue with hunger. My body wanted it all. I wanted pleasure from his hand and I wanted to see every part of him. It was this frantic need that made me shake.

His touch always seemed to take me to another place, where my worries and fears unraveled and slipped away from my body.

I pushed myself off of him and took off my dress.

He stared at me, his eyes blazing.

"You're gorgeous," he growled.

Right then, I felt it. *He* did that to me. Made me feel beautiful and confident and so powerful.

Max shed his shirt. It dropped next to my dress. My hands moved down his stomach, tracing the ridged muscles.

A sheen of sweat started to form on his brow as I touched him.

I finally reached his pants. I toyed with the button.

Max's breathing became heavy.

I unzipped his pants slowly, just like he did with my dress. His hips lifted instinctively. I shoved his pants and boxers down around his ankles. I looked down at him. I tingled with anticipation, and I reached out and curled my fingers around his dick.

My touch varied, switching between featherlight to holding him tight. I touched him with fascination. There's nothing like being free and having a man underneath you, losing control and giving it all to you.

He hissed in a sharp breath. His entire body was frozen, like it was carved from stone. While I continued to torture, I leaned over him. My left hand splayed against the sheets. His eyes opened long enough to meet my gaze. His pupils were dilated with lust and there was a dazed expression on his face. Knowing that I put that expression there made me damp in between my legs. I kissed him hard. He breathed through his nose and dropped his head against the mattress.

An anguished laugh escaped him. "You trying to kill me?" he groaned.

I leaned even closer. "You want me to stop?"

"Hell no."

I smiled against his lips and tightened my grip. When his

breathing started to turn into panting and his strong body jerked beneath me, I pulled away. I stood up to take off my underwear and bra.

Max lifted his head and stared at me. His eyes were hot, scanning every inch of my skin.

"Keep the heels on."

I lifted a brow.

"My heels, hmm?"

I watched as he put the condom on with quick, steady hands.

He sat back and opened up his arms. I crawled over him, my knees on either side of his body. The tip of him rubbed against me and if I rose a bit higher, he would slip inside of me and I would feel nothing but him.

"If you're going to kill me, do it right. Straddle me."

I paused. It was brief. A millisecond to brace myself for everything that was about to happen.

I straddled him.

His hands moved from my waist and curved around my breasts. His palms brushed against my nipples and a breathy moan escaped my lips.

"Rise up to your knees," he said.

I obeyed.

"Guide me inside that tight pussy. Go slowly. Sink down until you're wrapped around me as tight as a glove. And don't stop until you're screaming my name."

I felt a jolt go through my body.

I followed his directions and slid down his dick slowly. My eyes closed. My legs started to quiver. For the past few weeks I'd been drained of energy. But this . . . this changed everything.

I moved up and back down just as slowly. All those tingles that seemed to ricochet wildly beneath my skin, he felt too.

"Fuck!" he shouted, drawing out the word with anguish.

His hips lifted up, meeting me every time I moved back down. Our rhythm became faster and faster. Muscles started to burn, and right when those tingles in my body were about to burst open, he flipped me over.

Cold air touched my skin. And I didn't get a warning or head start. Max covered me in a half-tackle. One of his hands lay flat on the sheets, the other was wrapped around my waist. My hair pooled over the side of the bed.

Our lips collided as he moved into me powerfully, taking over, moving frantically. A wild look was in his eyes. All I could do was hold onto him tightly.

I was starting to slip under.

"I'm gonna . . ." I panted. My voice faded away as he thrust into me.

"What are you gonna do, love?" Max said gruffly, his eyes never leaving my face.

Come. That's what I wanted. That's what I was seconds away from. My eyes were close to shutting. I was ready to close out the world just for those few seconds of pure bliss.

But he held my jaw in between his thumb and index finger. Max wasn't demanding. He was *asking* me not to shut him out.

The headboard rattled. I could smell the tangy scent of our sweat. My fingertips sank into his skin, holding him as close to me as humanly possible. My body started to spasm and I kept my eyes open.

I would share this with him.

I didn't scream his name. I could barely breathe, let alone speak.

Max came seconds later. His jaw was slack and his eyes were heavy, but he kept them open.

My control and the solid ground beneath me slipped away. And I was falling, frantically reaching for something to break my fall. It was a fast descent. Lasted only a few seconds.

Max buried his face into the crook of my shoulder. Then my eyes finally closed as I realized that I didn't just love this man, I would give him everything . . . and if that wasn't enough I would let him take what he needed, just as long as he returned my love.

He shifted slightly. His eyelashes fluttered against my skin. His lips parted and grazed against my neck. And the next four words out of his mouth almost killed me.

"God, I love you."

23

COMPONENT

I WOKE UP TO AN EMPTY BED.

My head lifted from the pillow with my hair a wild mess. I peeked over at the vacant spot on the bed, where Max should have been.

I didn't know what time it was. My body was still worn out. I sat up. The mattress was crooked and the sheets were wrinkled and close to completely falling off the bed, and all I could think about were four amazing words.

"God, I love you."

I sat up and rubbed the sleep away from my eyes. Max's watch was on the nightstand. I picked it up. Two a.m. Where the hell was he?

When I stood up, my muscles protested. Yet I couldn't complain or regret a single second.

I walked across the room, grabbed a robe from his closet,

and walked out into the hall. I had no problem sleeping alone, but if I was going to stay here with Max, I wanted to be with him while I had the chance.

The house was quiet. Just a single lamp was on in the hallway. I heard his voice. It was muffled but definitely coming from downstairs, in his office.

I hadn't known him a long time, but I knew he worked hard at his job. I smiled to myself. But then his voice, which seconds ago was quiet, suddenly became harsh and demanding. I flinched and stopped in my tracks, waiting to see if he would explode again. A sick feeling of dread danced up my spine. The only time I'd ever heard Max lose his temper was because of Lana's dad.

I walked down the steps and pressed my ear against the door, straining to hear the conversation.

"You're threatening me?"

There was a long pause.

"Not a smart move," Max said darkly. "Just remember that up until now, I haven't done a damn thing when I could've destroyed your fucking career with one simple action. It's because of your daughter that I chose not to."

More silence.

I heard a chair creak. I could picture Max leaning forward, resting his elbows on his desk. "I'm hanging up. Don't ever call me at this hour again. And Michael? Just so you know, I'm a good friend . . . but I'm an even better enemy."

Seconds later, the phone hit the wall with enough force to make the heavy oak door shake.

I opened the door. It creaked loudly. Max was still sitting behind the desk. His head was bowed, fingers laced together, resting against his forehead. He instantly looked up, jumping to his feet.

I opened the door farther and walked inside. His phone was

in pieces: screen cracked, battery lying on the ground. I looked at Max. His jaw was clenched as he stared back at me.

"You were out of bed."

Max crossed his arms, staying stubborn and not saying a word.

"I was looking for you," I said dumbly.

His shoulders sagged as he leaned his palms against his desk. "I couldn't sleep," he finally replied.

I waited for him to elaborate. He never did.

"Is everything okay?" I asked carefully and stepped farther into the room.

"Absolutely." He turned away, shuffling papers on the desk. "Just dealing with some work bullshit."

I nodded and tapped my fingers against his desk. "That makes sense, because everyone knows all work bullshit happens at two in the morning."

Imperceptibly, his fingers tightened around the papers in his hands.

"Yes," Max said.

"You want to tell me what's really going on?"

Max rubbed a hand down his face. "No, Naomi. I don't."

"I heard you talking to him."

"I figured as much."

I walked to him and leaned against the desk. "Then why lie?"

He leaned back in his chair, his hands curling around the armrests, and looked up at me. "Why do you think?"

I stared at him quietly. "Why did he call?"

His eyes shut as he rubbed the bridge of his nose. "Ah, shit . . ." he muttered.

Suddenly he stood up and walked over to the window. He stared outside, his palms braced against the window frame.

Those strong shoulders were slumped, his spine slightly bent. His body could do so much damage, could put fear into some of the biggest men out there, but he'd had to sit back and let Lana's dad slip through his fingers. I knew it was weighing on him, but I didn't know it was this bad.

I wrapped my arms around his waist and rested my forehead on his back. We stood there quietly.

"He's panicking," Max said. "He knows he's losing control, so he's trying to take a swing at anyone to get his way."

"Tell me the truth."

He looked up and held my gaze in the window. "I am telling you the truth."

There were still more truths that needed to be said. He and I both knew that.

"Are you in danger?"

He opened his mouth. I interrupted him. "Don't try to protect me and hide the truth. Just be honest."

Max turned. My arms were still around him and his hands moved up to cradle my face. Very slowly he said, "I'm not in danger. And I'm not worried about Michael. People screw up when they're scared. They become careless."

He kissed me. Whether it was to silence me or take away all the tension from the room, I didn't know. He put everything into that kiss and I took every bit.

We went back to bed and fucked one more time. We took our time, touching, kissing, licking. But no matter how hard we tried to make our worries disappear, nothing worked.

Our fears loomed over us for the rest of the night.

24

TRUTH AND REPOSE

"I THINK IT'S GOING TO SNOW FOREVER," I SAY. MY LIPS ARE inches away from the window, making the glass fog up.

The sun is partially hidden by dim, gray clouds. Yet it still manages to reflect off the snow, making it sparkle.

No one answers me. Everyone in the rec room is swept up in their own minds, problems, and pain. They each have stories of their own. I pull my eyes away from the outdoors and look around.

There's a lady sitting across from me. The same lady that sat next to Pretend Mommy during the group therapy session. She stares outside. She hasn't opened her mouth since she sat down, which was three hours ago.

No smile.

No tears.

Nothing.

I want to know her story. I want to know what brought her here. I can guess all day, but I know I'll never know the truth.

I exhale and drum my fingers on the table. It's so quiet in here, and it's not the good kind of quiet. This is the type of quiet that makes your ears ache. It makes time move at an agonizingly slow rate, making you feel like you're going to lose your mind at any second.

"We're not going to get out of here," I say casually. The lady doesn't say a word, yet I continue our one-sided conversation. "All of us are losing so much time. We can never get it back."

She blinks, and call me crazy, but I think that's her way of showing she's listening. I think she agrees.

"What do you have out there?" I ask her.

No answer.

"Do you have any family? Any friends out there waiting for you?"

She blinks slowly. I'm getting tired of trying to decode her blinks, so I give up.

We sit there in silence.

"God offers to every mind its choice between truth and repose. Take which you please—you can never have both."

I turn. Pretend Mommy is sitting at the table across from me. She's staring at that damn plastic baby.

"Huh?"

"Ralph Waldo Emerson said that," she says as she caresses the baby's plastic cheek. "And he's right. We can't have both. We have to pick one."

I turn in my chair. My back touches the wall and I cross my arms. "And you think we all want both?"

"Well . . ." she says slowly. "We're all still here, aren't we?"

Her words make my heartbeat slow. I swallow. "How long have you been here?" I ask.

She looks up at me, and her cobalt-blue eyes are piercing. Even though she's crazy, I see knowledge far past my own. Knowledge that only experience and pain can give you.

"Three years," she says.

This place—this prison—is her home.

"Most people will only spend a few months here. They stop fighting their truths. They accept them for what they are and leave."

My chin lifts; I don't like where this conversation is going. "And what about you?" I ask. "Where's your truth?"

She points to the window. "My truth is somewhere out there. I didn't want it three years ago and I still don't want it."

I sit up straight in my chair. Only two steps away is the person I'm afraid of becoming. I don't want to be locked in Fairfax for the rest of my life. I refuse to let that happen.

Pretend Mommy smiles knowingly and leans close. I lean back. "Your truth is out there too, isn't it?" she says.

My chair squeaks loudly as I stand. Pretend Mommy looks down at her baby. Instead of singing a sweet lullaby to her plastic baby, she sings an old hymn that sends chills up and down my spine.

She's fucking crazy. Everyone around me is fucking crazy.

I walk out of the room slowly, and when I get to the hallway, I quicken my steps.

I'm not crazy like them.

I know I'm not.

My door slams behind me. I do a quick sweep of the room. Lana's dad isn't here today.

I pace, picturing the frozen icicle still hanging on to that weak, naked tree branch. Despite the freezing temps and strong winds, it refuses to drop.

I fall back onto my bed and stare at the ceiling. "You're not crazy," I say loudly. "You're not a lifer."

I inhale. "You're not one of them."

I think I'm finally starting to realize just how much time I've lost. I'd known it was passing me by, but the impact finally slams into me like a freight train.

I can dream. I can imagine and hope, but it will never change a thing. And the most terrifying thing is that I know, I *know* there's more to the story. There's another train coming straight at me, at full speed. Yet I can't see it. I can only hear the ground slightly tremble. The tracks rattling beneath my feet. I can hear the sound of a whistle blaring.

But I can't move.

All I can do is hope that when it does hit, I die within seconds.

"I'm not crazy," I repeat. "I'm not crazy. I'm not crazy . . ."

25

UNREEL

THAT NIGHT, I DON'T DREAM ABOUT LACHLAN. OR MAX.
I dream about Lana.

She's twelve. Her waist-length hair is in a French braid. She has just finished eating and is rinsing out her bowl. Her teacher will be there in ten minutes. Every day they would meet in the spare office upstairs for her lessons. Lana would start out with Social Studies and move on to Math. There would be a small break in the day for lunch, and after that she would have an hour of quiet reading. The last two classes would be English and then P.E., but Lana just saw that as extra time to ride her horse.

Her life may seem ridiculously boring to some. But she loves her simple routine.

She shakes the water from the bowl, turns off the tap, and puts the bowl on the drying rack. That's when she feels him.

Her body becomes frozen as her dad approaches. Her muscles lock up and all she can do is stare straight ahead. She counts the backsplash tiles as her dad stands behind her, his body against hers. He runs his fingers down her braid.

Forty-five, forty-six . . . she mouths. Her eyes run over every smooth tile piece. The square pieces are so small. She could count them for days.

"All that pretty hair," he says.

Sixty-five, sixty-six . . . Her mouth is moving frantically. Her hands are shaking, but she stands still, waiting for her dad to stop talking and touching.

She waits, but he never moves.

"You have lunch at eleven thirty, correct?" her dad says. His breath touches her skin. Tobacco mixed with coffee. It doesn't mix well.

Seventy-one, seventy-two, seventy-five . . . She messed up. It instantly throws her off. Her heart starts to thump wildly inside her chest. Her lungs begin to constrict, making her breathing shallow. She can't think straight.

"Lana?"

Lana swallows. "Yes, that's my lunch."

"Good." He steps back. "I'll see you then."

He walks away. The back door shuts behind him. Lana sags against the counter, feeling relief over his departure and dread for when he comes back.

My eyes burst open.

Twelve-year-old Lana is bent over me. Her eyes are bloodshot from crying. Her braid is loosened, with strands all around her face. She has on a pink shirt, with flowers all over it. A pair of jeans, slightly rolled up and with chalk fingerprints.

She's a genuine kid. Except for those eyes. They're a decade older.

My fingers curl around my sheets. She exhales, and it appears in the air like a fine mist. I gasp, sucking in the same air she's breathing.

"Will you still help me?" she whispers. Her voice is small and young and so scared.

I answer instinctively. "Of course."

Twelve-year-old Lana doesn't look convinced. She stares at me with distrust.

"I will. I promise to help you!" I sit up. My arms reach out in between us. I want to hold her. Console her. Reassure her that I will keep my promise. But my fingers slash into thin air.

She's gone.

I jump out of my bed, as if it's on fire. "No . . ." I drag out. I check under the bed. There's nothing. I stand up on shaky legs. "No, no, no. She was here. She was right here," I whisper out loud.

There's nothing in my room.

No Lana.

No voices.

No dark eyes in the corner.

I turn in a circle, looking over every inch of my room. Everything starts to spin. Something akin to desperation takes over my body. I stop. The room continues to move. There is double of my bed. The walls multiply. Yet there is no Lana.

I drag my hands through my hair and groan. "I'm sorry, Lana," I whisper. "I'm trying to get out of here."

There is only the sound of the wind hitting my window. I turn and stare at it, as if it's the reason for all my problems.

I become angry. At Fairfax. My inability to get out of here. And Lana's silence.

"I'm awake!" I yell inside my small room. "You have my attention! Why won't you talk to me?"

Silence fills my ears.

"Come and talk to me. I'm listening! Talk . . . please."

The light turns on. I whirl around. Mary is standing in my doorway. She's frowning at me.

Without thinking twice, I run to her. "Lana was here." My finger shakes as I point to my bed. "She was standing over me and she was asking me to help her."

The look in Mary's eyes makes my voice shake. Pity mixed with disappointment. That's never a good thing.

"I promise she was here," I insist. "She was."

Mary's hands are on my shoulders. She slowly guides me to my bed. "Of course she was."

I look over my shoulder. "You don't believe me."

"I do."

"You don't," I accuse. "She showed me what happened to her as a child, and it's a sign. She needs my help, and that was her way of reaching out."

There's that pity and disappointment. Maybe I really am insane. Maybe this place is where I belong. My legs buckle. I drop to the floor. My knees curl.

Mary doesn't call for assistance. She quietly sits down next to me. Through the blur of tears I see her stretch out her legs, her hands disappearing into the pockets on her shirt.

She lets me cry. I don't know why she's staying and what she plans on doing, but I'm grateful that she hasn't left. Her silent support makes my tears subside.

Mary speaks up. "There are so many people here. Every single one has a life and a story to tell. Each one worse than the last. I don't know your story, but I know it's bad, and I know you're terrified." She tilts her head, and the look she gives me is so motherly. "Naomi, I don't want Fairfax to become your home. You deserve so much more than this. You deserve to live a good life, because you only get one chance to live." She holds up a finger. "One chance. There are no returns. No redos, no matter how bad we want them." She pats me on the shoulder. "Please make your life worth living."

We sit there in silence. When I first came here, I thought Mary was some uptight nurse who couldn't care less what happened to me.

I realize now how wrong I was.

I tap my shoulder against hers. "Thank you," I whisper.

She smiles. Her hand disappears from my shoulder as she stands up.

"Where are you going?" I say.

I like her company. I love her words. I want more of both.

"You need something to make you sleep," Mary says.

She leaves. I sit there quietly. I stretch out my legs, just like Mary did. I don't have pockets, so I just cross my arms. I don't move a muscle. I'm hoping that if I mimic her movements, some of her strength will rub off on me.

It doesn't.

Mary comes in a few seconds later. Pills in one hand, a small cup of water in the other. She holds them out to me. "Here you go."

I take them numbly. Mary helps me up and I lie back down, waiting for the pills to do their job.

Mary walks to the door. Before she closes it, she says quietly, "Sleep well."

I turn on my side and stare at the wall.

Doesn't she know? I don't sleep.

I dream.

26

WHITE COTTAGE

3 YEARS AGO

I HAVEN'T SEEN LACHLAN IN A YEAR.

It felt like the life was being slowly sucked out of me. Most days I felt like I had no value, like I was a penny dropped on the sidewalk. When I felt that way I instinctively turned for Lachlan. Not having him there felt like I was missing a limb.

Last summer he came home for a quick weekend visit. Since he had graduated college, he'd stopped coming home for the holidays. His visits were next to none, and I was resentful. I was sad. I was jealous because I wanted all his time. He was busy with his internship and I knew that. He was working hard. He was making his own money, and saving every dollar.

"Don't be mad, kid," he had said to me.

Kid. When I was ten I used to like the nickname, but now I was starting to hate it.

I crossed my arms and looked up at him. "Can't you upgrade me to a different nickname? I've officially outgrown 'kid.'"

He glared at me, a hard look in his eyes. "That's all I call you!"

"Well, call me something different . . . oh . . . I don't know, call me by my name?"

He shrugged but looked away. Thirty minutes later he was getting back into his car and driving back to his job and his apartment and his single life. I hated that I would be reduced to e-mails, texts, and calls.

I watched him go and it felt like I had been standing here all 365 days, waiting for him to come back.

And now he was here. Finally.

I pulled on the reins of my horse and watched him. His back was turned as he talked with his dad. I wanted to call out his name right then, but I kept my mouth closed.

I tried to imagine what he would see if I did call out his name. Would he see young Naomi with braids hanging down her back and her knees scraped? Or would he see me as I was now? The braids were gone. I was taller. My legs were longer. My chest that used to have a "little something" had turned into a lot of something. My eyes that were once too big for my face now looked just right. My cheekbones, the ones that I thought were too sharp and awkward-looking on my face, now fit. I felt good about the girl who looked back at me in the mirror.

I knew that it was inevitable that Lachlan would also change. But he looked better than I could have ever imagined. His shoulders were broader. His hair was cut shorter. The longer strands on top were mussed from the wind. My heart twisted so tightly at the sight of him, I thought it would break into a million pieces. I vowed to myself right then and there that I would never let myself go this long without seeing him again.

When he crossed his arms and kicked his head back to laugh loudly, I couldn't hold my happiness in any longer.

"Lach!" I shouted.

I was off my horse in seconds and walking toward him with quick steps. I didn't care that my blond hair was probably crazy from the wind. Or that my cheeks were red from the cold air. None of that mattered, because he was finally back.

Lachlan turned with a bright smile on his face. My heart did a little flip and I smiled back. As I walked closer, though, his smile started to fade. He looked me up and down with his eyebrows drawn tight. When I stopped in front of him he said nothing. Just stared at me as though he had never seen me before.

"That you, kid?" he finally said.

I tilted my head up to look at him and frowned. I had barely said two words to him and something already felt different between us.

"Stop calling me that."

A faint smile was on his face, but it was strained. Tight and controlled. "You're different."

"I've grown up," I said.

"You have," he agreed.

Not for one second did I imagine that we would ever struggle to talk to each other. I'd just assumed we would pick up where we left off the last time. But the last time was long ago. *Too* long ago. There was a silence between us that had never been there. I wanted it gone. I hated it.

"I'm so happy to see you," I said in a rush.

I didn't wait for permission. I leaned forward and wrapped my arms around his waist. Lachlan's body tensed for a second before his arms hesitantly banded around my shoulders. We stood there, with our arms wrapped around each other. I had dreamed of being this close to him so many times and not letting go. He always hugged me, but it was always a friendly hug. More like a pat on the back. But we were past a few seconds and his arms were still around me. Butterflies that I always seemed to get when he was around had disappeared, and instead, my body just tingled in every single spot that was pressed close against Lachlan. My nose brushed his throat and I smelled his scent instantly. It was outdoors, mixed with cologne. It was a heady scent to me—one that drudged up memories and reminded me that Lachlan's arms were home for me. My fingers clutched the material of his jacket tightly.

My imagination was not limited when it came to Lachlan. I would think of the craziest scenarios of how he would suddenly fall for me. He would tell me how much he loved me. And then he would kiss me. It would be a kiss that could take every kiss and touch before him and make it disappear. But it always stopped there. Right now, my mind was giving me scenarios that involved more than kissing. My arms tightened around his stomach, inadvertently pressing him closer. My breasts were pressed against his body and I felt warmth in between my legs. It was like lighting a match. One instant there was nothing, and the next there was nothing but light and heat.

It scared me enough to make me pull away. Lachlan looked at the spot I had been in seconds ago with confusion before he cleared his throat and looked around. Only a few inches kept us apart. I took a step back. "Tell me everything!" I demanded with a squeak in my voice. "How's your new job? When are you moving back to McLean?"

So many questions. I couldn't contain any of them. Lachlan would always keep in touch via e-mail, but his e-mails were brief. Quiet. They were nothing like seeing him in person, where he would always go into great detail about his friends, school, or even something he had seen that was funny to him.

I lived off those stories.

Lachlan's shoulders visibly relaxed over my questions. "My new job is boring. I'm basically an errand boy, with a small cubicle as my 'office.' And my 'office' is right next to this guy. I think his name is Darin. He's a heavy breather. Creeps me the fuck out. I swear he does it to drive me insane."

I laughed. "It still sounds exciting. Even with Darin the Heavy Breather."

He hesitated before he slung a heavy arm over my shoulder. He used do this all the time, in a friendly way. But now my breasts were pressed against the side of his stomach and the heat of his body warmed me instantly. The tingles were back. He cleared his throat.

"Everything is exciting to you," Lachlan said. "I could tell you I'm getting a root canal tomorrow and you'd be jumping up and down with excitement."

I gave him a look as we walked toward the deck in the backyard. My hand had been hanging awkwardly at my side since we started walking. I wanted to reach out and touch him the way he was touching me. I hooked it around his waist.

"And as for moving back to McLean, I don't think that will ever happen."

My head whipped in his direction. "Why not?"

"There's more to this world than just McLean. A lot more. Trust me. Once you leave your home, you'll never turn back."

I nodded briskly, soaking in Lachlan's words like a sponge. But he didn't have to tell me twice about never coming back to McLean. I had no desire to stay here, but a part of me was scared at what else was out there.

"What about you? What's going on in your life?" Lachlan asked.

"You already know," I reminded him. "I tell you in every e-mail what I'm up to."

He nodded. "But you're still writing?"

"I am."

"That's great," he said with another strained smile on his face.

I wanted to shout at him, *"Where is my Lachlan? Where are you?"*

He talked to me, but his voice was tight, making me anxious. I didn't like this . . . awkwardness. I didn't know how to get rid of it.

I stepped away. His hand disappeared from my shoulder, making me feel cold and alone.

"I have to go home," I said. I stared down at the ground, kicking pieces of gravel around with my foot. "We're having guests over for dinner."

I looked up at him. His eyes remained on me. But there was a different look there. One that I had never seen. He would always look at me with amusement, like everything I did was guaranteed to bring a smile to his face. But now he just looked pensive, almost unsure of me.

"You'll still meet me tonight, right?" I asked.

There was that frown again. His shoulders tensed as he backed away.

"Yeah, tonight, Naomi." His voice was terse.

I would see him later. Like all the other million times I saw him, but this time, things would be different.

I walked away from him, back to my horse, replaying our conversation. I was too preoccupied to realize that he had finally called me Naomi.

"WHERE THE HELL ARE WE GOING?"

"Just wait," I said. "We're almost there."

"It's pouring-down rain. I'm getting ready to turn back home."

I didn't even bother turning around. "No, you're not. Just keep walking."

Miles away from our families' properties, hidden in the foliage of oak trees, was a white cottage that was all mine.

I'd stumbled across it by accident a few months ago.

The sunlight was out that day and in the corner of my eye, past the oak trees, something glinted. I walked deeper into the woods for what felt like miles before the trees finally thinned out. The ground was covered in old leaves and twigs, and in front of me was a cottage that was falling apart. The white paint was chipped off. The front deck was caving in slowly. A few windows were broken, or simply boarded up. All it would take was for one big gust of wind and this place would crumble in seconds. But I thought it was amazing. I thought it had potential. I looked past the damage and was determined to fix it. That night I wrote Lachlan an e-mail describing the cottage. He wrote back and said it sounded like the setting of a horror movie.

Tonight, I was determined to prove him wrong. This place was my personal haven. I saw the beauty of this cabin before it became weather-beaten and neglected. I saw a fresh coat of white paint, a new deck, brand-new windows, and flowers planted around the house. I saw the beautiful white cottage it used to be.

I parted the wet tree branches and stepped into the clearing. I shined my flashlight on the cottage. "Here it is," I sighed.

Lachlan stood beside me and stared. He was silent for a moment, then pointed his flashlight at the cottage. His eyes narrowed as he inspected what was in front of him carefully.

"Not too bad," he finally said.

I grinned at him. "Kind of cool, isn't it?"

"In a creepy kind of way, yes."

The rain continued to fall. Splashing onto my jacket, soaking my hair. I didn't care. I stepped closer to the cottage, letting the cool water pour down my face.

"Do you think we're the first people to find it?"

Lachlan moved closer. "Doubt it. The windows didn't board up themselves."

"I'm not talking about that. I'm saying, it's probably been sitting here for years and years without any of us knowing!"

"Is this your way of telling me that you're going to be one of those realtors that goes around looking for destroyed homes, buys them dirt cheap, and sells them for triple the value?"

I shrugged, turned my head, and smiled back at him. "Maybe."

He looked at me with an odd expression on his face.

The whole trip there, I'd tried so hard to act natural and pretend that there was no tension between us. But that one look ruined all my efforts.

Old Naomi and Lachlan were gone. Wherever they went, they were hiding so well that I doubted we would ever find them again.

Normally, words just poured of my mouth when I was around Lachlan. One simple subject would lead to a conversation that would split in half and keep multiplying until we were on a completely different subject than the one we began. Yet right now I was frantically trying to think of something we could talk about.

"I'm glad you're back," I finally said.

He smiled, although the smile was strained. "It's been a while, hasn't it?"

I pointed my flashlight to the damp ground, jerking it back and forth until it became a blur. "E-mails are nice, but seeing you in person is even better."

"That's your way of saying you missed me?"

I shined my flashlight over my face for a quick second. I wanted him to see the sincerity in my eyes. "You know I missed you."

"I've missed you too."

I couldn't see his face, but I heard the honesty in his voice and I saw a piece of the old Lachlan. The one that had been MIA the entire day.

"Lachlan . . ." I looked away.

"What?" He turned off his flashlight and took a step closer. "Why did you just say my name like that?"

"Like what?"

"Come on, I've known you long enough to have you figured out." He gave me a hard look. I stayed silent. "You don't believe that I've missed you?"

"Well, you sure have a hard way of showing it. You're barely home."

"What is the big deal?"

"The big deal is you've been gone for 365 days!" I shouted. "Not a week or a month. A whole year!"

His eyes widened and he whistled. "Keeping a tally?"

I was panting by this point. "Every day."

"We keep in touch," he argued. "I talk to you almost every day."

"E-mails aren't enough."

"If you thought that, you should have told me," he said

quickly. "You should've said, 'Lachlan, e-mails aren't enough. Come home. I miss seeing you.'"

"Lachlan!" I yelled. "E-mails aren't enough. Come home. I miss seeing you!"

He looked at me with shock. "What's gotten into you?"

"Nothing's gotten into me. I've always felt this way."

"No, you've changed. You've become . . ."

"What?" I advanced. "I've become louder? I've become older?"

Lachlan just stared at me. He was seeing a different side of me. One that was speaking its mind and revealing the truth. But everyone had a breaking point. You can only take so much until you have to get your words out before you explode.

I opened my mouth. "I—"

Could I do this? Could I actually go through with telling him how I felt? Once it was out there, I could never take it back.

"I love you!" I shouted. My feelings that had been so well hidden came to the surface. Lachlan looked blindsided. "And I shouldn't. I know I shouldn't. But I can't help it!" I tossed my hands in the air. "What am I gonna do, though? I need you when I know I shouldn't."

I turned off my flashlight and tossed it between my hands, waiting for him to answer. It seemed like years went by before Lachlan spoke.

"No, you don't," he said. He almost looked frightened.

"I do," I whispered.

He was older. Between the two of us, the world automatically deemed him the authority on love. But the world got it wrong. I knew better. I knew love was a spider web. Once you were caught, it was something you couldn't escape.

"You don't," he repeated.

I smiled sadly. It was all I could do.

Lachlan rubbed his eyes and groaned before he turned toward the trees. I stared at his back. His fingers were laced and resting on his head.

He whirled around. "I think you're confused," he said knowingly.

I was shaking my head before he even finished speaking.

"I'm right," he continued. "It's a little crush. Just an infatuation that you've had for years."

"You're wrong."

"I'm right."

He walked close enough for me to see the confusion in his eyes. And then he leaned in close. Closer than he'd ever been. His breath tickled my skin. I seized this moment. I looked at him. I mean, really looked, like I'd never done before. Water dripped down his face and curved around one cheekbone before it dropped onto his jacket. His lashes were spiky. There was dark stubble on his face. On the tip of his nose was a bead of water that dropped onto the groove above his upper lip and trickled down. Before I could watch that water drip disappear between his lips, he kissed me. I felt that bead of water against my lips and my eyes instantly closed. Even though I was drenched from head to toe, my skin felt like it was on fire. My blood roared through my veins, and I couldn't pull away if my life depended on it because Lachlan Halstead was finally kissing me.

I think he went into the kiss convinced that my "crush" would never be over until he put it to rest. He thought the kiss would be two pairs of lips meeting, and it would be flat and be over within seconds.

But it was so much more than a simple kiss.

Everything stopped: time, breathing, my mind.

All I could focus on was his lips pressed against mine. He

didn't move them away or increase the pressure. I was grateful for that, because even this one simple contact made all the tingling seem like it was nothing. Right when I was reaching up to wrap my arms around him, he pulled away.

All the warmth from his lips disappeared and it felt like cold water had been thrown onto me. My eyes fluttered open. I stumbled into him. He jumped back as though he'd been burned.

We stood there in silence, staring at each other in a half-daze.

I was the first to recover. "Do that again."

Lachlan said nothing. Just blinked rapidly at me as the rain fell down around us.

"Do it again." I couldn't stop staring at his lips.

"No."

"Do it." I stepped closer. "Kiss me. Show me what to do."

He took a step back and then another and another until he was pressed up against a tree. I saw just how unsure he was and I also saw lust. I wasn't imagining it. My eyes weren't playing tricks on me.

"You and I both know that was a really bad idea," he said, his voice strained.

"Was it, though?" I whispered.

He flinched as if I had struck him.

I stayed perfectly still and waited for Lachlan to do something, anything.

A deep, shuddering breath escaped him as he closed his eyes. He was at war with himself. And I saw the moment when he ignored that part that held him back. My pulse hammered as he leaned into me. This time his lips didn't just linger. They moved, slanting across mine slowly.

I followed his lead. I chased after his breath, opened my mouth. His lips were warm compared to the cold rain and softer than I'd expected. My heart was thundering so hard it felt like it was going to burst out of my chest. I pulled away slightly. The tip of his nose brushed against mine. His lips were a hair's breadth away from mine. The look in his eyes was powerful, showing me that if I hadn't pulled away we would still be kissing. I swallowed hard.

"You told me to never trust a guy," I said, my voice shaky.

"You were supposed to listen," he said against my lips.

We went back in at the same time. This kiss was even stronger than the last.

His fingers sank into my wet hair. My hands reached up, curling around his neck, holding on to him like he was my anchor. I stood on my tiptoes. My elbows rested on his shoulders and I reached behind my head, grabbed my hood, and pulled it up and over our heads. I had waited years to kiss him and I didn't want to share Lachlan. Not even with the rain.

It fell around us, hitting my hood as Lachlan gently tilted my head to the side. The kiss deepened. I felt his tongue against my lips. I opened my mouth. Lachlan hummed and I answered with a whimper. I didn't know if what I was doing was right. I just followed what made me feel good.

Slowly, my tongue touched his. Lachlan shifted close. I could feel him through his jeans. I breathed through my nose.

He ripped himself away.

Lachlan was breathing heavily. He rested his forehead against mine.

We didn't say a word.

27

RUNNING START

ANOTHER MORNING.

Another day in Dr. Rutledge's office.

Before she can ask me how I am and what happened next, my mouth is already open and the words are pouring from my mouth . . .

28

HAPPINESS

"I LOVE WHAT YOU'VE DONE."

"Really?" Lana said.

I turned and smiled. "Really."

I made a circle around Lana's living room, looking at the little touches she had put throughout the apartment to make this space hers.

Turns out you can find some good stuff at thrift stores. Or maybe Lana just had a good eye. She picked things out that by themselves just looked used and ugly. But together it all worked.

There was a large, off-white bookcase that flanked the entertainment center. A comfy, tan couch with a large, gilded mirror mounted on the wall behind it. And there were flowers on every available space. On the kitchen table, the end table. Real or fake, it didn't really matter to Lana. I asked her why she had so many. She said that when she looked at them her spirits would instantly lift.

Lana looked down at the pillow lying on her lap and picked at a loose thread. "It's been fun picking things out."

"And it's been fun going from store to store picking things out with you."

I made myself comfortable on the couch and took a good look at her.

"You're doing okay?" I asked.

"Yeah. I'm fine."

That was Lana's go-to answer. Every time she said it, her voice was hollow. But today I heard excitement and saw the small spark of hope in her eyes.

She drew her knees close to her chest and leaned in, as if she were sharing a secret.

"I signed up for some online college courses," she confessed.

"That's great!"

Lana shrugged and looked away, hiding her blushing face. "It's not much, but—"

I held up my hand. "Stop right there. Don't say it's not much. It's a huge step in the right direction."

"I knew you would say that."

"What are friends for?"

Lana smiled warmly. "I still want to look for a job."

"That's good," I said tentatively.

Lana had to do most everything on her own terms. Sure, I could encourage her until I was blue in the face, but ultimately, it had to be her that made the final choice.

"I guess so," she said as she trailed her fingers across the couch cushion. "I thought about what you said."

I nodded, urging her to continue.

"I went into the bookstore three times yesterday. I hung around the shelves, staring at the cash register, just waiting to get the courage to walk up there and ask for an application. I wimped out each time, and now everyone who works there probably thinks I'm a stalker."

She gave me a weak smile. I frowned.

"I told you I'd help you find a job."

"I know. But I wanted to get a head start. I can't live off my savings for the rest of my life."

"It'd be a nice way to live, though, right?" I teased.

"The best way."

"Look . . ." I said thoughtfully. "It's only been three weeks. You're getting used to this new change in your life. Give it some time."

"How much time will I need?"

"Doesn't matter. There's no cutoff point or expiration date. Just take all the time you need."

She glanced over at me and quietly asked, "How's Max?"

"He's good."

I never told her about the conversation I'd overheard between Max and her dad. I saw no reason to let her know. She was doing well, so why would I bring it up? It would take all the progress she had made and blow it to smithereens.

"Have you talked to Lachlan?" she asked. Her tone was carefree, but she watched me carefully.

I walked over to the patio doors, looking at the buildings around us. I didn't want to talk about him. He was a ghost that needed to be laid to rest. All those memories I had with him needed to stay buried with him. But just the mention of his name brought up those memories: lying flat on our backs in the tree house, talking and talking and talking. That very first kiss that turned my world upside down.

I swallowed and closed my eyes, trying to make those memories disappear.

My eyes opened. I was still standing in place. Still standing in Lana's apartment, yet my mind was rooted in the past. I swallowed past the lump in my throat. "Nope."

"Not once?"

"Nope," I repeated, my voice tight.

"That's . . . strange."

I turned. "Why is it strange?"

"He's been in your life for the past ten years."

"So?"

"It's just weird that you would cut him out."

"I haven't cut him out."

She tilted her head. "Then what do you call what you're doing?"

"Everything's changed, Lana."

"I know that better than anyone. But you can't just—"

My gut started to twist painfully. This was a conversation I wasn't ready for.

"Stop," I interrupted.

"What is this?" There was a small smile on Lana's face as she waved a hand in between us. "Normally, you're the one handing out advice and leading *me* in the right direction."

Is that what Lana thought she was doing? She thought Lachlan was the right direction?

"There's no need for leading, Lana. I'm just fine," I said softly.

My breathing became shallow. I crossed my arms, but it was only to hide my shaking hands. I didn't want to shut her out, but I refused to talk about Lachlan. I exhaled loudly and picked up my purse.

"I gotta go. I'll see you later?"

Lana looked at me for a long second. For a moment, I was afraid that she could see the truth.

"Yeah," she said slowly. "I'll see you later."

I DROVE DOWN LINCOLN ROAD. IT WAS A FIVE-MILE STRETCH that led to Max's house.

My window was open, letting in the smell of firewood. It was slightly overcast, but that didn't stop a few kids from playing with a sprinkler in their front yard. I drove past them with a fleeting glance.

All I could think about was Lachlan.

I hadn't expected Lana to mention his name. He was a subject that we hardly brought up.

He came into my life at the right time. And when he left, I knew it was for a reason. But I also knew we weren't finished. I knew he would come back into my life. I just wasn't ready.

I pulled into Max's driveway. His car was parked in front of the garage. A silver Beamer was parked in the circular drive. I ignored the pounding in my ears and gripped the steering wheel, trying to get a good look at the car.

"Shit," I whispered.

That was Lana's dad's car.

I pulled up beside Max's car. My hands were still grasping the steering wheel in a white-knuckled grip. I tried to imagine why Lana's dad was here. Maybe it was innocent. Maybe it was for work. It didn't really matter; every scenario ended badly.

"Shit," I repeated.

First instinct: Turn my car around. Get the hell out of Dodge. Far away from Lana's dad.

What I would actually do: Stay.

I had to know what was being said.

I walked up the sidewalk. My legs were threatening to give out on me. I went to ring the doorbell, but at the last minute I stopped. Now that I knew Lana's dad was here, I wanted to be as inconspicuous as possible. Like a spy who sneaks in and out without anyone noticing.

I stepped inside and scanned the foyer. Lucy, Max's housekeeper, was turning to walk up the stairs with a laundry basket in hand. She stopped and stared at me with wide eyes. She was in her mid-fifties. Her brown hair was graying at the temples. She came here three days a week.

I pressed my index finger against my lips before I motioned for her to come closer.

"How long have they been in there?" I whispered.

"Not long. Maybe five minutes."

"Okay. Good. I—" I stopped talking when I saw the look on her face. She would cover for Max if anything happened. But I was a different story.

"Naomi, you shouldn't be here," she whispered back.

"I'll leave in a few minutes."

I patted her shoulder, gave her a reassuring grin, and tiptoed to Max's office door. Lucy's footsteps sounded above my head.

My palms laid flat against the door and I focused hard on what was being said.

"Why are you here? You're angry that your daughter is gone?" Max's voice was tense with anger. "Help me out here. Tell me what's really going on."

"I know you're a sensible man, my boy."

I closed my eyes and gently rested my forehead against the door. That was Michael.

The purpose was to listen to their conversation for a few minutes and get out of there before either one saw me. Yet I found myself turning the doorknob. It was barely an inch, but it was enough to see inside. I closed my left eye and turned my face, peeking inside with my right.

Lana's dad walked the length of the room. He had on black dress pants, a white dress shirt, and a navy-blue tie. His light brown hair was combed over to the side. Not a hair was out of place.

"I just came here to speak with you," her dad reasoned. "Man to man."

Max snorted and leaned back in his chair. He watched Lana's dad with a sharp eye. "Just say what you need to say and leave."

Her dad stopped walking and faced Max head-on. I didn't see his face, but I watched his body language. The way he stood, how he crossed his arms. "Whatever my daughter told you, it's not true."

Max said nothing.

"I understand that you think you're doing the right thing. You think you're protecting her, trying to be a hero. And I find that admirable." He flashed Max his politician smile. The one that always put everyone at ease. "But there's no one to save here. Everything is all right."

Max didn't buy into his words or his smile. He rested his elbows on his desk. Both of his hands were curled into fists and pressed against his lips. He sat there, the clock ticking the time away, just looking at Lana's dad with a cold stare. Finally he moved. One hand lay flat on the desk; the other was pointed right at Lana's dad.

"You can sit there and smile and tell me that nothing has happened. And you can try to tell me that you would never do anything to hurt your daughter. But we both know it's a fucking act."

Her dad's shoulders stiffened.

"I wonder what everyone in McLean would do if they knew what you really were."

"I'm nothing but a loving husband and father," her dad said firmly.

The anger was spreading into Max's eyes, making him shake. He was a ticking time bomb, ready to go off at any second.

"I don't give a fuck who you think you are! In my book you're a fucking rapist!" Max roared.

"That's a big accusation to make and a huge hit at my character."

Max smiled darkly. "It's not an accusation if it's the truth."

"Were you there? Did you see whatever my daughter told you I did with your own eyes?"

My gut twisted over his condescending tone.

"I didn't have to be anywhere to know it was the truth," Max responded. "Since the day I met you, I knew something wasn't right. You always have an answer for everything. That smile of yours never slips from your face. You go out of your way to be nice. I should've realized that smile was to hide some fucked-up shit."

"Enough!" her dad snapped.

He turned away from Max. I got a good look at him. His hands were braced on his hips. His jaw was clenched, and his skin was pale and clammy. He took a few breaths as he stared down at the floor. I could see him scrambling to get his bearings. Max sideswiped him and even though I was scared shitless right now, I couldn't stop the smile that came across my face.

Lana's dad took a deep breath. A smile was already on his face as he rotated back to Max.

"We're getting off on the wrong foot here. I just came here to fix the damage between us," he said as he sat down in the seat

across from Max. His body slightly bent, his elbows on his knees
and his fingers steepled. "Your eye for buying and selling stocks
is unrivaled. We may no longer be working together, but that
doesn't mean I can't recommend you to fellow businessmen."

"Is this a joke?"

"No."

"I drop you as a client and as a thank you, you recommend
me to your fellow 'businessmen'?" Max asked in disbelief.

"I am a fair man."

"No, you aren't. You're a desperate man. And you're here to
make sure that I keep quiet and don't ruin that perfect reputa-
tion of yours."

Lana's dad didn't say a word.

Max lifted a brow, that dark smile still on his face. "Am I
right?"

Lana's dad leaned close. The chair creaked beneath him.
"You don't know what you're doing. You're making a bad
choice." That calm tone had disappeared from his voice and it
became low and ominous. His true colors were showing.

Max spread his palms out. "I'll take my chances. Now go.
Get the fuck out."

Lana's dad tapped both armrests before he stood. Max stood
at the same time, ready to see him out.

But I saw the smile on her dad's face. It was cunning, and I
knew he had something up his sleeve. When Max walked around
his desk, Lana's dad stopped him by putting a hand on his arm.
Max looked at it with indignation and pure rage. Michael
stepped into Max's personal space and said in a dark voice:
"Son, your expiration date in this town is coming up. But I'll
still be here, and everything that's been mine will still be mine."

Max's eyes became shuttered and I wanted to step forward.
I'd never seen that look on his face. It was hatred. A blinding

rage that put everything within reach in danger. He stopped thinking with a clear head and moved so fast, Lana's dad never had a chance to react.

His hand curled around Lana's dad's neck. In one quick move, he slammed his face against the edge of the desk. I heard the telltale sound of bones cracking. Lana's dad screamed. The sound was filled with pain and made me shudder. One hit was good enough, but Max didn't stop. His grip on Lana's dad's neck tightened. Max slammed his face against the desk two more times, and I realized he wasn't going to stop until her dad was dead. I pushed open the door and ran into the room. "Stop!"

Max didn't stop. He didn't look up at me. His jaw was locked, nostrils flared. He moved like he was in a trance.

I grabbed onto Max's arm and pulled. "Stop it. You're going to kill him!" I yelled.

Max looked at me. There was a wild look his eyes that made my skin break out in goose bumps. He panted, and his shoulders rose and fell rapidly. He still gripped Lana's dad by the back of the neck in an ironclad grasp. I pleaded with my eyes for him to let go of Michael and walk away.

Max dropped him. The man fell like a rag doll. He was groaning, holding onto his bleeding nose. Blood seeped in between his fingers, dripping onto the floor. I ignored him, stepped around him, and placed my hands on Max's face. I got him to take a few steps back, but his eyes were rooted to Lana's dad on the floor. His entire body was stiff, practically shaking with anger.

"Don't," I whispered fiercely.

I waited for the anger to clear from his eyes, for a bit of sanity to return. He finally swallowed and looked at me. Some of his anger seemed to fade and I saw a small piece of the Max I knew.

Lana's dad groaned as he gripped the desk and stood up.

Max's eyes flicked over to him. In a low voice he said, "Go."

I kept my hold on Max. I didn't trust him. He might have calmed down some, but it wasn't enough for me to let go. I looked over my shoulder at Lana's dad. He reached into his back pocket and grabbed a monogrammed handkerchief and wiped away the blood on his face. He laughed derisively as he looked down at the blood staining his shirt. Instead of looking at Max, the person who did this to him, he looked directly at me.

I'd never understood Lana's refusal to tell everyone what her dad had done to her. But having those cold, dead eyes directed at me made me understand why she had so much fear. His lips curled into a knowing smile, as though he knew exactly what I was thinking. My breath started to quicken. It felt like the air was slowly being let out of the room. Little spots started to form behind my eyes.

Max muttered a curse underneath his breath. Our roles switched. He stepped in front of me and pointed at the door. "I said *go!*" he bellowed. Even bruised and bloodied, Lana's dad still had the nerve to smirk at me. His face sobered when he looked at Max with a sharp look in his eyes. "Think about what I said."

With those words, he walked away, whistling a tune that I didn't know. His footsteps echoed in the hall. Max and I were frozen in place, waiting for him to leave. The front door slammed seconds later. The windows rattled, and Max and I were surrounded by heavy tension.

I let go of his arm. He walked away, his hands clasped behind his head. He stared up at the ceiling.

Moment later, there were footsteps coming down the stairs. Lucy stood in the doorway. I'd forgotten she was even in the house. She gasped as she took in Max. Lana's dad's blood was on his shirt and hands, and even a little on his face. She didn't say a word.

"You can leave for the day," I told her quietly.

She looked at Max. He kept his eyes rooted upward but nodded bluntly. She left moments later.

The house was completely quiet. It was finally just the two of us.

"What are you doing here, Naomi?" Max said gruffly.

"What am I—" I shook my head in disbelief. "What am *I* doing here? What the hell was *he* doing here?"

"I don't know," Max said. He still wouldn't look at me. "I opened the fucking door and there he was. I still had stuff I wanted to say to him, so I let him in."

"Was busting his face up what you needed to say?"

His hands dropped. He turned to look at me, his eyes flashing. "I'm not going to say *sorry*! I did what I've been dreaming of doing to that fucker since I found out the truth!"

"I'm not asking you to say *sorry*. I'm asking you to think!" I shouted. "He was trying to provoke you. All he was waiting for was that one moment. The one where you react. And you gave him what he wanted." I held out my hand and jabbed a finger in the middle of my palm. "He had you eating right here. Right in the palm of his hand!"

"Everyone in this fucking town is eating out of his fucking palm!" Max exploded. "He's used to calling the shots and no one going up against him. Today he got a very small dose of reality. Next time it won't be very small."

My nerves were shot. And Max's had fried and blown up in flames minutes ago. We stared at each other, both out of breath.

Some of his anger started to crumble. He looked away and spotted Michael's blood sprayed across his collar.

"Fuck," he breathed.

He walked out of the room, unbuttoning his shirt as he went. I followed him up the stairs.

I shut the door to his room and leaned against the wall. Max took off his shirt, wadded it up in a ball, and threw it in the corner. He paced the room like a caged animal.

"You should've let me finish him," he said.

"Okay. You finish him. What happens after that?"

"He's dead and no one has to deal with him again!"

"No. He's dead and you're behind bars. And then who do I have?"

That sobered him up. He dropped his hands as he walked over to me. "I'm sorry," he said, his voice soft. "I'm sorry I did that in front of you."

His fingers combed through my hair. He looked at me thoughtfully, staring at every single feature before he kissed me. His lips stay pressed against mine. Not moving . . . just there.

My hands gripped his face and I tried to deepen the kiss, but he wouldn't move. Adrenaline was still coursing through me. I wanted to transfer all that energy into kissing Max rather than arguing with him. I inhaled through my nose as I moved my lips against his. Max didn't budge. My head tilted to the side and I dragged my tongue across the seam of his lips. Not a thing.

He held back on purpose. He didn't allow lust to take over.

I hated that. I wanted to forget what happened downstairs.

Max's grip on my face tightened as his lips slowly started to move against mine, his tongue slipping inside my mouth. I gasped.

I could feel what was behind this kiss: desperation, fear, and ultimately, loss. And that scared me more than anything. I gripped his shoulders, my grip bordering on painful.

We had nothing to worry about. We would be fine. I wanted to tell him just that, but I didn't pull away long enough to say it.

I made my way to the bed, and Max followed. The pace of his kiss may have quickened, but his hands hadn't and were not near fast enough for me. I hurriedly undressed him, and he took his time taking each article of my clothing off.

And when we were both naked, with me draped over him, he let me take the lead. Yet everything was still different. I kissed his strong jaw, then moved down his body, his skin warm against my lips. I kissed the side of his pecs. My teeth grazed against the cut of his abs.

Max's hand curled around my skull. He lifted me up until we were face-to-face and kissed me in a way that would leave my lips bruised. I moaned and slid him inside me in one fluid motion.

I moved up and down slowly, watching him the entire time. Each time his hips lifted, his arms, which were wrapped around my waist, would tighten.

I held on right back.

29

TIME'S UP

ON AN EARLY FRIDAY MORNING, AT THE BEGINNING OF AUGUST, I suddenly woke up.

There was no crazy dream with me plummeting to my death and waking up seconds before I landed. I was wide-awake and alert, for no good reason.

I looked at the time. Five thirty-two a.m.

Lana's apartment was quiet. I shot out of bed and jerked open the blinds. It was the start of a new day. The sky was painted pale gray as the sun was getting ready to rise. Most of the city was still asleep. The streets were cloaked in fog.

I crossed my arms and leaned against the window. Everything was so peaceful and quiet, but my gut told me something was wrong. This felt like the calm before the storm.

That instantly brought me to Lana's dad. Weeks had passed

since the altercation between Max and him. Max and I had waited for her dad to retaliate. To call. Harass. Press charges. Or even to go so far as to have someone do his dirty work.

But nothing happened. Not a damn thing.

In a few weeks I would go back to school. My parents would be home within a few days. My old, normal life was waiting for me. Yet it seemed impossible that I could ever slip back into that life. How could I, knowing what I knew?

The lack of retaliation from Lana's dad should have made me feel at ease. But it didn't. I was incredibly anxious. He had the upper hand right now. I knew it. He knew it. He was waiting for that perfect moment to strike back.

Lana knew what had happened. It was too big of a scene for me not to tell her. She reacted just like I expected. Withdrew from me and Max. Blamed herself for what happened, holed herself away in her apartment. It took a few days for her to return to normal. Whenever I saw her I would look at her searchingly, trying to see if there was any clue to show she had talked to her dad. She would stare right back and shake her head.

That gut feeling refused to leave and the longer I stood there, watching the sun slowly rise over the city, the more anxious and scared I became.

I closed the curtains and left the bedroom. I made my way over to the fridge, searching for something to eat. I tried to tell myself that I was overreacting and that this feeling stemmed from my paranoia. My fingers drummed against the edge of the fridge when I heard the thump of the newspaper hitting the front door. My back became erect. I slowly turned.

I couldn't say that I watched the news, let alone read the newspaper. The most I ever did was scan the front page before walking away, going about my business. But right now, the clock ticked and the fridge hummed and I stayed still, my gaze directed at the door. I walked over and opened it. The newspaper was rolled up and held together with a green rubber band.

I didn't reach for the paper. I just stared down at the small piece of the front page. What I saw was a profile of a face: one eye, the sharp line of a nose, and lips pulled into a thin line. My heart slowed and my entire body felt numb.

"Oh, God," I whispered.

Everything became hazy as I picked up the paper and walked into the living room. I read the words over and over, but nothing would stick in my brain. Just the words *arrested* and *insider trading*. Blood rushed through my ears. It became hard to stand.

With the paper in hand, I walked to Lana's bedroom. I knocked a few times. No one opened the door. I grew impatient and walked in. Her bed was made. The lights were turned off and there was no Lana.

I stood there completely stunned before I ran out of the room, changed my shirt, snatched up my keys, and left the apartment.

I CALLED MAX. ALL MY CALLS WENT STRAIGHT TO VOICEMAIL.

In a desperate attempt to prove the newspaper wrong, I drove to his house. I didn't even bother pulling into his driveway. I just pressed the brakes and peered through the passenger-side window. There were cars parked that I'd never seen there. Maybe his parents?

There was no point stopping by if he wasn't there, and I knew he wasn't.

I drove to Lana's parents' house next.

If Lana knew what had happened to Max, and I think she did, then she would be here. She would retreat into her parents' hold. Partially out of fear, and to be reassured that everything could be smoothed over if she came back.

I sat in my car, parked in their driveway. The newspaper sat in the passenger seat like an ominous being, waiting to attack. The sun had risen, but clouds had moved in, creating a gray veil over McLean.

The longer I sat here, doing nothing, the more time was wasted. What was I waiting for? I snatched up the newspaper and scanned the front page.

The short version?

Max was accused of insider trading for six of his clients. None of those clients' names were listed. The article didn't say what proof they had or the person behind the accusations. But at the very end it said that anyone accused of insider trading could face up to twenty years behind bars and a ridiculous amount in fines.

This entire story was cloaked in mystery. None of it was true. I knew that. I knew that Max was smart enough not to go down the road of insider trading, but not everyone else would. Even if the charges were dropped, it didn't matter, because it would blow up into this huge scandal that would ruin Max and his family's company.

Lana's dad had a hand behind this. I was positive.

With the paper in my hands, I got out of my car. I had no idea what the hell I was going to do. I just knew I had to do something.

I barely thought twice about barging into Lana's family's house. There were voices coming from the kitchen and upstairs. They'd soundproofed the entrance well enough that Lana and her mom didn't look up when I walked in. They were in the formal living room. Lana was sitting on the couch and her mom was sitting across from her in the Louis XV armchair. Her mom's back was straight; her feet leaned to the right with one tucked behind the other. Lana had her hands on her lap. Her right knee wouldn't stop bobbing.

I slid into the dining room, opposite the formal living room.

Neither one said a word. Her mom reached for her coffee on the polished table in front of her. She held the saucer and stirred the spoon slowly, staring down at the liquid. Lana watched her with a nervous look in her eyes.

"Stop moving," her mom lashed out.

Lana stilled.

Her mom took a sip of her coffee before she placed it back on the table. She leaned back in her chair and crossed her legs. Her fingers curled around the edges of the arm of the chair. She looked regal and proud, like a queen sitting on her throne, knowing that no one would speak or move until she moved first.

Her mom cleared her throat and looked at her only child. "You know your dad didn't want to have to do this."

"But he did."

Her mom's eyes narrowed as she leaned close. "And do you know why? You fabricated a lie. The only reason this boy is in the position he's in right now is because of you. No one else but you."

"I didn't fabricate anything!"

Her mom laughed mockingly. "Of course you didn't."

Lana ignored her mom's words. "He was just trying to help me."

"But you're lying," her mom said vehemently. "You've always imagined things that were never there."

A wounded look crossed Lana's face. Her leg started to bobble again. "You know Dad did it. I know you do."

Her mom didn't say a word. She just sat there, staring at Lana with an unreadable expression.

Lana stood up and walked around the coffee table. "I can never understand why you avoided what's been going on. Or how you can sweep it all under the rug, trying to pretend that nothing is wrong. How could you ignore me when I needed you the most?"

"Enough!" Lana's mom lashed out. She quickly stood. I could see her hands shaking with anger.

It would take only three steps for her mom to walk forward and embrace her. But Lana's mom treated the space between them as if it were miles. As long as Lana lived, her mom would never be the one to take that step forward.

"Accept your life," her mom said.

"What?"

Her mom lifted her chin. "Do not play the victim and sit here with that pitiful look on your face, hoping that someone will feel sorry for you. You have to accept this life you have."

"What kind of life is this?" Lana whispered.

Her words were pointless. She was just talking to her mom's back. Lana stood in the room alone. Her mom entered the foyer, humming a pretty tune. A maid walked up to her with a bouquet of flowers in her hands. Lana's mom smiled brilliantly and bent her face to smell them.

"They are beautiful," she said approvingly. "Just beautiful."

With a pat on the maid's shoulder, she continued to walk down the hall, her heels echoing loudly.

I turned back to Lana. She stared in my direction for a moment. It took her a while to notice I was staring back at her.

She blinked furiously before she hurried across the foyer.

"What are you doing here?" she whispered.

I pulled out the paper and held it in between us. She didn't grab for it. Just stared at Max's face with blank eyes.

"You know already, don't you?"

She looked down the hall for a second before she nudged her head at the front door. "Outside?"

I nodded and followed behind her. The door shut with a firm click. Instead of diving right into the conversation, Lana sighed and sat on the top step, staring at the long, winding driveway with a contemplative expression.

"I found out last night," Lana said. "You were asleep and I didn't want to wake you. You needed a break from everything. I came back home to find out what was going on."

"Why . . . why didn't you wake me up?"

"Because you need a break from everything. Look at what this has done to your life. Your entire summer went to shit."

"You think that's your fault?"

"I know it is. Just like you think it's your job to be there for me. It's my job to protect you from my life."

"That's not true!"

"Everything is ruined," she whispered brokenly.

It was as though she couldn't even hear me.

A chill went down my spine.

"No, it's not. The charges will be dropped and everything will smooth itself back out."

"Can you stop?" Lana exploded. I pulled away. She laughed sadly and stared down at the grass. "You heard my mom back there. None of this would've happened to Max if I hadn't been involved!"

"Your mom is also the same person that chooses to believe her husband over her daughter. Don't listen to her. She has no idea what she's talking about."

Lana hugged her knees close to her chest. There was a defeated look in her eye. It was the same one she'd had the night I found her in the barn.

"You're not moving back home, are you?" I said with alarm.

She didn't say a word. I had my answer.

"You're not going to do that." I grabbed onto her arm, my grip tight. "You're going to go back to your apartment. You know why?"

She looked over at me; her eyes were glassy.

"Because you've made so much progress." I smiled encouragingly. "Come on, Lana. You have your own apartment. Your very own that allows you to come and go as you please! You're creating a life built around your own choices. Last year, would you have been able to do that?"

"No," she whispered.

"You think you have to move back because everything feels so hopeless right now, and you don't think you can be on your own, but you *can*."

I stood up and held out my hand. "What do you say? Are you ready to go back home?"

"Yeah." She took my hand. "I'll do it."

"What will happen to Max?" she asked me as we got inside the car.

I stared at the steering wheel. "He'll get out on bail. The charges will be dropped and everything will be okay again. I promise."

Lana looked at me doubtfully. And could I blame her? I didn't believe it myself.

30

BREAKING

"We can stop there for today."

I look at Dr. Rutledge. My pulse hammers against my skin. My voice is starting to shake as I further explain my story.

Instead of asking me questions, Dr. Rutledge doesn't say a thing. She sits back in her chair, her pen tapping against her notebook.

She sits up straight and laces her fingers together. "You know what I think?"

"What?" I ask wearily.

"I think you should take a weekend pass."

"A weekend pass," I repeat.

"I know these sessions have been wearing you down, but you're making significant improvement. I think a weekend pass would be beneficial for you."

When Lachlan first mentioned the idea of a weekend pass, I

didn't store too much faith in the idea. And when I broke down in group therapy, I thought my chances of ever having my freedom had disintegrated into thin air. But here I am, given a chance to have my freedom. Even if it does have an expiration date.

I stare at her skeptically. It feels like there's a catch that comes along with this opportunity.

"Would you like that?"

I nod. "Y-yes!" I stutter.

"If you don't think you're ready for it, you don't have to take it."

"I am," I say quickly. "I am. I'm just skeptical."

"There's nothing to be skeptical about. Everyone needs a break." She shrugs. "This is your break."

I exhale loudly. "I'll do it."

"Great!" she says triumphantly as she stands up. "Mary will help you pack your bag tomorrow and you can be on your way."

One small, but very important, factor finally hits me. "Who's picking me up?" I ask.

"Lachlan."

My fears slam into me swiftly. I can picture Dr. Rutledge talking to Lachlan, telling him that I truly am insane and that I will never get out of this place. Even though Dr. Rutledge has proven herself to me, it doesn't matter when old insecurities never die.

I think she sees the fear in my eyes. She lays a hand on my shoulder and looks at me with concern.

"I've spoken to him once," she says gently. "He spoke to me last week about a weekend pass, and that's it. You have nothing to worry about."

I swallow. "Thanks," I whisper.

"Now," she grins, "get some rest. Tomorrow is a big day."

31

MATCHES

THE NEXT EVENING, I'M WALKING DOWN THE HALL WITH MY overnight bag in hand. Mary is right next to me; Lachlan is in front of me. His back is facing me and he's talking to Dr. Rutledge.

I revert to teenage Naomi. The one that turns red around him. Whose lips split into a ridiculously bright smile while her heart flips wildly in her chest.

Dr. Rutledge looks over Lachlan's shoulder at me. Her brows lift and she smiles. "Good morning, Naomi."

Lachlan turns and looks at me. He gives me a one-sided grin. I think my heart just dropped down to my stomach.

He's dressed in a simple pair of jeans, a dark blue shirt, and a brown jacket. He looks so relaxed and at ease. He's never looked sexier. "Look at you," he says, and reaches to take my bag.

"I know. Can you believe it?" I lift my foot. "I have laces on my shoes."

Mary actually laughs. Holy shit. Who knew she had a drop of humor inside of her? But in all seriousness, putting on clothes—that weren't sweats—and wearing shoes makes me feel as if a piece of myself is clicking right back into place.

Lachlan's grin stays in place as his eyes sweep me from head to toe. There's a heavy sense of anticipation in my stomach be-cause the minute we walked out the front doors he would be all mine. There would be no nurses checking up on us, or telling him that it was time to go.

I pull my eyes away from him and glance at Dr. Rutledge. "Am I good to go?"

She holds a clipboard between us. "You just have to sign off on a few papers." She puts it on the counter next to me and hands me a pen.

I scan the contents of the page quickly. It's basically a sign-out form saying that I, as the patient, or the guardian of the patient, understand what a weekend pass entails.

I glance at Dr. Rutledge. "I don't need my parents' signa-ture?"

She clears her throat and looks over my shoulder at the pa-perwork. "No. It's a weekend pass," she says quietly. "I just need your signature."

I wasn't going to challenge her. I quickly scribble my name on the bottom of the paper and step back. I shift my feet and stare at Dr. Rutledge.

"That's it," she says happily. "Have a fun weekend, Naomi." Lachlan and I walk out the door. I take a deep breath of the fresh air. I scan the cars in the parking lot. There are high piles of snow in the corner of the lot from the snowplow. Salt is pep-pered along the sidewalk to prevent falling. And I'm glad, because today I'm so excited and anxious to get out of here I would have run ahead to Lachlan's car and busted my ass.

I put one foot in front of the other, reminding myself that I need to look like a normal person. One that walks outside and interacts with people in the real world daily. I look over at Lachlan. His walk is confident. Shoulders straight. Chin slightly lifted, daring anyone to step in his way.

When I get into his car, I breathe into my hands as we wait for the car to warm up. Lachlan places a warm hand on my thigh and smiles at me. "Are you ready?"

"Absolutely."

"Good," he says, and pulls out of the parking spot. "That's exactly what I wanted to hear."

He pulls out onto the road and presses the gas.

The temptation to turn in my seat and wave at Fairfax is strong, but if I do, my gaze will wander to the ghost of myself staring longingly outside, putting another tally on the window. So I stare straight ahead as the dry, frozen grass flies past us.

"You might as well relax; it's a two-hour drive to my house," Lachlan says.

"How do you expect me to relax?" I wave my hand around. "I haven't been in a car in months. I need to take everything in! Today's been pure torture. I sat in the rec room the whole day, staring at the clock."

"If it makes you feel any better, there's a pile of paperwork on my desk because I couldn't concentrate. I ended up leaving work an hour early." Lachlan gives me such a raw, personal smile, I almost clutch my chest in pain. "But if you want to keep looking around, then by all means . . . don't let me interrupt."

"Nah." I shift in my seat. "Tell me about your house."

"What do you want to know?"

"What's it like?"

He shrugs. "It's a house."

"Come on," I coax. "Give me your best description."

"It's small. Two bedrooms, one bathroom. There's a small kitchen and living room. The carpet is outdated, along with the appliances, but I like it."

"Did you decorate?"

He gives me a look that says, "What do you think?"

I grin and watch as dusk paints the sky.

We take the highway, bypassing McLean. I watch my hometown fly past me from my window and it looks like a blur of lights. I should probably feel some pull to the town I grew up in, but I don't. The only pull that I have is the memories with Lana. Those memories tug at my heart, screaming at me that Lana is out there. Maybe not in McLean, but somewhere close.

We turn here and there and the two-hour drive flies by, and soon we're driving into the outskirts of Charlottesville. We stop by a fast-food restaurant and order greasy food that makes my stomach rumble.

"We're almost there," Lachlan says.

"It's okay," I reassure him. "I'm having fun."

"Just sitting in a car?"

I shrug and sneak a few French fries. "I'm getting a glimpse at your new life in this town."

"I'm still adjusting," Lachlan admits. "But it's nice having no one know your name." He looks over at me. "You'd love it."

"If I ever get out of Fairfax," I murmur.

"You will," Lachlan says firmly.

We drive out of the city. Cars start to become sparse and the road becomes smaller and more compact. Lachlan has to slow down to avoid the potholes. Excitement courses through my veins when he pulls onto a gravel driveway. It started to snow when we left Charlottesville. The headlights illuminate the frozen grains, making them look like they're dancing in the air.

The ride up his driveway is rough. I jostle around in my seat and grab the handle above my head to hang on.

"You drive up and down this daily?"

"Yep."

"How does your car even have shocks?"

"It's just a little bumpy," Lachlan argues.

I shoot him a look.

"Okay . . ." he says slowly. "It's really bumpy. But I'll get it fixed soon."

A moment later he parks the car. I stare at the house in front of us. "So this is your house."

It *is* small. White paint is chipping on the side. There's a small porch with just a broom leaning against the side of the house. There's no grandeur. No over-the-top design. It is the exact opposite of how we grew up.

I couldn't love it more. It reminds me of the cottage out in the woods.

Lachlan tilts his head, giving me a boyish smile that reminds me of the fifteen-year-old boy I fell in love with. "This is it. Does it meet your expectations?"

My opinion matters to him. And even as a kid it had mattered. That's what makes Lachlan my safety net—I will always matter to him.

"Of course! I love it."

We both get out of the car. He goes to the trunk and grabs my bag. "What made you choose this place?" I ask.

He slings my bag over his shoulder and grabs my hand. We walk to his house, side by side. "Small. Surrounded by solitude. What's not to love?"

We stomp the snow away from our shoes as we walk across the porch. Lachlan unlocks the front door and flips the light on next to it.

There's a small entryway that leads directly into the kitchen. Probably one of the smallest kitchens I've seen, with old appliances the color of avocado.

He drops his keys on the counter and wordlessly guides me to the living room. It's the biggest room in the house. There is just a beige rug, with a brown leather couch, a chair, and an end table around it and a television in the corner. The last piece of decoration is a dozen boxes shoved against the wall.

I point at the boxes. "I love the way you've decorated the place." Lachlan leans against the wall and grins. "It took me a long time."

I walk forward, looking at each piece of furniture. "I can tell."

"Tell me, Interior Decorator Naomi, what would you do differently?"

"Well, for one thing, I would put curtains up." I point to the bay window. "And they would be lace curtains. I would paint the walls a pale yellow. I would keep the rug you have now. Hang some pictures up. Find some beautiful flowers, and I would make sure that the bay window was filled with pillows, so I could relax and stare outdoors anytime I wanted."

"That sounds like a lot of work."

For him, yes. But if I lived with him, I would do it myself and I would do it with the biggest smile on my face.

"You're thinking," Lachlan says.

I correct him. "I'm imagining."

"Same thing."

He walks into the kitchen. I hear cabinets open and close. "I knew you would love this place," he calls out.

I follow Lachlan. "You did?"

He grabs two plates and fills them up with food.

"Of course," he says absently. "The realtor showed me the house and when I saw the bay window, I remembered you talking about that as a kid."

"So technically this house is half mine," I tease.

Lachlan hands me my plate. I try to take it away. Lachlan keeps his grip. He won't let go until I look at him. When I finally do, I see the intense look in his eyes.

"Half yours? It's all yours."

I just stare at him. He isn't lying.

"Come on," Lachlan says. "Let's eat in the living room."

We sit in companionable silence and eat our food.

"Are you excited to be out of there?" he asks.

"I can't believe it," I confess. "There's no twenty-minute outside breaks. Or a nurse knocking on your door every hour on the hour. I don't have to hear the constant sound of voices outside my door, and I don't have to sleep in that terrible room. Plus, the food is much, much better."

"Yeah?" he asks with a small grin.

I nod. "Burned meatloaf and runny mac and cheese are about as good as it gets there."

Lachlan swallows. "Does everyone eat together?"

"Mostly. Unless you've done something wrong. Then you eat in your room."

Beneath his slanted brows, his eyes turn hard. I know I've said too much. He's thinking about Fairfax. I'm thinking about Fairfax and I don't want to. His house was a place that was free from all the dark things looming over me. It should stay that way.

I want to take my words back and start over. I look down at my food, suddenly not feeling hungry at all. I stand up and walk back to the kitchen, putting my plate on the counter. When I walk back into the living room, Lachlan stares straight at me with confusion. I stare at him for a second before I turn off the lights. Slowly making my way to the large window, I cross my arms and stare outside.

Lachlan's house sits on a hill. From here, I can see the lights of the city flickering bright. I picture people inside their houses, all relaxed and calm. It puts me at peace. It makes me want to stay right here forever.

"What are you doing?" Lachlan asks.

I tap my nail against the glass. "Looking at the view."

"With the lights off?"

"It's the best way to see."

If I were at Fairfax, I wouldn't see this picture in front of me and I wouldn't feel this way. Right now, if I want to, I can reach out and touch and experience the world I'm looking at.

Lachlan scoots his chair back. I hear his footsteps, and drawers opening and shutting.

Snick. Snick.

It's a familiar sound that makes my heart speed up.

It takes only seconds for an amber glow to light the room. I look over my shoulder and see Lachlan holding a match in between his fingers. Lit not with a lighter, but a simple matchbook. Just like the ones we used to light off fireworks.

He smirks at me mischievously. His eyes glow brightly from the flame. There is enough heat in his eyes to make me swallow loudly.

"What are you doing?" I ask.

"Playing with fire." He jerks his wrist and the fire dies out. "I'm trying to lighten the mood." His deep voice is closer and my heart starts to speed up. "Remember how you used to always blow the matches out?"

"I remember," I say softly.

I look at the open living room and in the dark I picture all the furniture gone. The wood floor drops out and is replaced with fresh, green grass. Two young people appear. Their heads are bent, backs bowed, as they huddle together. Their lips move rapidly. I can't hear them. And I don't need to. Their words are seared into my brain. I watch with rapt attention as the boy says, "I got one more firework. Wanna light up the sky?" He holds a match in between them.

And the girl nods and smiles at him. Her heart shines in her eyes. He hands her the match. She takes it.

I close my eyes. When they open, Lachlan has a lit match in his hands. The boy and girl are gone. The furniture is back in place. Those two people have evolved. That girl can now act out her feelings. And that guy still smirks at her, but his eyes are white hot.

Something settles deep inside me. It spreads throughout me, making my blood hum and my body tingle. Lachlan keeps walking until I'm pressed up against the window, the cold glass on my back and his body warming me from the front. I tilt my head back to look at him. He lifts a single brow, daring me not to touch him. That's the last thing I see before he blows out the match.

I know this is a little game that was meant to lighten the mood, but now a sexual tension has filled the room. I know Lachlan isn't done and I know he won't be done until I'm practically a puddle on the floor.

His cheek brushes against mine. I hear the match drag against a coarse surface. My hands curl into fists against my thighs. My fingernails sink into my palms, creating crescent-moon indents.

The match is the one thing keeping us separated. It lights up his features. His lips are sensuous and his eyes are brilliant. The stubble on his face looks almost golden.

"You're perfect," I say very quietly.

Lachlan tilts his head and smirks. "No, I'm not. It's just the lighting."

"You are," I insist.

He brushes his hand across my throat. My pulse jumps wildly against my skin.

"You wanna know how you look right now?"

I nod.

I thought he would blow out the match, but he doesn't. He brings the match close to my face, going over every feature slowly.

"Your eyes are bright. The fire almost makes them look violet. Your cheeks are red. And all that blond hair looks golden"— his hand drags through my hair—"hanging around your shoulders. And your lips are wet and slightly parted." A single finger grazes my lip. "If I move my face just an inch closer, I could suck on that bottom lip . . ." And right when I think he's going to do just that, the room goes black.

His hand drops from my face. The two of us are quiet. Both of us breathing rapidly.

"This is my last match," he says in a sexy whisper. "Do you want me to light it?"

My breath comes out shaky. "Yes."

The match drags across the matchbox slowly. And then there's an amber glow. Lachlan holds the flame between us. "Hold it, Naomi."

The flame travels downward, racing toward his fingertips. He still holds it, waiting patiently for me to respond. He'd let the fire reach his fingers. He'd take the pain for me.

My hand shakes as it reaches out. Lachlan's eyes go half-mast the minute I grip the match.

"Now take a breath and blow it out," he says gruffly.

He's not asking me to blow out the flame. Lachlan wants me to blow out the pain, tears, and destruction from my life. And more than anything, I want to do the same thing. So I lean my face closer to the flame. I look Lachlan in the eye, and with one big gust, I blow the flame out.

The room goes dark.

The match drops to the floor.

The sound echoes around the room. I stand perfectly still, breathing rapidly. The room may be dark but the fire hasn't died. It's just transferred to my body. It spreads throughout my veins. It suffocates my fears. My insecurities. My sadness.

I find myself shifting closer.

And then I feel his lips touch mine. His mouth moves so slowly. My eyes close. Lachlan's hands gently rest against my neck. His tongue glides along my lips. My lips part. His thumbs brush against my throat.

This kiss is gentle yet firm.

This kiss demands to be felt.

This kiss makes up for all the time lost that I'll never get back.

He moves back an inch. I can't see his face, but I can feel his eyes on me. "Let me touch you," he says.

I'd do anything he asks of me. I tell him yes and before I've even finished speaking, he reaches out and hooks his index fingers through my belt loops. He doesn't stop guiding me forward until our bodies are touching. I feel his fingers encircle my wrist. I spread my hand, palm up, waiting for his hand to lace with mine, but his lips make contact with my palm, moving to my wrist, where my pulse pounds against my skin. His fingers move up my arm and grip my elbows. He guides my hands to his neck.

I've grown confident underneath his touch and I kiss him. I kiss him knowing that he is the best kind of therapy I will ever have.

Lachlan guides us across the room. We move down the hallway and through a doorway. Out of the corner of my eye I see a large bed. I sit on the edge and raise my eyes to his. He reaches behind his back and grips a handful of his shirt and pulls it over his head.

It was a brisk action and yet my hands jerk at my sides, wanting to reach out and touch him. Lust simmers in my stomach. My fingers curl around the sheets as I carefully look at him. Everything I want is right in front of me.

Light comes in through the window, casting his skin in a blue hue. Highlighting the tendons that travel up his arms and his powerful biceps. I can make out the contours of his stomach, and the sharp-muscled V that disappears underneath his jeans. He could wrap himself around me and I would disappear from sight.

"You can do whatever you want," he says, his voice not quite steady. "I'm all yours."

My hand reaches out like it has a mind of its own. I touch the side of his pec before my eyes drift south. I've touched him like this before, but it never gets old. I always find something new and fascinating when I touch Lachlan.

I watch Lachlan suck in a breath. I move down his stomach. His skin tightens and the outline of his abs appears. My blood roars through my veins as my fingers drift down to his jeans hanging low on his hips.

I feel courageous and lean forward, my teeth grazing the skin above his jeans. My fingers find the button to his jeans. His eyes are hot, watching every single thing I do. I pull his jeans down, and then his boxers. I wrap my hand around his cock. It's thrilling how when I touch him, I have all the control. He closes his eyes. His mouth opens.

He mutters a curse and his hands reach up and grip the back of my head, holding me in place.

"Naomi," he groans. "Slow down."

"What if I don't want to slow down?"

I know I should savor every touch, kiss, and bite. When I'm back at Fairfax I'll have this memory to hang onto. But I'm so far past the slow-down option, it's now a distant memory. It's been too long since I've had Lachlan all to myself.

Mine, mine, mine, I chant in my mind.

My hand tightens around him. He sucks in a sharp breath.

"If you don't stop," Lachlan pants, "this will all be over way too quickly."

I want him inside of me. I want him to fuck me. That's the ultimate goal. That's the only reason I let go of him.

I lean back and take off my shirt. It drops onto the bed and I wait expectantly. But Lachlan doesn't touch me. He is frozen, with only his eyes sweeping me from head to toe.

"What are you thinking?" I breathe.

My body is perfectly still, but I have to stop myself from pulling him to me.

"I'm thinking," he says slowly as he looms over me so I'm forced to tilt my head back to look at him, "I'd do anything with you . . . for you . . . to you." He leans down, his eyes level with mine. "I'm thinking you have me under a spell."

He kisses my open mouth. I breathe through my nose as he unzips my pants. We break apart for only a second. My pants

come off. My underwear quickly follows. All that's left is my
bra. A small scrap of material. The look in Lachlan's eyes shows
he wants it gone. I reach my arms behind my back to unhook it.
Lachlan beats me to it. He rises onto his knees. I tilt my head
back to watch him. My bra comes undone in seconds. He keeps
his eyes on mine as he slowly pulls the straps down my arms.
The cold air touches my breasts. My nipples harden. I smile
faintly as I watch Lachlan take me in. I move across the bed.
Lachlan follows me. When my head touches the pillow he dips
his head. Lips circle around an areola slowly before they wrap
around my nipple. My back arches as my hands grip his shoulders, nails digging into his skin. I forgot that this is how it is with
Lachlan. I forgot how my body can go from cold to on fire
within seconds. I forgot how he knows just how to touch me,
kiss me, hold me in a way that drives me crazy.

He switches between both breasts and I'm panting.

"I've fucking missed you," he groans against my skin. He's
still touching me, as if he's afraid I'm going to disappear. "I've
missed all of you."

His lips move away from my breast and drift down.

I keep my eyes open and watch him. The temptation to close
my eyes is there, but I want to be wide awake for this. I want to
watch everything.

His head drifts farther down my body. His hands tighten
against my hips imperceptibly.

I feel his breath against my stomach. I move restlessly against
the sheets. Teeth scrape against the curve of my hip. By this point
I'm trembling. Lachlan stops and lifts his head.

"Do you want me to keep touching you?" he asks, his voice
a low growl.

"Why ask me that?" I pant. "You know I do."

"When I touch you, I want you to always remember it comes from me and no one else." His fingers drift over my hips, across my inner thighs. "I want you to never forget me."

He leans in, his lips inches away, but he doesn't move. He hasn't even started and I'm already trembling.

Lachlan leans in and kisses me in between my legs. Even though I've been bracing myself for him to touch me, my back arches up off the bed. It's impossible to stay perfectly still. As his mouth moves over me, he watches me the whole time. But I can't keep his gaze. My eyes close and my head falls back.

My hands curl into fists. I want to grab him. I want to tilt my hips this way and that, to find the perfect angle, but I know he's building me up. His tongue moves in one quick sweep upward. I gasp. My body jerks. He hits the perfect spot at the perfect time. It is almost vicious, what he's doing to me. My legs keep moving against the sheets. One leg is angled outward; the other curves around his shoulder. I'll find any way to get closer to him.

Up and down his tongue brushes against me, driving me into a complete frenzy. I try to keep up with him for as long as I can. This uncontrollable feeling sweeps through me. My blood roars in my veins, feeling like tiny pinpricks moving underneath my skin, and my control breaks in half.

I grab the back of Lachlan's head, my fingers curling into his hair. I move my hips, finding my rhythm. It creates a friction that makes me hook my legs over his shoulders.

His hands curve around my thighs, his fingers tighten, and he presses me closer to his mouth.

Every muscle in my body tightens. I'm tingling everywhere. My hips lift up. Lachlan holds on, his mouth quickly moving against my skin.

There's this amazing second where I'm blissfully numb. I scream out his name.

My body drops to the mattress. I stare up at the ceiling in a complete daze. I'm panting, relishing the sensation in the aftermath. Pure bliss. That's the only way to describe it.

Lachlan lifts his head and gives me a come-hither smile. His hands move up my thighs and back down. I watch him with heavy-lidded eyes.

He sits up and reaches for a condom. I prop myself on my elbows and watch as he puts it on. His hands are quick. He meets my gaze. His hair is mussed from my hands. His eyes are wide and shining with lust. His chest is heaving. He has this wicked grin on his face as he looks over my body.

He doesn't ask or wait. His elbows fall on either side of my head, knees touching mine, and he surges into me.

"God, you feel good," he whispers hoarsely.

Those first few seconds my body stretches and I can barely breathe. It's delicious agony. His hand wraps around my neck gently and when he's fully inside me, his forehead rests against my own.

His hips start to move in a semicircle. The entire time, his gaze remains fixed on mine.

He pushes deeper. My legs lift. My shins brush against the sides of his ribs as I tighten my grip around him, pushing him deeper inside of me. My eyes almost roll into the back of my head.

"Who's with you right now?" he demands.

"You are," I pant.

"Good. Remember that," he says gruffly before he switches our positions. He's beneath me, and I'm above him. My palms lay flat against the hard wall of his chest.

"Who's in control right now?"

I look down at our bodies.

"Me."

"Yes, you." His hands curl around my hips, gripping me tightly. "You have me where you want me."

His words are thrilling and send a quick jolt of lust throughout my body.

I move slowly at first, watching his face. Just like he had watched mine.

His fingers dig into my skin. But he doesn't guide. He lets me have all the control.

I feel myself tighten around him, and he groans.

I start to move faster and my muscles start to ache. My pulse feels like it's vibrating against my skin.

His large hand travels from my neck to the back of my head, bringing me down to his face. His hips are thrusting frantically.

The bed squeaks.

The two of us are panting.

Sweat coats our skin.

The sheets rustle beneath us.

All these sounds are amplified until Lachlan gives one final thrust and calls out my name.

"Naomi!"

I will always remember the way he said my name. His voice was so raw. His feelings were exposed and out for the entire world to see. This is a man who will take all my pain, gather it up, and shoulder it as his own.

I collapse on top of him. My forehead rests against his shoulder. His chest heaves. We stay like that until our heartbeats slow down.

I don't know what to say. I'm speechless. So I move off him. Lachlan is lying there, with his forearm draped across his eyes, but when I move, he lifts his arm and blinks rapidly.

He takes the condom off, tossing it aside, and reaches for me. "Come here," he growls.

I love the deep timbre of his voice, raw from shouting. It makes my lips split into a lazy, satisfied grin. He wraps his arms around me, holding me so tightly against him.

Sex.

Love.

Fucking.

Call it what you want, but they are all the same. Each one requires you to give a piece of yourself that you can never get back.

But with the right person, everything will align perfectly. The world stops turning on its axis, time slows, and you realize that while you're losing a piece of yourself, you're also gaining something in return. What that person gives you fits you just right.

That's how I will always feel with Lachlan.

He holds me and I know I'm safe.

32

FIRE

I'VE DECIDED THAT LOVE IS A SICKNESS.

But not at first.

At first it's delicious. Just like a dessert. Nothing compares to that first bite. And you don't savor it, but you become ravenous. You know this could be the best thing you've ever had, so you keep tasting, you keep taking. Your greed clouds reason and by the time you realize you've gone too far, it's too late. The love is gone and you're left with nothing but pain.

If I knew all this, why was I setting myself up for the pain?

Twigs snapped underneath my shoes as I paced. The moon was out, chasing away the heat. In the distance I could hear crickets. I didn't stop to appreciate the sounds or the peacefulness of this moment. I was too angry at myself. Angry that I had answered Lachlan's call last night. Angry that I had agreed to meet him here.

He said that he'd be flying in today and staying for a week. Once upon a time, Lachlan coming back home would have made my entire year. But after that kiss, everything had changed. I thought things would remain the same, but I was wrong. The summer I turned eighteen, I waited and waited for him, but he never came home. He'd said that it was a busy summer with his internship and he said that with his carefree voice, like he knew that I would always be in McLean, waiting for him. But could I blame him?

If the past showed us anything, it was that I was standing there, always waiting for him. But all of that was about to change. Maybe he knew I would be leaving here. Maybe that's what made him come home.

He still e-mailed me and I got calls from him daily. Technically, I knew more about him than ever before. But I wanted to see him face-to-face. I needed his physical presence just as bad as his words.

I heard the sound of footsteps and turned. Lachlan was walking this way. His gaze was on the ground and his hands were pushing branches away from his face. He finally glanced up and stopped in his tracks.

We took each other in.

He was wearing jeans, and a gray T-shirt that was loose around his stomach and stretched tight around the shoulders.

I wiped my palms on my shorts as he came closer. My heart was drumming in my chest. The sun tinted his hair a golden brown. It was longer than normal, with strands brushing against his forehead. There was stubble on his cheeks and jaw. And those eyes that drove me crazy were less playful and more serious.

I skipped formalities, just like I always did with him. "Did you just get in?"

He nodded and took a step forward. "Landed an hour ago."

I looked around. "How was your flight?"

He looked at me carefully and took a step forward. "It was boring. I planned on getting some paperwork done, but I was seated next to a guy who talked to me the whole time," he said conversationally.

I smirked. Right about now would be the time I would ask for the entire story. But right now I had too much I needed to get off my chest.

"Have you been waiting long?" he asked.

I walked around slowly, kicking an acorn back and forth. "I haven't been here too long."

"Good. I was—"

I didn't want to stand here and pretend that everything was the same. I stopped short and quickly turned around.

"I'm getting out of here, Lach," I said in a rush.

Not a sound was made. It was as though my words sucked the air around us.

Lachlan stood perfectly still. "What?"

"I got accepted to Millikin University." I smiled, but Lachlan didn't return my smile. "It's a private college in central Illinois. I-I've always wanted to apply there, and I finally got the courage."

I waited for him to say something, but he never did. He tucked his hands into his pockets, rocked back on his heels. His eyes became fixated on the trees behind me.

"When are you leaving?" he finally asked.

I watched him carefully. "In a few weeks."

He looked at me and I saw the misery in his eyes. "That's great."

"Is it?"

Lachlan nodded.

I stepped forward. "What's wrong?"

"Nothing. I'm happy for you, Naomi." He smiled, but the smile never reached his eyes.

"Are you?"

"Of course." He crossed his arms and looked back at the trail.

I placed my hand on his arm. "You always told me to dream and to want something outside of McLean. So I did. And now I'm getting out of here and you look . . ."

His chin lifted. He looked me square in the eye. "I look what?"

"You look angry," I said very quietly.

"I'm . . . frustrated. Just when I'm coming back home for good, you're up and leaving."

If this weren't happening to me I would have laughed at the irony, but all I could do was breathe through the pain of knowing that the world was against us. The thought occurred to me then that we would probably never have the perfect opportunity to be together.

"I knew someday you were going to get the hell out of this place. I just didn't expect it to be now."

Before he came here I'd had every intention of letting him know just how angry I was. I planned on yelling at him. So where was that anger now?

"I've been here the entire time. What stopped you from coming home?"

"You were seventeen!"

"So?"

He tilted his head to the side. "You were just a—"

I backed away. "I swear to God if you say *kid* I will lose it!" I yelled. "You've known for a long time that the years have caught up with us. The age gap isn't so wide anymore. You knew it last year and you knew it a few years ago when you kissed me!"

His shoulders straightened defiantly. His lips were in a tight line. He wanted to deny my words so much. Instead of shouting and letting the truth free he took a step back, and then another.

"I'm not going to stand here and fight with you," he finally said.

"So you're going to leave?" I said to his retreating figure.

"It's better than this!" he shouted over his shoulder.

"I told you a long time ago that I love you. I still do."

He stopped and turned. I licked my lips nervously.

"Are you leaving because you're angry with me or because what you're feeling scares you?" I asked.

His hands were on his hips and his jaw ticked. His eyes swept over everything but me. "Naomi . . ."

"Well?" I persisted.

I stood there, my hands clenched at my sides, waiting for him to answer my question. I told him the truth long ago. I deserved the same. I deserved to have him look me in the eye when he finally did.

Seconds ticked by. It felt like years. And then his hazel eyes locked with mine.

"Do you love me?" I asked.

Lachlan was rigid, not saying a word. My heart pounded in my chest with fear.

He took that step forward. A step I had been waiting on for years. He ate the distance between us, and when he reached me, he gripped my face with both hands. His lips touched mine.

You know that one-of-a-kind kiss? The one that takes all your pain, fear, insecurities, and sadness and destroys it within seconds? The kiss that brings you back to life?

That was this kiss.

I stood on my tiptoes. I gripped his shirt with one hand and wrapped the other around his neck.

He backed me up until my shoulders touched the tree. I forgot about the world around us. Everything was put on pause and it was just the two of us.

Our hands reached for each other's clothes at the same time with quick, impatient jerks. He fumbled with the buttons on my dress. He worked his way down, the material loosening around my body. His finger grazed my stomach as the last button popped free. My dress parted, exposing my pale pink bra. My nerves were tingling. I wanted him to touch me, but I took this chance to grab the hem of his shirt. His arms lifted. Up and over his shirt went.

We didn't reach for each other. We stood there, taking each other in. I had waited years for this moment and it was finally here. My eyes traveled down his body. The smooth skin of his chest. His abs tightened, becoming ridged with each heavy breath he took. My hands curled into tight fists when I looked at the muscle above his hips, the one that forms a V and makes my brain go haywire.

My hands were shaking as I reached for the clasp in between my breasts. It unhooked and the material of my bra parted, grazing against my ribs.

I stayed in place, wanting him to have time to look at me. Just like I did with him.

I looked at him and my heart started to frantically beat. His eyes were more than intense. They were almost desperate and showed me that maybe I hadn't been the only one waiting for this to happen.

Lachlan swore before he crashed into me. The skin-to-skin contact made me gasp. His mouth moved over mine. I tilted my head back, my fingers digging into his biceps.

His hands drifted across my skin and his lips followed. I felt his warm breath on my breast, felt his tongue flick against my nipple.

"Keep going," I urged.

I'd never felt so much heat in my body. It felt like I was seconds away from bursting into flames. I didn't want it to stop.

He curled one hand into my hair. The other gathered the material of my dress, bunching it around my waist before he cupped my ass. He held me against him and I could feel just how hard he was.

I breathed through my nose and traced the taut muscles of his stomach.

Lachlan hissed through his teeth. He rested his forehead against mine as I unbuttoned his pants. My thumbs slipped past the material of his boxers. My hands were shaking, and I started to breathe hard. I was ready to see and feel him.

That's when Lachlan jerked away, as if a bucket of cold water had been poured over his head.

He stood there panting, with his pants dangerously close to falling off his hips. I knew I didn't look any better. My hair was messy from his hands and my lips were bruised from his kisses. I held my dress together with one hand.

"I'm not going to do this here." His voice was raw.

"Why not?" I breathed.

His eyes were still white hot, but they softened as he looked me up and down. "You're Naomi," he said, as if it explained everything.

"I don't care where we do this." I meant that.

On the floor, in a bed, or even against a tree. It didn't matter where; I just needed him and I needed my arms around him. I was back to square one with love. Where I was oblivious to the pain and completely starving.

"Touch me right now," I whispered, and let go of my dress. The material slid down my arms. My nipples hardened. Goose bumps covered my skin.

His mouth opened, but not a sound came out.

He came back to me before the last word had slipped from my mouth. His hands gripped the back of my thighs, lifting me up.

"Wrap yourself around me," he said.

I eagerly hooked my legs around him.

"But my underwear," I protested.

I grabbed the waistband, intent on pulling them down, but he beat me to it. Material ripped and fluttered to the ground. I watched, breathlessly, as he reached for his wallet from his back pocket and grabbed a square foil packet. The wallet dropped to the grass. He lowered his boxers. He was stiff, inches away from my thighs. I watched, my body shaking, and he put the condom on.

He moved slowly and I swear he did it on purpose, letting me take a good look at him. I wanted to wrap my hands around him, the skin looked so soft. I reached out. Lachlan intercepted my hand, holding my wrist gently. He looked at me, his lips curved in a wicked smile.

I lifted my hips. His dick brushed against my thigh.

That wicked smile faded.

He pushed himself inside me slowly. Making me feel every single inch. My mouth parted. My eyelids fluttered shut. This felt too good.

I waited for him to move, but he stopped. His hand curved around my jaw, forcing me to look at him. And I realized he wanted to watch me. He wanted to watch my reaction as he moved inside me for the first time.

"Move," I panted. "You have to move."

I thought he was going to make me beg. And, honestly, I knew I would. Lachlan could get me to do just about anything.

"Lachlan," I gasped. "Move."

He finally gave me what I wanted. I felt relief, but only for a second. He started to slide in and out of me faster. Just when I would start to find his rhythm, he would move his hips and my mind would black out.

He kissed me hard on the mouth in a kiss that wasn't meant to be sweet, but a kiss that was meant to brand me forever.

I was his.

The tree bark dug into my skin, and it fueled me to arch my back and tighten my legs.

My head turned. I saw our shadows slanted across the grass. I blinked a few times, finding it impossible to accept that this was us. The man's hands were above her head, leaning against the tree for leverage. His knees were slightly bent as he rocked into her. They found a rhythm. Her head tipped back and she tightened her body around him like a second skin. Her hand curved around his neck before they drifted over broad shoulders and to his back. Her fingers sank into his skin and when he withdrew, she dragged them across his skin, knowing that there would be claw marks left behind. Their bodies never broke contact.

The scent of sweat lingered in the air. That didn't stop them. Nothing would stop them. They would keep moving, keep finding new places to touch each other just as long as this feeling never faded away. "God, I love you," he said in a low voice.

His words slipped past my skin, ran through my veins, and went straight to my heart.

My skin started to tingle, until it felt alive. Tears welled up in my eyes. *Stay, stay, stay,* I thought to myself frantically. I didn't want this feeling to leave me. I tried to pace myself, but it was futile. I was past that mark. My muscles tightened and my eyes shot open, and above me, the sky blurred into a gray mist. My body felt incredible, almost weightless.

The sensations started to ebb, making me feel boneless.

My head dropped to his shoulder and I held on as Lachlan moved inside me with frantic thrusts before the heels of his feet lifted off the ground and held his body in place for a second. His head was back, giving me a view of his jaw and neck. He shouted incoherently, his body shuddering. I smiled faintly and kissed his shoulder.

I felt his heart beating violently.

His head dropped onto my shoulder. I heard him say again against my skin, "God, I love you." I curled my fingers into his hair.

He held me because I couldn't move. I felt like a rag doll, my legs and arms still dangling around him.

When my heartbeat started to slow, he finally released me. My feet touched the ground. I stumbled a few steps away, as though I had forgotten how to walk.

I fixed my clothes, and the whole time, Lachlan stood perfectly still. His chest heaved and his head rested against the tree.

I slid the last button in place and swallowed. "Please don't tell me you regret it," I said tentatively.

His eyes closed as if he were in pain. He straightened and tossed the condom off and buttoned up his pants. He finally saw his wallet on the ground. He frowned at it like he had no idea how it got there.

"I probably should, shouldn't I? But I can't." He pointed to where the two of us had been entwined. "I'll never regret that."

"Then why do you look like that?"

He grabbed his shirt and put it on with quick, angry jerks. It slid in place and he stared at me with shock.

"I'm not finished!" he exploded.

I stopped in my tracks, my eyes wide.

"You're leaving here and I'm so fucking proud of you," he whispered. "But if tonight showed me anything, it's that I love you and I'm never going to get you out of my system."

My lips parted but I didn't say a thing. I was still reeling from his words. *I love you* coming from Lachlan would never get old. Those three words sent a jolt through my body.

He laughed humorlessly. "I don't want to let you go."

I didn't want him to let me go. I wanted to stay beside him for the rest of my life. I didn't tell him how I felt, though. That small voice in my head whispered to me, telling me that the minute I said what I wanted, it would never come true.

I walked over to him, my arms wrapping around his waist, and looked up at him. He leaned down, his lips moving slowly over mine. Everything I didn't say, I poured into that kiss. Lachlan responded, holding me so tightly I could barely breathe.

I pulled back first.

"We should get back," I said with regret.

I held out my hand. He grabbed it, swallowing it within his own. I always had to keep up with his long strides, but tonight he walked slowly. The grass crunched underneath our feet.

"I'm nervous," I said.

"About leaving McLean?"

"About leaving you. McLean. Everything I know," I admitted.

He squeezed my hand. "Don't worry, you're gonna be fine."

"I don't know if it's normal to feel this nervous."

"You're starting a new chapter; of course it's normal."

I wanted to ask him if he would visit me.

I was afraid to be somewhere without him. Even when he

was away from McLean, I still had the comfort of the tree house and the memories of us. If I left, I was afraid my memories would stay behind.

His house came into sight. The lights were on and I saw shadows moving within. My grip tightened. I wasn't ready for him to go. "Have you seen your parents yet?"

"Just for a second. I dropped my bags off and came to you."

I smiled. I was his first priority.

We reached the tall oak tree. Both of us stared up at the tree house. Throughout the years Lachlan's dad had replaced rotted-out boards, but the years were starting to take their toll.

Something was so final about tonight. It felt like I was closing a chapter of my childhood. No more late nights, sitting in the tree house and spilling my heart out to Lachlan.

The wind picked up. I blamed it for the tears in my eyes.

"Lachlan?" his mom said.

Lachlan shot me a look. We didn't want tonight to end and we definitely didn't want someone else interrupting us.

Lachlan let go of my hand. "Stay," he mouthed before he walked up to the deck. I stood behind the oak tree, like an escapee. I peeked and watched Lachlan and Magy.

"Mama," he greeted.

The two of them hugged and she gave him a kiss on the cheek before she pulled back to look at him.

I loved the way Magy Halstead loved her son. It shined in her eyes and in the way she talked to him. She was a small woman who only came up to Lachlan's shoulders. But even though she was small, she was fierce. No one went up against her.

Every time I saw her, she always said hi, but she would look at me very carefully, as though she could see past my eyes to what was really inside of me.

It always scared the shit out of me.

"Your dad said your flight landed hours ago," Magy said. "Where have you been?"

"I was with Naomi."

Magy said nothing. I watched as her lips thinned in disapproval. "How is she?" she asked tightly.

"Good." Lachlan crossed his arms and leaned back against the railing. "She's leaving for college soon."

"That's great," she murmured.

Great for Magy, maybe.

"Of course," Lachlan said. "I'm really proud of her."

The two of them were silent. Magy stared out before she walked over to him and mimicked her son's actions.

"I remember how she would always be up in the tree house, always creating stories about getting away."

Lachlan looked over at his mom. "You heard all that?"

"Of course. My bedroom window was open in the summer. I always heard you two."

Lachlan grinned. I tapped my head against the tree and grimaced with embarrassment.

"You didn't think she would get out of McLean?"

"I had my doubts," she said honestly.

I watched Lachlan's shoulders stiffen.

"Why?" he said.

"Lachlan . . ." she sighed. "I don't know if she can stay that far from you. From the minute she saw you she instantly had a crush on you that's grown into love and a level of attachment that sometimes makes me wonder."

Lachlan stood straighter. His head tilted imperceptibly in my direction. "Yeah?"

"Yeah." Magy looked at her son carefully. "And I think somehow along the way she got ahold of you." She reached out and tapped her hand on Lachlan's chest, right where his heart beats. "She still has a piece of you."

He didn't lie or make up excuses. He faced his mom and said in a deep and steady voice, "I love her."

She didn't argue or try to prove Lachlan wrong. Instead, she nodded and pursed her lips in thought.

"Describe it to me," she said suddenly. "Describe your love for her."

"Mama . . ." Lachlan said. Magy wouldn't budge. She stood there, waiting for her son to answer. "What you're asking me to describe . . . I can't. It's like asking me to describe fresh water. I need it to live. I need her to live."

Magy took a deep breath. "I like Naomi," she said casually.

I wanted to snort. Even Lachlan looked at his mom skeptically.

"I do," she insisted. "But this has nothing to do with liking her. It's the fact that she has a level of need for you that is so intense and powerful, nothing can shake it. I just don't think you realize how much of yourself you'll have to give to be with her."

"Why are you saying this?"

Magy was silent. She crossed her arms and leaned against the rail. "When you really love someone . . . you're in it for life. It's so easy to use that four-letter word at the beginning, where everything is so simple and perfect. If Naomi loves you like I think she does, then you need to be there no matter what. Her happiness, fear, and pain—even her thoughts—become yours and you need to do everything to make sure it stays that way."

My eyes widened, completely shocked that Magy Halstead had just uttered those words.

"I'm not going to run," Lachlan vowed.

"Good." As an afterthought she added, "Don't let her down."

"I won't."

Her lips pulled up at the corners and she hugged Lachlan. "Good to have you home, honey." Before she turned away, she looked over Lachlan's shoulder, and directly at me.

I stood there, just waiting for her to call out my name. But she turned and walked inside.

The door clicked shut.

Lachlan was frozen, as if he were carved from stone. I came out from my hiding place and walked toward him. He stared out into the fields with a faraway look in his eyes. I stood next to him and rested my head against his arm.

"I know you heard," he said.

"Every single word."

He looked at me with regret. "My mom, she was just—"

"Being a mom," I finished for him. "She was right in everything she said."

He looked at me thoughtfully and said very quietly, "I do love you."

I smiled faintly. "I love you too . . . but love doesn't solve everything. So where do we go from here?"

Lachlan closed his eyes and rubbed the bridge of his nose. "I can't ask you to stay in McLean. You deserve to get away and have that college experience . . ." He let his words linger. And I hoped that whatever he said next wouldn't tear my heart to shreds.

"So you're going to go off to college, and I'm going to be here, waiting."

"In McLean?"

Lachlan nodded. "After my internship, I was only supposed to be in Pittsburgh for a year. That year is almost over with, and then I'll come back home."

I knew the first part. I just didn't know the part about

McLean. I laughed at the irony. The world was playing a cruel joke on the two of us. Right when we decide to give this—*us*—a try, one of us has to leave.

My laughter died and my heart ached. I stared at him with a look of devastation. He opened his arms and I walked into his embrace willingly.

"I promise," he whispered into my ear, "I'll be here."

33

ASHES

Late Sunday night, Lachlan drops me back off at Fairfax. We sit in his car, right outside of the front doors. I stare down at my hands, not wanting to go inside.

This weekend has been exhilarating, a breath of fresh air for me that I didn't think I would ever have. It was ending too quickly. It felt like Lachlan was picking me up for the weekend only a few minutes ago.

"I don't want to do this," Lachlan mutters.

My hands are shaking. I bite down on my lower lip and try my hardest not to cry.

"This was good for you, right?" Lachlan pivots in his seat and it causes his scent to drift over me. My resolve crumbles. A tear slides down my cheek. "Getting away was nice?" he says.

"I loved every second," I whisper brokenly.

"So did I." Lachlan leans closer, reaches out and grabs my hand. "I need you to go back in there and get better. You have no idea how bad I want to drive away right now with you in the car. Last night I thought about where we could go. Maybe go all the way to Maine. Or Florida?" He smiles. "But I could never finish the thought. I'd be too fucking selfish to take you away right now. I know you can do this. Okay?"

"What if I can't?" My voice breaks. "What if I'm really fading away and there's nothing left of me?"

"Impossible." He wraps his hand around the back of my neck. Our foreheads touch and our eyes are inches apart. "People can only fade away if there's nothing left for them. But there's me and you. We'll always be something strong enough to keep you going."

Tears fall from my face and onto the leather of the seat. Lachlan doesn't brush them away and I don't want him to brush them away.

I dry my face with the back of my hand and sniffle. I look over at Fairfax with dread. "The last two days I actually felt normal. I want to always feel that way."

"You're going to feel that way again. Really soon."

Lachlan pulls me back into a tight hug. This is the last one. It's the good-bye hug that I've been dreading all day. His grip is tight, and it's as if he's hoping he can press the pieces of my life back together.

I wish he could. I wish it were that simple.

I pull away first and grab the door handle before the second round of tears comes. Before I get out and walk away, I kiss Lachlan hard on the lips. My eyes squeeze shut and I grip his shirt. I let my lips linger for a few seconds before I rip myself away.

I jump out of the car and grab my bag. The bitter air makes the warm tears pooling at the edge of my eyes frigid, like a frozen icicle. I think of that icicle on the tree, my icicle, and it gives me enough strength to trudge forward and not look over my shoulder.

Back to hell I go.

34

IMPASSE

"DID YOU HAVE A FUN WEEKEND?"

"I did," I say, as I close her office door.

Thankfully, she doesn't ask what I did. I wouldn't have told her. I sit down across from her.

Dr. Rutledge smiles. "I can tell. You look . . . refreshed."

"I feel refreshed," I admit. I turn my head and stare out the window. It snowed overnight, and now there's a fresh blanket of snow over the land.

"I know you miss him."

I stare at Dr. Rutledge. Right now, I want to lean forward and ask her who do I miss . . . Lachlan or Max? Because my heart misses both of them. It is slowly ripping, straight down the middle, and there's nothing I can do about it.

I knew that after I came back to Fairfax I would have to explain the rest of my story. I didn't sleep last night because of it. I didn't see Lana's dad in my room; I just replayed everything I've told Rutledge and the small piece that was left to tell. I don't know if I'm ready.

Dr. Rutledge opens her notebook and grabs a pen and leans back in her chair. Her lips pull up into a smile. "Are you ready?"

"To tell you the rest of my story?"

She nods.

"I don't know," I whisper.

She lays her pen back down. "What are you thinking, Naomi?"

"That I've never gotten this far in telling my story."

"Does that scare you?"

I shrug. "Maybe."

"I think I would be scared too." She rests her chin on her palm and drums her fingers against her cheek, staring down at her desk thoughtfully. "Having to hold all this to yourself is a large burden to carry. To give it all up would be even harder."

Hesitantly, I nod, unsure what to do or say.

"We don't have to do this today," Dr. Rutledge says. "We can go at your pace. I'm happy with the progress you've made."

So am I. All my progress took long enough, but at least it's happening. I know Dr. Rutledge is right. I know that giving it all up is hard, but it's what is after my story—the unknown—that is much scarier to me. I feel like I've reached an impasse.

I rub my damp palms against the material of my sweatpants, until I create a friction that makes my skin tingle. Yesterday, Lachlan told me to be strong.

Be strong, be strong, be strong, I whisper over and over to myself until I finally look up at Dr. Rutledge and lift my chin, in what I hope shows my determination.

"I can keep going," I finally say.

Dr. Rutledge tilts her head, staring. "Are you sure?"

I nod briskly. "I will tell you the rest."

35

GONE

It was raining. Hundreds of raindrops beaded on the window and dripped down slowly like tears. The red stoplight shone through my windshield and onto my face. I rested my forehead against the cold window and looked out at the street. Right across from me, placed on a newspaper stand, was another article with Max on the front page.

He was released on bail over a month ago and it was still an ongoing scandal in McLean. Clients had left his family's company and their good name was dragged through the mud. Everyone has their own thoughts and speculation. The majority believe the accusation is true and say they aren't surprised. A smaller lot are baffled, shocked that Max would ever do such a scandalous thing. But they all have one thing in common: none have reached out to Max or defended him.

The light turned green and I quickly sped away, my tires hissing on the wet pavement. I drove out of McLean and when I pulled into my family's driveway, I did a quick sweep to make sure no one was home. I didn't resume college like I was supposed to in August. I told myself that I was just taking a semester off and when everything with Max and Lana died down, I would go back. That didn't sit well with my parents. They looked at me with disappointment in their eyes. Every time they talked to me, their words were heavy and it was impossible not to hear the accusation in their voices. I was failing, and to them that just wasn't an option.

It was a strange feeling, knowing that I was disappointing them. It had happened in the past, but all my past failures were made up in due time. I didn't know how to fix this failure, short of going back to school. Everything felt like it was a mess and I was slowly sinking.

Before I got out of my car, I quickly typed out a text message to Max that I was going to change real quick and then I would meet him at his house. I held my purse over my head as I ran to the back door. Dozens of birds flew above me. I looked up at them. They formed a sharp V. I watched as they drifted farther away, looking like little black dots. I wished I could toss all my problems up in the air and have the birds take them away.

I snorted at my ridiculous thought and glanced at the long stretch of land and trees around me. Nestled within those trees was my cottage. The roof was probably covered by wet leaves the shades of burnt orange and red. Summer disappeared for good a few weeks ago. It took the hot, sunny days and bright colors with it and left the world with falling leaves, cloudy skies, frost-tipped grass, and chilly days. It also took my optimistic spirit and gave me confusion and pain.

But the cottage hadn't changed. It still held some memories that nothing and no one could take away from me. If I closed my eyes I would remember the way Lachlan had held me and looked at me a year ago. How he had told me he loved me and the way it made me feel like everything would be okay. I wanted that feeling back.

I forgot about changing my clothes. I tossed my purse inside the house. I walked off the porch as if I were in a trance. My feet slipped a few times on the slick grass, but before I knew it, I was running. Strands of my hair blowing behind me. The cold wind whipping against my face, making my eyes water. My fingertips were tinged pink by the cold. I quickened my speed and my body started to slowly warm. Adrenaline started to course through me. I smiled as I approached the thick swarm of trees.

The closer I got, I swear I heard Lachlan's voice. *God, I love you, Naomi.*

I picked up the pace and his voice became louder. *I promise I'll be here.*

I ran through the trees. I pushed branch after branch away from my face. The trees shielded most of the rain above me, but dozens of raindrops still slipped past them and dropped down on my head. I finally reached the clearing and stopped. I was panting as I rested my hands on my knees and stared at the cottage.

It was older and more weather-beaten than before. But it was still the same. I smiled and laughed breathlessly.

"You okay?" someone asked behind me.

I gasped and turned.

Lachlan stood there, staring at me thoughtfully. He was drenched from the rain, making his coat look more like a heavy weight than a comfort. His hair was stuck to his neck and his cheeks were slightly red from the cold. He looked out of breath like me.

No hello. No greeting of any kind.

I just said, "How did you find me?"

"I saw you running and followed you."

We stood there in silence. I was practically numb to the rain falling down around me. This was the first time I was seeing him all summer. I was stunned. I didn't know whether to break down and cry or run into his arms. I looked at him with a critical eye, searching for any noticeable changes. He was the same.

The last time I had spoken to Lachlan had been on the phone. I had been two days away from leaving campus. Two days away from summer break and driving back to McLean to see Lana. We spoke every day, but there was a mounting tension surrounding us. I had pressure from school. Lachlan wanted to know what was wrong; he wanted to help me. Only I couldn't tell him what was wrong. And I was mad because there was no way for him to help me, either.

Before we got off the phone, he had told me he would see me when I got back. I said okay. He said "I love you." I loved him right back.

But what happened between then and now? What had the power to pull us apart so vigorously?

"Are you okay?" Lachlan asked.

I blinked away the rain and the past. "I'm fine," I said faintly.

Lachlan still looked doubtful. He took a step in my direction. "What's wrong?"

"Nothing."

"You're not acting like it's nothing."

Lachlan stared at me, searching for a clue that would prove him right, and if I continued to look at him, he would find it. He stepped forward and reached a hand out. I dodged that hand like it was poison and made sure to keep a good distance between us, but it was killing me.

Lachlan stared at me with a hurt expression.

"Do you know I'm with someone?"

My words were punctuated by the rain that was falling in big, angry drops from the sky. Lachlan stopped walking and was perfectly still. He said nothing, and at first, I thought he didn't register what I'd said. His eyes narrowed and his jaw became clenched so tight, a small muscle became visible around his cheek. His head turned a fraction of an inch.

"What?" he said slowly. He didn't raise his voice over the rain, but I heard him.

"His name is Max. I met him at the beginning of the summer, at a party he was hosting."

His eyes merely widened.

"Lana was with me," I rushed. "I mean . . . I went with her. She had to go because her parents were there, and—"

I was rambling and I knew it. Yet it was the blank expression on Lachlan's face that made me stop talking. His eyebrows were pinched together. Eyes scrunched as if he was trying to peer very carefully at me.

"What are you talking about?" he asked in a low voice.

I stared at him miserably; it was all I could do.

"It's *me* . . ." He pushed away part of his jacket and gripped the material of his shirt. "Lachlan."

"I know that," I said a little defensively.

"Do you?"

"Of course I do!" I shot back. "I've known you practically my entire life!"

Lachlan shook his head. "Are you sure you're okay?"

I opened my mouth, but not a word came out. Lachlan was making me doubt myself. He was making me feel like I was losing my mind. I hated that.

Then he opened his arms up to me. I thought having Max in my life would be enough for me.

I was wrong. I needed them both.

I went to Lachlan willingly. He was so warm and solid and stable. I told myself to breathe in and out, but it wasn't working. My breathing was harsh, coming out in convulsive gasps. I wished that I could tell him everything that had been happening. I would start from the beginning and tell him Lana's story. I pictured the pain falling away from my body. Lachlan would listen and I could lay all my fears to rest and things just might be okay.

I said into his chest, "I'm not okay."

36

MIRROR

LANA AND I REACTED TO MAX'S ARREST IN OUR OWN WAYS. I shared her sadness and despair, but it didn't pull me under. I had too much anger and aggression inside of me to let that happen. She felt responsible for it all.

I hadn't seen Lachlan in a week. It didn't matter, though, because nothing had been the same since. Throughout the summer I had done a good job of pushing him to the back of my mind, but seeing him made all my efforts evaporate. My head felt compressed and weighed down, like I was on the verge of a painful headache. Even now, I rubbed my temples methodically.

Lana lay on the couch. A throw draped over her body. Hair pulled up into a greasy bun. She had a waxy, pale look to her skin that most people get when they haven't been outside in a while. I felt restless energy building up inside of me. I couldn't sit here idly, doing nothing. I jumped out of my chair and clapped my hands.

"You gotta get up," I announced. "You have to eat something."

Lana looked over at me like she had forgotten I was even in the room. "I ate." She pointed at the empty plate on the floor.

"Yeah, but a piece of toast is not going to cut it. You see, your body needs this thing called energy to keep going."

Lana gave me a heavy-lidded look, then looked back at the television behind me.

I grabbed the remote and turned it off. She gave a small protest as I sat next to her. I exhaled loudly and leaned against her legs.

"Come on," Lana said. "Get it out."

I looked at her, my eyebrows knitted together.

"I know you want to tell me off right now."

I sighed. "I don't want to tell you off. I just want you to cheer up. Things are . . . weird right now."

"You told me that a month ago." Lana wrung her hands. "Are you going back to school?"

I stiffened slightly. "Next semester I am. I mean . . . there's nothing else for me to do, right?" I looked over at Lana and smiled weakly. She never smiled back. "My parents expect me to go back."

"But do you want to go back?"

"I think so," I said quietly.

I stood up and paced the room. I tugged at the collar of my shirt, suddenly feeling like I was being choked. "How can I focus on anything else right now? It feels like my world is crashing down around me."

"Maybe it's been crashing down around us the whole time."

I wanted to tell her to save her breath. It was nothing new to hear Lana talking so cryptically; she had been doing that for weeks. Yet her words were starting to eat at my conscience, making me paranoid and sending a cold feeling up and down my spine.

"What's that supposed to mean?" I said.

Lana shrugged, but she didn't avert her eyes. She looked me straight in the face. "I just think that the truth is finally catching up to you, to the both of us, and that's what I wanted to avoid. The very thing I wished would never happen . . . did. People are being crushed because of my dad."

When she finished talking the apartment was so quiet, you could have heard a pin drop.

We didn't say anything. I had nothing but the sound of her words echoing in my head.

I got up and left the room.

We avoided each other the rest of the day.

I WOKE UP TO THE SOUND OF A CRASH.

I sat up instantly, feeling like I was being ripped out of a dream. It took me a while to come back to reality and when I did, I looked over at the clock. It was almost six in the morning.

The disorientation wouldn't leave. I had to stop my body from lurching forward. I felt almost numb, yet there was an organ inside of me, about the size of my fist, that wouldn't stop frantically beating. I placed my palm over my heart and took a few deep breaths. After a few minutes, my heart rate still wouldn't go back to normal and I gave up. I got out of bed. My legs were shaking as I opened my door and peeked my head into the dark hallway. Light seeped out from under the bathroom door. I called out Lana's name. My voice was crystal clear and steady, but she never answered me.

I finally walked across the hall. The apartment was dead quiet. I could hear everything: the blood roaring through my veins, my labored breathing, and my footsteps against the carpeted floor.

When I reached the door I went to knock, but hesitated for a millisecond. There was the smallest part of me that urgently told me not to go in.

I knocked lightly. My eyes closed when there was no response.

"Lana?" I said.

On the other side I heard drawers opening and shutting and the sound of sniffling.

"Lana, I'm coming in," I said as I opened the door.

I was only one step forward when I stopped short. Lana was staring at her reflection with a knife pressed against her left wrist.

I approached very carefully and said her name. She didn't look at me.

"What are you doing?" I said.

She blinked before she resumed staring at herself. Turning her head this way and that, looking over her features with a critical eye.

"My skin is perfect," she said, and grazed the blade against her wrist. Her hand started to shake. I sucked in a sharp breath. "But you know what?" She tilted her head to the side and stared at me through the mirror. I stared back. Lana may think she's hopeless, but I see a person there. One who's had to fight to survive her entire life. If she made it past this hurdle in her life she would be unstoppable.

"Inside I have so much pain," she said. "It just keeps multiplying."

"And you think cutting yourself will fix that?"

"Yes."

I tried to reason with her. I told her we could go somewhere—anywhere—that would make her feel better. Was she hungry?

Lana said no to all the above.

I tried again. "What about something to make you sleep? You'll take it, fall asleep, and tomorrow will be a better day. You'll be able to think everything through!"

Lana looked at me, still through the mirror, as if I were insane. "I don't need anything to make me sleep. I know how to make my pain disappear." Lana held up the knife. The blade glinted in the light and my breath became stuck in my throat.

"Just hand the knife to me," I pleaded.

But Lana wasn't with me anymore. I could see in her eyes that she was stuck in the recesses of her memory. Drifting farther and farther away from reality.

"You don't get it," Lana said.

"Explain it to me." I took another step into the bathroom and shut the door behind me. We were the only two people in the apartment, but I still felt the need to close the door. It felt like I was closing the world off from this extremely private conversation. "Make me understand."

She looked at me like I was the crazy one. "This," she waved the knife in the air, "is the only way to get the pain out of me."

"No, it's not," I said quickly.

The knife went back to her wrist and even though she had a white-knuckled grip on the metal, her fingers shook uncontrollably. I was waiting for that perfect moment to lunge forward and grab it from her without either of us getting hurt.

"Lana, if you just—"

"Will you let me talk?" she shouted.

I flattened myself against the door. I'd never heard her raise her voice to anyone.

I held my hands up in surrender. "Yeah. Yeah. You can talk. The floor is yours."

She was breathing hard, staring down at her wrist as if it were speaking to her.

"Once . . ." Lana started out slowly. "When I was twelve, my grandma had a lady over from her church. They were sitting in my grandma's living room and I was eavesdropping outside the door. My grandma asked her how she was. The lady, who was in her mid-thirties, had a small packet of tissues on her lap. She had just lost her baby at twenty weeks. She said, 'He's still in here.' She rubbed her stomach. 'Even though he's gone, I feel him every day.' She went on to tell my grandma that sometimes she lifts her shirt up expecting to see a swollen stomach and when she sees nothing there, she just wants to die. My grandma told her not to think like that, said suicide was a sin."

Lana continued to stare down at the knife with laser-sharp intensity. I finally took a step forward, my hand outstretched in front of me.

"But you know what that woman said? She said, 'Is suicide a sin? I know my son's safe now. Safe and happy. I just want to be with him. I want death.'

"At first I thought, who wants death?" Lana looked at me, really looked at me, past my outstretched hand and cautious gaze. She laughed breathlessly as she said, "To me, death was terrifying. Most people fight it off for as long as they can. Yet this woman craved it. But then I thought of something. Maybe this lady understood something that we all will later on. When the tears and anger aren't enough, maybe dying is the only guaranteed way to end your pain."

Lana had tears in her eyes.

"I used to think that the abuse and humiliation would stop.

But now I realize that it never will. So why am I putting myself through this pain? Why not end it all?"

Tears dropped onto her wrist. There was a small second where the two of us both looked down at that perfect wrist, marred only by a single teardrop.

Lana pressed down. The skin around the blade turned white. I lurched forward. It was too late. She dragged the blade across that wrist and then the other.

It took her only two seconds to cut open both wrists. There wasn't even a drop of blood on the blade.

The knife dropped to the floor. Lana gasped and stared at me. I expected to see terror in her eyes over what she had done, but she looked happy, almost relieved.

She smiled and gazed down at the blood that was slowly but steadily starting to rise to the surface and trickle down her hands, falling onto the floor. It looked like colored teardrops.

"Holy shit," I breathed. I stared between her and the blood. I felt numb.

The life was slowly draining out of her and she still managed to lift her hand in the air, watching those teardrops trickle down her ghost-white skin.

"It's all fading," she said with awe.

My breath was coming out in short gasps. The blood was making me queasy. I held my breath as I stepped forward. I kept my gaze on Lana's face and I focused on her lips. They were curled up in a small smile. I tried to picture happiness and laughter, instead of the hopelessness and despair around me.

"Lana, what did you just do?" I said, my voice a little faint.

Her body sagged against mine like dead weight. I reached for a towel, and when I did, I slipped on her blood. We both lurched back and hit the wall with a loud thump.

Lana rested her head against my shoulder. I breathed slowly and stared up at the ceiling in a daze. My head throbbed and the light above me blurred in and out.

The two of us sat there in complete silence. There was only the sound of my labored breathing and Lana's very faint breaths.

"She was right," Lana finally whispered. "You're really only safe when you're dead."

37

SCARS

I HEARD THE MONITORS BEEPING, STEADILY BREAKING THROUGH the silence. Lana lay in bed, staring at the television with a far-away look in her eyes.

I stood outside her room. The only thing that stopped me from walking into her room was her parents. They arrived promptly at ten in the morning and had been with Lana ever since. It was going on two hours. Instead of loving and fretting over their daughter with concern, they said nothing. Disgust and disappointment was written all over them. Her mom clutched her purse and touched the pearls around her neck. Her dad wasn't much better. His lips were in a thin line, eyes hardened, as he looked at Lana as if she were the weakest person he'd ever seen.

I peeked into the room and as I did, my foot tapped impatiently. They flanked her bed, both sitting down and both staring at the television across from them. They blinked every few seconds like robots that were trained to act human-like.

The television cut to a commercial. Lana's mom cleared her throat. Her hand went back to the pearls.

"Well . . . was it worth it?" her mom asked her.

Lana turned her head, blinked, and said in a very slow but sure voice, "Every single inch."

"Is this a joke to you?"

"Absolutely not," Lana said. "I can think of funnier, less painful ways to crack a joke."

"I'm serious."

"So am I."

"It's a joke to her, Michael!" her mom ranted. She breathed through her nose and stood up. "All of this is a joke to her. She doesn't care about how this will look for the family. I shouldn't be surprised. If she doesn't care about her own life, why would she care for ours?"

"Mom—"

"I can't do this." She grabbed her purse. Before she walked out the door she looked back at her husband, not her only child. "I'll be in the waiting room."

She fixed the strap of her purse and ran a hand down her hair, like she was getting ready for a show. If you really thought about it, she was. The minute she stepped outside of this room, she was onstage. She had the main role of being Lana's loving mom. It took a lot of work for her to get into character.

The door slammed behind her. I flattened myself against the wall but there was no need; Lana's mom never once looked my way. She walked ahead, head held high, her heels echoing in the hallway.

I looked back in the room.

Lana was staring at the television. She appeared unaffected by her mom, but I noticed the slight tremor in her hands.

Her dad didn't get up from his chair. He was close enough to her that his knees pressed against her bed.

"Your doctor said that you should be out of here in a few days," her dad said.

Lana just nodded.

"You'll just have to see a therapist a few times a week, but everything can go back to normal. And when I mean normal, I mean you back home . . . where you should be."

Lana glanced at her dad. "What?"

"You need to be at home, where your mom and I can watch you and make sure that this never happens again."

She blinked, and when her eyes focused on her dad, there was nothing but revulsion in her gaze. I knew it was the first time Lana was openly rejecting him.

I didn't know why she chose that moment to be the time. Maybe last night's attempt had not only brought her to the brink of death, but it had also made her fears disappear.

"Fuck you," she whispered coldly.

His head tilted to the side, as if he had heard her wrong. "What did you say?"

"I said, *fuck you.* I did what I did because of you." She looked down at her bed. "Now get out."

"Your mother and I are trying to help."

"Mom left the room a few minutes ago because she couldn't look at me. She doesn't want to help, and neither do you. Get out."

Her dad didn't appear to be in any rush. His cheeks were flushed, undoubtedly from anger and embarrassment. He stared at his daughter, his eyes filled with unearned hate. His daughter stared back at him, her eyes blank and unflinching.

"I can press this button," Lana said, "and a nurse will be here within minutes."

Her dad stood up.

I hurried away from her room. A few seconds later I heard the door creak open. Footsteps sounded. Her dad didn't scurry away like her mom did. He waited for a few moments, leaning against the wall, staring down at the waxed floor thoughtfully before he pulled out his phone.

"Tim, how are you? It's Michael. Listen." Her dad cleared his throat and started to walk down the hall. "I need a favor from you . . ."

I wanted to follow behind him and listen to every single word. The nurse had just stepped into Lana's room. She would take her blood pressure, check her temperature, and ask if Lana needed anything. I'd be back in plenty of time to slip into Lana's room and finally be able to talk with her, but I stayed where I was and watched her dad walk farther away, until he turned the corner and disappeared.

Something was up his sleeve. I didn't know what, but I knew it had to involve Lana. I knew that Lana's parents were desperate to hide her suicide attempt as quickly as possible.

The nurse finally left the room. I walked in after her and softly closed the door behind me. Lana kept her eyes glued to the television. It was a rerun of an old sitcom, complete with a laugh track, houses that never got dirty, and a household that hugged every chance they got.

"I wish my problems could be solved in thirty minutes or less," Lana said quietly.

"Me too," I sighed, and curled up at the edge of her bed, acting like this wasn't a hospital room that smelled like disinfectant, but her room back in her apartment that smelled like lilacs.

I watched the show for a few seconds before I looked over at Lana. "How are you?"

"If I told you I was okay, or fine, would you believe me?"

"No."

"Then I'll tell you the truth." She swallowed. "I feel terrible."

I looked Lana over. Her face, which normally looked so smooth and clean, was pale, almost translucent, with a sheen of sweat around her forehead and upper lip. Her lips were chapped. She had the prettiest hair. Pin-straight and silky, like a child's. It ran down the length of her back, stopping at her waist. The ends were always neatly trimmed. But today her hair was messy, pulled back into a lopsided ponytail. The worst part was her wrists. They were heavily bandaged, lying on the bed like dead weights.

"I think the pain is stronger now," she said gravely.

I stood up, thinking that she needed a nurse or doctor to come into the room and help her. "What?"

She held up her bandaged wrists, staring at them with a mixture of resentment and sadness. "My pain. It's stronger. I think the pain has been in my body for too long. I could keep cutting away at my skin, but it will never matter." She stared me straight in the eye. "The pain's never gonna leave."

I slowly sat back down.

What could I say to that?

I tried to think of some inspirational quote. Something, *anything*, that would give her hope. I had nothing.

We both knew that.

Her hands dropped heavily onto the bed.

"For a second, though, it was bliss," she confessed. "I know that's fucked up to say. It's the truth, though. I thought for a second that all my problems were going away. But for each drop of blood I lost, gallons of pain were waiting to fill me back up."

"I wish I knew what to say," I said sadly. "But nothing I say will ever make it right."

"I'm not asking for you to make it right. No one can."

"So what happens from here?" I asked.

"I don't know. My doctor keeps saying that I'm leaving in a few days so my parents can help me 'recover.'"

I flinched.

She smirked. "Ironic, right?"

"You're not going home with them, are you?"

"No," Lana said firmly.

I opened my mouth to voice my opinion.

"Can I just have a moment alone, please?" Lana said.

"Sure." I stood up and said good-bye, even though it was the last thing I wanted to do. The door shut behind me. I sagged against it, my hands on my knees, taking deep breaths.

I left moments later. My legs were shaking and it felt like I was going to collapse at any moment. I quickened my pace. The elevator was in sight, but I felt like I was in a fun house. It became farther and farther away until it felt like I was never going to reach it.

I started to run, but the hallway became narrower and longer, stretching for miles. Nurses and visiting family members were all around. I could hear their hushed voices. I'm sure all of them had their own problems to deal with, but I would have done anything at that moment to trade lives with them.

I realized, then, that seeing Lana being raped had created a small crack in my sanity. Each event after that made the crack spread. A network of veins appeared, making me fragile. I was finally starting to shatter. Everything was catching up to me and I broke into millions of pieces.

I crumbled to the ground and screamed, trying to erase Lana's words.

"The pain's never gonna leave."

Her voice kept getting stronger and the world slowly faded
to black.

When I woke up, I was at Fairfax.

38

CHANGE

THE CLOCK ON DR. RUTLEDGE'S DESK CLICKS. MUCH LIKE THE monitors did at the hospital. I stare at Dr. Rutledge, waiting for a new, radical change to happen.

Here it is.

Here's my story. It's out in the open and there's nothing left for me to say. So what happens now?

Will I slowly transform back into the person I once was? Or maybe Dr. Rutledge will snap her fingers and I'll realize this has all been a dream.

I don't care what really happens as long as *something* happens.

We sit there, staring at each other. The clock continues to click and I start to become impatient. I deserve—no, *earned*—this change. So where is it?

"Do you get it now?" I ask impatiently.

Dr. Rutledge nods. "I do."

My eyes narrow. "Please don't humor me."

"I'm not. I understand you went through a terrible situation."

"If you understand, then explain to me why I'm here. Tell me how someone who was just trying to help her friend ends up in a mental institution."

Dr. Rutledge continues to look at me, saying nothing, offering me nothing.

"I didn't try to kill myself. That was Lana." I jerk my sleeves up and hold both wrists out. "See? No scars. Nothing."

She looks down at my wrists. My pale, scar-free wrists.

"See?" I'm practically shoving them at her. "See those veins? I know I have blood in them and I know I have a soul inside of me and I know I have a life worth living. Although . . . right now it's not much. But I know I have it."

She looks away from my flawless wrists and into my eyes. I drop my arms and sit back down. We're surrounded by silence. Except for that clock. That stupid, fucking clock. I want to pick it up and smash it into pieces. I rub my temples.

"Tell me," I beg. "Please tell me why I'm here."

She drops her pen onto her desk. She leans forward and says in a gentle yet firm voice, "You're here because you broke down. Everything with Lana was too much to take."

"That doesn't warrant someone who's been completely normal and healthy to be sent here," I argue.

She smiles sadly. "When someone has the breakdown you had, and experienced what you did, it does."

My lips quiver. I feel foolish. I feel ashamed. And that is ridiculous. "I want to go home," I say.

Is home even home anymore? Will my parents let me come back?

"No. You're not ready to be released yet."

I drop my head into my hands. Weep or scream? I don't know. I wait for the big, knotted ball to burst free from my throat, but nothing happens.

"What are you feeling, Naomi?"

"I feel like I just took one step forward and twenty steps back," I say into my hands.

"You think you're getting nowhere?"

I nod and look at her, blinking back tears of frustration.

"I just want answers," I say hopelessly.

"As much as we want it to happen in a flash, that's not the way it works."

My eyes flutter shut and I listen to her, feeling rejected.

"Tomorrow's a new day."

I'm tired of new days and the fresh new optimism that comes with them, because hours later, when the sun sets, it steals my optimism and it's back to feeling so alone.

Mary opens the door. My session is up. Dr. Rutledge says she'll see me tomorrow. She gives me one of her uplifting smiles.

I don't tell her what I'm feeling or thinking. I just stand up and walk out the door with Mary.

39

GENEVIEVE

"Dr. Rutledge, may I have a word?"

I lift my head. Dr. Woods, Naomi's old psychiatrist, is standing in the doorway.

Tim Woods is fifty-eight years old, with black hair that's peppered with gray. Lines are forming around his eyes and, not surprisingly, around his lips. He never smiles. He is straight to the point—a factual kind of person. He's at the end of his career, biding his time until he can retire. Maybe he once cared, but he doesn't now.

It's a fleeting thought, but I wonder if this career will siphon the determination out of me like it has Tim Woods. Will I, too, stop caring?

I shut the medical textbook in front of me and wave him in. "Of course."

He glances at my book. "Were you busy?"

"Not at all."

Tim takes a seat. I hardly speak to Dr. Woods, so seeing him in my office is a surprise, to say the least.

"What can I help you with?" I say with a smile.

His fingers drum on the armrest. His eyes are somber. My smile starts to fade and my stomach starts to churn. Something's wrong.

"I wanted to talk to you about Naomi Carradine."

My gaze drifts to her file sitting on the corner of my desk. In the upper right-hand corner her name is written in black marker: CARRADINE, NAOMI.

"What about her?" I ask, my eyes on her file.

"I thought you should know that her mother signed her out of Fairfax."

My head lifts slowly. I stare at Tim with disbelief. Did I just hear him right?

Tim watches me, his fingers steepled against his lips.

"What?" I ask faintly.

"As of today, Naomi is no longer a patient of Fairfax."

Four years of college.

Four years of medical school.

Four years of residency.

Hours upon hours of studying. I trudged through all those years remembering why I wanted to be a psychiatrist: to help people.

Before I came to Fairfax, I worked for a small private practice for two years. I would see moms stretched thin. A few teenagers down and in a hormonal rut they couldn't get out of. There was nothing over the top. The opportunity to work here was my chance and I took it, anxious to show what I was really capable of.

I didn't know what being a psychiatrist was until I arrived here. Until I took Naomi Carradine on as a patient. Every time I looked at Naomi, I saw a girl that when she looked in the mirror saw nothing but darkness. I couldn't ignore that.

"Why?" All I can come up with are one-word questions. I see all the progress that Naomi was making and it makes me feel sick to think that it's all been a waste.

Tim shrugs. "Her parents believe that her medications will be of more help."

"You don't agree with that, do you?"

"She's getting better," he argues weakly.

"She is. But not good enough to leave!" I explode. So unexpected. So unlike me. But my patience has snapped in half. "My sessions were going somewhere. She was so close to having a breakthrough. A few more sessions and she could've been released within six months."

"Her mother doesn't want a few more sessions. Time's up."

Dr. Woods watches me carefully. I stare down at my desk.

"I've barely had her," I say quietly. "We were just now getting to the root of the problems!"

"We're not against Naomi. We—"

My head shoots up. I pounce on his words. "Who's 'we'?"

Tim balks. "Me and her parents."

I've been so focused on Naomi leaving that I didn't even think about how Tim even *knew* she was leaving.

"When did you speak with them?"

"I spoke to them just yesterday."

"About what?" I fire back.

"I'm not your patient, Dr. Rutledge. There is no need to talk to me like one."

"But she's no longer your patient."

"I understand that. But I felt her parents had a right to know what's going on," he says with a sharp edge to his voice.

"Absolutely. But if they wanted to know her progress, they

could have called and talked to me. I would have gladly updated them on everything." I look him in the eye. "You're not her doctor. It wasn't your place."

Tim gives me a hard look. "I spoke with them because, quite honestly, you're too close to Naomi."

"Excuse me?" I say very slowly.

"You seem to have a gray area with her. You are entirely too involved. You—"

"I know what you mean," I say impatiently. "Don't diagnose me."

"Perhaps someone should, though. It's very simple: You never become attached to your patients. You're supposed to be the doctor in this situation, but you ignored that. You felt for this girl and cared for her when all you have to do is treat her and let her be on her way."

When I leave at the end of the day, I make sure to leave my work in my office. But Naomi's voice echoes in my head all the way home. Her face flashes through my mind as I eat dinner and get ready for bed. When I'm lying in bed, I see her file with her name printed in the right-hand corner in clear, black letters on my ceiling.

Those letters start to mesh together and I lie there, hoping that they'll stop moving and reveal the answer to Naomi's problem.

Clearly that's just me, though. Tim Woods has no such problem. He sits here with such ease, handing out biting insults like they're candy.

"I'm trying to be a good doctor to her," I say.

"What about her weekend pass last weekend? Were you being a good doctor then?"

I sit up straighter in my chair. "What?"

"Why weren't her parents notified?"

"Is this why she was released, because I gave her a small break?"

"Naomi is not allowed to take a weekend pass. She can't sign in and out of Fairfax. That decision isn't hers to make. Yet you allowed her to sign herself out and Lachlan Halstead to pick her up."

"She's a patient. Not a prisoner."

Dr. Woods's lips are in a thin line. His disapproval is apparent. I suppose I broke some moral code for doctors by hiding the weekend pass from her parents. They put her in our care, and they were supposed to be notified if she was leaving Fairfax. No matter how short the time was. But I can't feel guilt over what I did. I know it was the right thing. Naomi came back from her weekend pass with a bright light in her eye. She was recharged. It was a boost that she needed.

"How did her parents even find out?" I ask suspiciously. "Wait," I hold up a hand, "let me guess. You told them?"

Tim says nothing. In fact, the longer we talk, the more uncomfortable he becomes: shifting in his seat, adjusting his glasses every few seconds, clearing his throat like he's trying to get something out. My eyes narrow on him.

"What do you know that I don't?" I ask quietly.

"Nothing," he says, his voice stiff and cold.

Liar, I think.

"Come on," I coax. "Tell me the truth. Tell me why you accuse me of being too close to *my* patient, yet you take it upon yourself to call her parents and update them on everything that I'm doing. Again, this is with *my* patient."

"You're forgetting that she was my patient before you."

I give him a hard look. "Outside of Fairfax, do you know her family?"

He answers way too quickly. "No!"

"Liar." This time I say my thought out loud.

We look at each other for a moment. I have no intent of backing down. He came into my office. He told me she was leaving. He needs to explain it all to me.

Tim exhales loudly and rubs the bridge of his nose. "Naomi's parents are . . . close friends of mine. Her dad expressed concern over Naomi's behavior. I encouraged him to seek involuntary commitment so she could be admitted here. The plan was for her to stay here for just a few months to give Naomi a chance at getting better."

I sit back heavily in my chair, feeling like I was just kicked in the stomach.

"So you did a," I make quotation marks, " 'favor' for them."

"You could call it that," he says carefully.

"And her parents were just buying time so they could figure out what they could do with her. Am I right?"

"I didn't say that."

"But you didn't have to say that. I'm not an idiot, Tim. Her parents never came to visit her. Not once. In fact, I don't think I've ever spoken to her parents before."

"Hold your judgment," Tim says sharply.

"Can you blame me for judging? This is their daughter." I can't hide the disdain from my voice. "So you pulled some strings to get her in here. Did you do the same to get her released?"

"Of course not!"

"Of course not," I repeat slowly. "Never mind the fact that Naomi's mom signed her into Fairfax, giving us consent to care for her daughter! And then she magically shows up and signs her daughter out because she feels like it!"

"Don't tell me how this place runs," he says harshly. "I've been practicing much longer than you."

My palms are splayed on the desk as I lean close and say very slowly, "Then act like it."

His eyes narrow into thin slits.

I grab my coat from the back of my chair and my purse from the floor. Anger makes my blood boil, and if I'm being honest, there's a small bit of fear there, too. I make my way to the door.

Tim shifts in the chair. "Where are you going?"

I hold the door open with my foot. "To talk to the facility director to put a stop to this."

Tim takes off his glasses, inspects the lenses, and cleans them with his white coat. "Naomi left with her mom an hour ago."

I gape openly at him. His indifference to this entire situation speaks volumes. I realize that I would rather feel too much for my patients than nothing at all. I never want to turn into Tim Woods.

I look at him with disgust. "She's not ready to go back into the world. If you were any kind of doctor, you would have pushed aside your relationship with her parents to do what's right for her."

I walk out of the room, not caring what he has to say.

"She's just a patient. That's it, Genevieve!" Tim yells. "Stop treating this girl like family!"

A nurse and two patients stop in the hall and stare at him with shock. I ignore all of them. As I hurry toward the entrance, I dig through my purse, searching for my keys.

"I'm just here to see Naomi," a deep, male voice says.

I stop short and see Lachlan Halstead standing there.

I forget about my keys and make my way over to him. I interrupt his conversation with the nurse. "Have you talked to Naomi?" I ask impatiently.

I don't have time to make polite conversation. Time is against me.

His brows furrow. He stands up straight. Those hazel eyes instantly become alert, as though Naomi's name is a switch for him. Every single powerful memory in Naomi's life comes from this man.

"No. Why? What's going on? Where is she?"

I go to answer him, when I notice the nurse behind the counter staring at us. I guide him away. "Her mom signed her out today."

Blood drains from his face. He clenches his jaw, closes his eyes, and turns his head away. There's a terrifying second where I think he's going to explode and lash out right in front of me.

"Lachlan, did you hear me?"

He nods and turns back to me.

"Did you—"

I speak up. "It wasn't me who released her. I would've never let that happen. I just found out that her mom picked her up over an hour ago."

He rubs a hand across his face. "Shit," he whispers heatedly. "So who did?"

Lachlan has this look in his eye. Blank and void. It's a look that people have when they are driven by their anger. They won't stop until they get to act out their aggression.

"That doesn't matter," I say smoothly. "I just need to find Naomi. Right now."

Lachlan stares at me a second longer before he gestures toward the parking lot. "Just follow me."

I give him a grateful smile. My heart calms down and for a second I think everything will be okay. Lachlan and I are almost out the door. Just a few more steps. Then I hear Dr. Woods's voice. So does Lachlan. He stops walking and whips his body around. I also turn. Dr. Woods walks into the reception area, laughing with the nurse next to him. He looks at the front doors, his gaze flitting away before he does a double take. His eyes widen, not at the sight of me, but at Lachlan. I realize these two know each other outside of Fairfax.

Lachlan advances. He doesn't stop until he corners Dr. Woods, completely towering over him.

"Do you know what you just did?" Lachlan roars.

Dr. Woods turns pale. The nurse behind the front desk stands up. A few patients stop their activities and stare.

I run over to Lachlan and grab his arm, trying to push him back. Not in Dr. Woods's interest, but in Naomi's, because the quicker we get out of here with everyone scratch free, the better.

"You've turned a blind eye to everything. Fuckin' makes me sick!" Lachlan's voice is starting to turn hoarse.

I've got him a few steps away. A few more tugs and he would be out the door. But then Dr. Woods speaks.

"Lachlan, I did what was right. Her parents were concerned about her—"

"You're a motherfucker!" Lachlan continues. "Do you hear me?"

"Now wait a minute, I—"

I pivot around and glare at Dr. Woods. "Just shut up," I hiss.

My back has been turned no more than a few seconds, but by the time I turn around, Lachlan is already peeling out of the parking lot.

I swear underneath my breath and run back to the front desk. The nurse is sitting there with a shocked look on her face.

"Give me Naomi Carradine's address!" I say to her.

Her eyes widen. "Dr. Rutledge, I don't think that's the best idea."

"Just give it to me!" I snap.

She quickly looks up Naomi's file and rattles off the address. I write it down, my hand shaking the entire time.

Dr. Woods steps into my way, holding his hands out. "Genevieve, calm down. You and Lachlan are clearly upset and—"

"Do you know Lachlan outside of Fairfax?"

He stares at me, saying nothing, before he nods. "I know his parents."

I mutter a curse and walk around him.

"Think about what you're doing!" Dr. Woods calls out behind me.

I whirl around, walking backwards and pointing my finger directly at him. "I'm doing this because of what you allowed to happen this morning. Whatever happens is on you!"

I turn back around and run to my car. I can feel everyone's eyes on my back. It occurs to me that more than just my job is on the line. I can just about kiss my career good-bye. Even with that depressing thought looming above my head, I still slam my car door and follow Lachlan. I finally realize that I probably am too close to Naomi and her story. I pushed myself into her world, where the truth was hidden by lies. The option to step back and do nothing has disappeared.

My mistake, but my choice.

40

CONVERGE

FREEDOM IS A HEADY THING.

When it's been absent from your life for so long you become obsessed with it. You think of all the things you'll do when you get it back. Maybe stand outside and breathe in all the fresh air you can. Or maybe you'll lie in the grass and watch as the sky above and the white, puffy clouds slowly drift by, knowing that you have nowhere to go. The more time that passes, the more you envision what you would do. And then, when you are handed your freedom, so easily and so quickly, you almost don't know what to do with yourself.

That's exactly how I felt when Mary came into my room and told me I was going home. She had my suitcase in hand and a solemn expression on her face as she packed up my stuff. It was so unexpected, and completely out of the blue, that I could only stare with shock. I quietly got dressed, looking over at her every few minutes.

Before we left my room she handed me back my shoelaces. A bag of makeup. A nail file. One pen. And my cell phone. I had stared down at the items with shock. Was this really happening? I kept thinking. Or was this some kind of elaborate prank at my expense?

When we walked down the hallway, I braced myself for Mary to pull back and tell me that this was just a practice run for when I really was released and that I had to go back to my cold, lonely room.

I finally saw my mom by the front doors, standing next to Dr. Woods. I quickly realized that this wasn't a joke. I was actually leaving. So where was my excitement? Why couldn't it walk on up to my fear and kick it aside and fill me up with hope? It was there when Lachlan picked me up, and that freedom was only temporary.

My mom turned around when she heard our approaching footsteps. She walked over to me. I instantly got a whiff of her perfume.

"Ah, there she is." She hugged me.

"Mom?" I frowned over her shoulder as she patted my back. "What's going on?"

She pulled me back, holding me at arm's length. Perfectly straight, white teeth appeared when she smiled. "You're going home."

"I know that . . . but why?" Nothing was making sense.

"You need to be home, that's why."

That was probably the only explanation I would get.

"Are you ready to go?" she asked.

It didn't feel right. Just yesterday, I had left Dr. Rutledge's office feeling worn down. She had told me I wasn't ready to go home yet, and now here my mom was, right out of the blue? My gut twisted tightly. I swallowed down the lump in my throat and nodded.

"Yeah, I'm ready."

I reached for my bag. Mary was still holding it, both hands tightly gripping the strap. I didn't want to look her in the eye. I don't know why. I just knew that if I did, tears would ensue. Mary was always so stern and stoic, but I was used to her. She had become a consistent part of my life and I didn't know what I would do without her.

She reached out and hugged me. Her grip was tight. I had to pull away first.

"Take care of yourself," she said into my ear and smoothed my hair. The whole time she had a smile on her face and tears brimming in her eyes.

"I will," I said.

A few minutes later, my mom and I were walking out the front doors. Before I got into the car, I spotted that naked tree next to the rec room window. That frozen icicle was melting. Water slowly dripped down onto the soggy ground.

It felt like an omen—the ending of my time here.

I spent the entire drive home trying to figure out if that was a good or a bad thing.

When my mom parked in front of the house, neither one of us made any attempt to get out of the car. She grabbed her purse and exhaled loudly. I just sat there, completely frozen over.

"You're home," she said slowly, staring at the steering wheel. "It's time to move past your stay at Fairfax." She looked over at me. "We need to be a family again."

No *welcome home*! Or hugs. Just the cold, hard facts.

Instead of relaxing when I got home, I dropped my bags off in my room and walked right back out the door with just my keys in hand.

An hour later, I'm still driving.

I have no idea where I'm going and I don't care. I follow the twists and turns of the road, trying to ignore the restless feeling taking root in my gut. It makes my fingers tap anxiously against the steering wheel. A few minutes later, I park the car and get out. The air rushes into me, making me shiver. I cross my arms and turn in a circle, staring at the barren earth.

When I left Fairfax, I didn't look at my discharge papers. I was just happy to be leaving. I assumed that it was deemed safe for me enter the world again. Right?

Everything seems harmless enough. The sky's a cloudless gray. The temperature is warm, considering the bitter-cold weather that's been happening. The ground is soggy. Potholes filled with water pepper the road.

That icicle runs past my memory. I bend down, my back resting against the car door, and drop my head into my waiting palms. I picture the water dripping onto the ground.

Drip, drip, drip.

I bet it's gone. I bet there's nothing left of the frozen water drop. Why does that fill me with so much despair? Because it meant more to me. It represented my life and everything I was fighting for. It's gone, and I still haven't figured out a damn thing. If anything, I am even more lost. Even more broken.

When I was in Fairfax I had one singular goal: to get out and get answers. That goal would keep me going, even when it felt like I was running on empty. To get out and still have no answers makes me feel hopeless. Tears of frustration slip down my cheeks and onto the black asphalt. I wipe my face, stand up, and take a deep breath. No matter what I feel, I know one thing is for sure. Lana is out there somewhere. I know it sounds impossible and crazy, but I feel her heartbeat echo in my ears.

Not my own.

Just hers.

I get back in my car, do a U-turn, and try to find a road that looks familiar. A few minutes later I finally do. The houses rushing past me are ones that I've seen for years. But I ignore them. I focus on only one thing: the heartbeat echoing in my ears. In fact, the closer I get to Lana's house, the more prominent her heartbeat becomes. I press my hand against my heart. My heartbeat is calm and steady and very quiet up against Lana's, which is loud, with a short, staccato beat.

Dr. Rutledge once told me that Lana is safe and that her dad could no longer hurt her. So why, when I get to her house, does the echo burst from my ears? Why do I feel her all around me?

I run toward the front door, knowing with a sickening gut that Lana is here. Maybe Dr. Rutledge thought Lana was safe, but she's wrong. She's been wrong the entire time. That thought alone is powerful enough to make my legs buckle.

I make it to the front door and burst into the house. I'm panting, looking frantically around. There's a candle burning somewhere; the scent meets my nose. I can hear the sound of the grandfather clock clicking in the dining room.

I just want to find Lana. Instead I find Max. I freeze in my tracks. He's pounding on Lana's dad's office door.

"Michael!" he screams. "Open up!"

His hands are frantically beating against the hard oak. A crash sounds from behind the closed doors. Fear shoots down my spine.

I walk down the hall, closer to Max.

"No, no, no," I whisper faintly.

Max doesn't see me come closer. He takes a step back and kicks the door down. The wood splinters and the door hangs from the hinges.

He runs into the room. But I can't. I'm too afraid to go forward. I already know what I'm going to see and I don't want to see it. Once is enough.

The only reason I step forward is because of Lana. I can hear her voice. I can hear her crying and moaning. I walk into the room and the blinds are closed, shutting the world out. Only the light on her dad's desk is on. And on the floor, right across from her dad's desk, is Lana, being held down by her dad.

I think I scream, but no one notices.

Lana's dad holds her hands above her head with one hand and covers her mouth with the other. His pants are down and so are her jeans.

Her eyes are wide and frantic. They find mine and she looks at me with alarm.

"No," I whisper.

"I own you," her dad pants. "Your life is mine."

"No," I groan.

Her dad turns and looks at Max. He yells something. I can't make it out. The volume has been turned down. All I can hear is the sound of Lana's heavy breathing.

Max's mouth moves rapidly. Lana's dad lets go of Lana, leans back on his knees. He's getting up.

That's when I notice Max reaching into his back pocket and pulling out a gun.

"Stop!" I scream.

Max keeps walking and his index finger wraps around the trigger. He's pointing it directly at Lana's dad.

I run up behind him. "Don't!" I yell.

Lana stares at Max, trying to warn him with her eyes to stop. She covers her face; her cries are muffled against her hand. Her dad pivots his body and goes to stand up.

Max pulls the trigger.

Everything happens so slowly, as if time is resisting, trying to stay in place, yet our actions are moving it forward.

The bullet releases from the chamber. It circles out into the air slowly. The aim is perfect, going directly to Lana's dad's head. It hits him. "Go," Lana mouths to me. Her eyes are wide open, pleading and begging for me to leave the room.

The black pinpricks of her pupils draw me in and I'm pulled into a vortex so powerful, there's no getting out. Everything changes in that second. Lana's brown irises that made her always look so vulnerable and quiet. The irises that hid so much are now dark, cobalt blue.

The exact shade of my eyes.

I drop to the ground and moan. It feels like someone is reaching into my chest and ripping the very life out of me. My breath comes out in shallow gasps as pain starts to radiate throughout me.

My body is leaden. Walking seems like too much effort. Yet, somehow, I'm moving. I stare down at my body as it's pushed across the room by some unseen force. I hover right above Lana and her dad. Her eyes, that are now identical to mine, meet my gaze. The pain throughout me starts to double.

The first bullet punctures her dad's skin. I watch in horror as his body jerks once before he falls backwards onto his daughter.

That's when the impossible happens: my body merges with Lana's.

It's so painful, as if I'm being squeezed through a small open-

ing. My skin pulling, resisting. Nerves are tingling. I scream at
the top of my lungs. My body starts to twitch. I grasp the air
above me frantically.

Reach, reach, reach. I'm trying to grab onto anything to get
me out of here. The pain inside of Lana is soul destroying, filled
with demons waiting to smother me. It becomes too much and
my hands drop limply to the floor.

My eyes feel heavy and swollen from tears. I blink a few
times, trying to adjust. But reality doesn't give me time to adjust.
It slams into me.

I'm not Lana. I'm not Lana. I'M NOT HER! my mind
screams.

I'm too numb to hold onto anything, except for the fact that
I can't breathe.

"Get him off," I pant. "Get him off me."

There's too much going on. My brain is on overload. It's
ready to explode. I feel so much pain. Little moans escape my
mouth.

I feel a wet, sticky substance on my fingers. When I lift my
hands, I see that my skin is paler and on my wrists are horizontal
scars about four inches long. The skin is red and puckered.

My lips quiver.

"I'm not her," I croak.

I turn my hand around and can see the bluish veins running
underneath my skin. That sticky substance? It's dark, warm
blood and it's on my fingers, slowly traveling down my hand,
onto my arms. "Naomi."

I look up at Max. He's pushing Lana's dad off me. When his
weight is off me, I greedily suck up all the oxygen I can. Max
drops the gun and stares down at me. His face is pale and his
eyes are wild. There are flecks of Lana's dad's blood on his
cheeks.

Not my dad. My dad wouldn't hurt me like this, I think.

Max holds my face and looks into my eyes, saying my name again, this time with more concern.

"Talk to me," he pleads.

And then I blink. It's just one simple blink. But when I open my eyes back up, Max is Lachlan.

Impossible.

My mind is playing tricks on me. Or maybe the world is playing one big trick on me? Either way, I blink frantically, hoping that I'm wrong.

But Lachlan is still here, dressed in the clothes that Max had been wearing seconds ago and with flecks of blood on his face. His hands hook underneath my arms. He pulls me onto his lap, cradling my head. I lie there like a rag doll, my arms hanging at my sides. My eyes close and when they do, I see a memory.

It's reeled in front of me slowly, giving me no choice but to absorb everything that happened. Lana is playing on the black asphalt, but it can't be her because I remember sitting there and drawing. I remember the pieces of chalk spread out around me. I hum a song that my nanny had taught me. I was only eleven. The sun is hot on my back but it feels good. I continue to draw and trace and when my creation is just right, I curl up in a ball, right in the middle of my creation, on that hot asphalt, and fall asleep. The memory ends there. I remember it being a good summer day. But Lana gives me the rest of the memory. She shows my dad finding me later on. He is furious. He asks what the fuck I was doing. I nervously tell him that I was sleeping. His eyes narrow slightly. He looks down at my creation and asks what I created. I move off my creation and look down. On the black asphalt is the outline of a body. I didn't give it eyes, nose, mouth, or even hair. But I gave it a heart. Because in my eleven-year-old mind, that was all that it needed, and it had been holding me tightly in its arms. On this black asphalt is a parent I had always wanted. It accepted my love, and in return loved me unconditionally. On this black asphalt is something I could never have.

My dad had screamed at the mess I made on the driveway. Told me to get a hose, clean it up, and then to go clean myself up. When I was clean, he raped me.

My body starts to shake.

All the pain I felt was one dark soul unraveling and intertwining itself around the other soul—the clean soul. The darkness hands over its black memories, hoping that the purity of the clean will obscure all its pain.

I feel arms squeeze me tighter. *Keep pressing, keep holding,* I think to myself. Maybe then all this pain and agony will leave my body.

I look down and finally accept that it's my own dad's blood spreading across the ground, seeping into the cracks of the wood floor.

The body holding me pulls away. I'm looking into the eyes of Lachlan.

"I'm so sorry," Lachlan whispers hoarsely.

This pain is mine and only mine. My body starts to shake until I'm practically convulsing.

Time speeds up right after that and I see Dr. Rutledge standing in the doorway. Her face instantly pales as she takes in the room. Her eyes go from the gun to Lachlan. She's putting the pieces together quickly.

Then she looks at me. Not with her doctor eyes; she looks at me with so much sorrow and understanding. I realize then that she knew all along. She walks into the room, kicking pieces of splintered wood aside.

"What happened?" she asks.

Lachlan doesn't turn around. His lips are in a flat line, his nostrils flared, and his eyes flat. "I caught him. I—" He tightens his grip on me. "I saw him. I saw him—" His voice croaks and fades.

Dr. Rutledge approaches us slowly. She touches Lachlan's shoulder and he tenses up. She backs away and quickly speaks. "This was self-defense, okay? He was going to come after you and you had to protect yourself."

Lachlan turns and looks over at Dr. Rutledge. "That's not what—"

"Lachlan, you had to protect yourself and Naomi," Dr. Rutledge utters meaningfully.

Lachlan nods.

"It's done," she whispers. And I want to know who she's talking to, me or Lachlan?

I hear footsteps outside the door and the murmur of voices. My mom walks into the room. All kinds of emotions run through her eyes as she stares at my dad's lifeless body. Her face crumbles. She runs over to him and drapes herself over him. She's sobbing so loudly my ears ring.

In the midst of her tears, Dr. Rutledge is on her phone, speaking frantically. I know that cops and EMTs will be here soon. I know they're going to ask me questions. Ask Lachlan questions. I know they're going to take my dad away in a black bag, placed on a gurney.

What I don't know is how I'm going to survive all the pain Lana has given me.

AN HOUR LATER, I'M SITTING OUTSIDE ON THE FRONT STEPS with a blanket draped around my shoulders. Cop lights are flashing. Five cops are here. Three of them are walking in and out of the house. The other two are talking to Dr. Rutledge and

Lachlan. They've talked to me a few times and I know it won't be the last. Two EMTs walk down the sidewalk, flanking a stretcher. My mom's still inside, still sobbing. I haven't talked to her. And she hasn't looked at me once. If she did, I don't think much would pass between us. With Lana's memories, *my* memories, slowly coming to me, I see there was nothing there to begin with.

I look ahead. Lachlan is walking this way. This whole time he's been Max. I still can't wrap my head around it. There's a lot I can't wrap my head around.

He stops in front of me. "I'm going in for questioning."

My eyes widen. I go to stand up, but he places his hands on my shoulders and kneels next to me. "It's standard procedure."

"I want to go," I say, my voice hoarse and scratchy from all the screams.

Lachlan smiles, but it never quite reaches his eyes. He's trying to make this entire situation appear better than it looks. It's a waste of time, though, because I know it's bad. I know that what happened inside that office will have serious consequences for him.

"Lachlan, I—"

"Naomi, it's okay," he says, his voice steady.

Dr. Rutledge walks over and sits down next to me. She places an arm around me. "I'm going with Lachlan. I promise everything will be fine."

My eyes are wide, frantic. "I'm not staying here by myself!"

"No, you're not staying here." Dr. Rutledge looks at Lachlan and back to me. "You're going to the hospital to get checked out."

"I'm not—I'm not ready . . ." My voice wavers and veers off because I can't form the right words. I don't know how to tell them that I'm ready for nothing. Haven't I been through enough in one day? Questions have been answered, but there are a whole slew still waiting to be answered. Those answers are in my head, waiting to be uncovered. I'm too scared to reveal them.

My body starts to shake. Behind Lachlan, two police officers are walking over. I grip his arm tightly. He leans his head against mine. One by one his fingers curl around the back of my neck. "He can't hurt you anymore, Naomi."

He kisses my forehead and stands up. I stare down at the sidewalk, refusing to watch him leave. I want to feel numb right now, but I feel everything. Isn't that what Lana was so good at: being numb? Keeping the pain at bay? I now realize just how endless her pain was. I place a hand over my heart, as if that will make the ache lessen.

A car door slams and then another. I hear a car pull away.

"Miss?"

I look up. An EMT is staring down at me with a calm expression. "Are you ready to go?"

Freedom is heady, yes, but as my life falls down around me I see the underlying truth: freedom has a price.

I just wish someone had told me it was my life.

UNVEIL

1 YEAR LATER

"When a person is lucky enough to live inside a story, to live inside an imaginary world, the pains of this world disappear. For as long as the story goes on, reality no longer exists."

—PAUL AUSTER

LIFE MOVES FORWARD WHETHER YOU'RE OKAY OR NOT.

The ground is frozen, with a blanket of snow covering it. It's a freezing winter night, where the stars are out, twinkling brightly. I watch all of this with a smile on my face, grateful that for once, I'm on the okay side. Once, there used to be a barrier between me and the outside world. That barrier was once the truth, and it held me back from so much.

For decades, my life had been put on pause. I stopped breathing, living. To put it simply, I stopped existing. But for the past year, I have been trying to exist, all the while knowing everything that has happened to me and not letting that define me.

"You ready?"

I look over at Lachlan Maximilian Halstead. "I'm ready."

"We need to hurry up," he says, his breath appearing in the air like puffs of smoke. "My fingers are going to freeze."

He kneels down and drags a match across the coarse matchbox surface. The flame comes alive. He looks over at me and smiles before he places the flame against the tip of the rocket.

There are times I catch him watching me, and before he can recover, I see the concern and sadness in his eyes. My past still weighs on him . . . on us. But it's getting better. Every day the wounds are less painful and noticeable.

The fuse glows amber and we instantly back away. I curl my hand around Lachlan's arm and lean into him and think about everything I've been through in the past year.

I was diagnosed with dissociative identity disorder. It's also called multiple personality disorder and is better known as split personality. In most cases there is more than one personality.

But Lana was my only personality.

My only alter.

My only part.

And creating Max? Well, that was a whole other twist that baffled Dr. Rutledge and the rest of the doctors. I know I can't go back and change what I thought and who I created. I just know that I did it to survive.

I direct my attention at the array of colors in the sky. For the next twenty minutes we light off rocket after rocket. Soon, I forget about the bitter wind hitting my cheeks. I just live in the moment and enjoy the show.

Everything that we've been through makes me realize that love is about finding the right person in this cold, oppressive world that loves all the wrong things about you. Everything you try to hide, that person accepts. And I know he accepts me.

He puts the matches in his back pocket and looks over at me. "Did you like the show?"

"It was beautiful."

Lachlan stands up and holds out his hand. "You ready to go home?"

I nod and take his hand.

ACKNOWLEDGMENTS

A huge thanks to a group of amazing ladies who read through *Unravel* when it was in its roughest form: Tosha, Melissa, Vanessa, Jessica, Nina, Claribel, and Darla. I can't thank you enough!

Thank you to Natasha for the beautiful graphics.

Christine, thank you for everything. For supporting me and believing in this story.

Thanks to Sheena for being one of the first to read those first few chapters.

Regina Wamba, my cover designer. Thank you for creating one of the most beautiful covers I have ever seen. I still get chills when I look at it.

Angela, my formatter. Thank you for making my book all pretty!

Lori Sabin, my wonderful editor. Thank you for everything you do. I could never go through the publishing process without you!

Thank you to my husband, Joshua. For your unwavering support. For every single thing you do.